FOLLOWING THE WAKE

The fallout from Evangeline Walter's murder touched everyone who knew her, as if her venom had poisoned their happiness. Even her cousin, Murray McGraw, who had a genuine affection for her, was not immune, and neither was Smiler O'Dowd, who loved her; but none suffered more than the wife and son of VJ Sweeney, who drowned at sea before he could be charged with her killing. Was it all too neat? Ten years on, the sense of unfinished business lingers, and Gil Sweeney has become obsessed with finding out what really happened when he was a little boy of eight.

FOLLOWING THE WAKE

FOLLOWING THE WAKE

by

Gemma O'Connor

Magna Large Print Books
Long Preston, North Yorkshire,
BD23 4ND, England.

British Library Cataloguing in Publication Data.

O'Connor, Gemma
  Following the wake.

    A catalogue record of this book is
    available from the British Library

    ISBN   0-7505-2065-5

First published in Great Britain in 2002 by Bantam Press
a division of Transworld Publishers

Published in Large Print 2003 by arrangement with
Transworld Publishers Ltd.

Magna Large Print is an imprint of Library Magna Books Ltd.

Printed and bound in Great Britain by
T.J. (International) Ltd., Cornwall, PL28 8RW

For Pauline

Acknowledgements

Following the Wake takes up the story – ten years on – from *Walking on Water*, though neither is dependent on the other. The geography and place names, like the characters, are imagined.

Neither this nor any of my previous books could have been written without John, and the unfailing support of our family; they have all my love and thanks.

Behind every writer there is a large production team; I am very fortunate indeed in my publishers at Transworld, whom I want to thank, especially my wonderful editor and friend, Francesca Liversidge.
    I would also like to thank the following: Brian and Kate Pattinson for unfailing support and encouragement; my god-daughter Liadain O'Driscoll for helping me realize the character of Shay; to my agent, Catherine Clarke, for keeping my spirits up and spreading the word, and to John Hamwee for keeping my foot on the ground.

See him! Whom?...
See him! How?...
See it! What? His innocence.
Look! Look where? On our offence.
See him filled with love...

Break in grief, thou loving heart;
For a child whom thou didst nourish,
Yea, a friend whom thou didst cherish,
Gathers wicked foes around thee
And doth like a serpent wound thee.

Chorus 1, Aria 12; from
J.S. Bach: *St Matthew Passion*
Edited in English by Neil Jenkins

Irish Daily News, Thursday 12 September
The tragic and untimely death is announced of award-winning journalist Fiona Moore who was fatally injured in a hit-and-run incident in Dublin city centre. Ms Moore worked for this newspaper for the past five years and won the coveted Columnist of the Year award last year. Forty-eight and recently divorced, she leaves a nineteen-year-old son and a ten-year-old daughter.

Comment, page 4; Obituary, page 6

Duncreagh Listening Post
PASSAGE SOUTH ANNUAL REGATTA.
The Baltiboys Race was won this year by
English businessman VJ Sweeney of Coribeen
on his ketch Azurra. *Mr Sweeney has recently*
joined the board of the Atlantis Hotel in Passage
South. The runner-up was Mrs Evangeline
Walter of Trianach on Cynara. *Attendance at*
this year's regatta was well up on any previous
year.
Twelve-year-old report found by Gil
Recaldo in newspaper archive

Regression 1

The waters of the Glár river are black and
peaty. Opaque, yet where it runs over the
rounded pebbles of the estuary it appears
quite clear. When I plunged my hand in I
could see tiny particles suspended in the
pale water, and if I let my feet sink into the
slimy brown silt, the colour oozed out and
swirled around, hiding them. The river was
my refuge. Once, I fell into the space
between my father's boat and the dock
when the tide was in and the water was
deep. I remember thinking, as I floated
down, down, how calm it was, how cool,

mysterious and silent. I touched the bottom before I made any attempt to surface, kicking away my waterlogged shoes as I rose. I wasn't in a hurry. The water enfolded me, kept me safe, and I knew that whenever things got too bad I could always slip off the dock and tread water under the slatted planks until my father went up to the house. I don't think it ever occurred to me that he might pull me out of danger. Or that he would notice if I drowned. I must have reckoned he'd be glad to see the back of me.

By contrast, my mother never allowed me out of her sight. Her comforting presence is what I remember. She was as terrified of my father as I was, but when she was with me I had no fear. She fended off the bad stuff. Most of it, anyway. Papa was always irritated and angry; with her, with me, with the whole goddamn world. He had a nasty habit of grinding his teeth just before he exploded. His temper was vicious and he didn't seem to care which of us he had a go at. It was all the same to him if she put herself between us. I don't think she ever knew how much I was taking in, how I willed her to clock him one, make him disappear. I used to drum the floor with my heels wishing it was him I was pounding. Now that I've grown up everyone believes I'm a pushover, but I think maybe I've inherited his foul moods and it scares me. Sometimes I have to sit on my hands to stop myself lashing out. I'm not sure anyone realizes. Certainly not my mother, who often misses the point, being a bit vague. Though that might be an act. Maybe, like me, she has things to hide.

Cressie worried about me all the time. That's what I call her now, though when I was little I called her 'Mama'. It was the first word she taught me and for a long time the only word I could say. My earliest memory is of the two of us sitting on the floor of an empty room, her clutching me in her arms. She is holding a warm, damp washcloth to the side of my face and it is slowly dripping blood, which disappears into old rough quarry tiles. Mama is weeping. The tears roll slowly down her face. Silently. I want her to stop. I can see our dog, Finnegan, keeping guard at the door. His tail is down but his mouth opens and shuts. There is no sound.

I tagged along beside my mother every-where she went. People smiled when they talked to her and patted my head and tried to make me smile as well. Others – I suppose they must have been our neighbours – waved when we passed in the car but I don't remember anyone clearly except old John Spain who was our friend. I called him 'Tar' – not because he was a sailor, which he was, but because anything beginning with T was easiest for me to say when I first began to talk. Frank Recaldo, who eventually became my stepfather, was 'Tank' for the same reason.

Every day, rain or shine, Tar went out fishing in his boat. Usually he rowed; he hardly ever used the outboard motor. He always wore bright yellow oilskin overalls and jacket with the hood up, or sometimes a navy cloth cap. He was famous for his lobsters and often brought us one, or a crab. I loved watching the lobster turn from dark blue to pink when it was dropped into boiling water. He was also famous because he'd once been a priest. I don't remember if someone told me that or if I just picked it up along the way. Tar didn't have many friends – at least, I don't remember him talking to anyone except us and an American woman, who lived near him on the far side of the river. I remember her because she always laughed whenever she saw me with John Spain. The way her red, red lips stretched over her long white teeth fascinated me. She was horrible; I hated her. My father must have liked her, though, because sometimes I saw her on his yacht *Azurra*.

John Spain. The man and the place became so entangled that I thought of the river as Spain. I used to dream I was back there. Always the same age, about six or seven, wearing a blue jersey and shorts with yellow wellies, plodding along the waterline. Sometimes I am sitting in the prow of Tar's boat, trailing my hand in the water until a fish surfaces and snaps it off. I watch the blood boiling on the surface, pouring from my upheld arm.

Tar taught me to swim. It amused him that I had no fear of the cold water. I suppose I was too young to understand or explain that, under water, hearing didn't matter; I felt normal. Looking was the thing, and learning when to hold your breath and when to expand your lungs. I remember him standing patiently, in his waders, by the edge of the water, while I dived in and out of the rising tide, pretending I was a dolphin. Sometimes he tied a long strip torn from an old sheet under my armpits and let me slip off the side of the boat. We didn't let on to my mother or she'd have stopped it, and I would never have learned Tar's great lesson: how to listen. Really listen. One day he asked me what it felt like to have water in my ears. To make me understand he cupped his hand in the water and let it flow into his own ear. I laughed and drummed the surface with my hand. I wanted to say it gurgled – which was odd because I hadn't the word. If I couldn't hear, how could I know something so complicated? Tar looked at me a long time as if he was trying to figure something out. Then, without warning, he tipped me over the side again and when I surfaced he had his mouth on the surface, saying my name: Gil, Gil. I felt it rippling and vibrating through the water. Gil, Gi, Gi, Gi. I held on to the edge of the boat and tried to copy him. Gi, Gi, Gi, Gil.

Tar gave me his quiet smile, hauled me aboard and sat me on the bench beside him. 'You Gil, me Tar,' he said, and I could feel the rumble of his strong, deep voice vibrate through the wooden seat-back. When we got back to his cottage he wrote *Gil* and then *Tar* in big letters on a sheet of yellow paper and stuck it on the wall. That was how he began to teach me to speak and read. As far as I know, he didn't mention the incident to my mother and never again to me. We just fell into a way of communicating which some-how allowed that, in certain circumstances, I was not totally deaf.

I loved being on the boat with Tar. There was something written in tiny gold letters on the inside of the prow. Tar told me it was his dead wife's name and that when he was alone he talked to her. I liked that. I liked the thought that even when you were dead someone still loved you. He was brilliant, the only person besides Cressie with whom I felt truly safe. And *no*, he did *not* touch me up, though someone told my father he did. How do I know that? I've no idea, I just do. It happened just before we left the estuary. I sometimes wonder if that is why John Spain died.

My parents were always fighting, and my father didn't seem able to walk past me without taking a sneaky sideswipe. When Cressie tried to protect me he'd turn on her. Sometimes she was black and blue all over. I watched her all the time. I could tell she was hurting by the way she walked. Knew when she wore her hair loose that she was hiding a black eye. Once, towards the end, I saw him burn the back of her hand with a cigarette – he just stubbed it out, casually. Three times. He didn't stop talking even when she opened her mouth in a scream. They were at the kitchen table. I was standing beside her, as usual. I believe now that he was trying to drive us away, though of course I didn't understand any of that at the time. It made sense once I discovered the house belonged to my mother's family. My parents only went to Ireland when my mother inherited Coribeen.

My father is dead and my memory of what he looked like is vague. I cannot see his face, just a blurred image of long legs and blond hair – like mine. I still find it unbelievable that I knew so little about him until I was fourteen, when Grandfather Hollingsworth dragged my mother to Oxford to look after him. 'You look just like your father,' was pretty well the first thing he ever said to me. 'Strange chap, Sweeney. Good-looking, athletic. Successful. Never figured out what he saw in your poor mother.' I ignored that little crack and asked if his name had been Gil. Grandfather gave me a strange look. 'No,' he said. 'It was Valentine Jason Sweeney.' All I could think of was that such a poncy name didn't tally with the ogre in my head. So my real name was Gil Sweeney, was it? After that, I used secretly to write 'Gil Sweeney, Spain/ Ireland/The World/The Universe' on my schoolbooks and it was the beginning of trying to piece together my father's history and the reasons why we left the estuary.

Frank adopted me at about the same time my little sister Katie May was born. But even before then I thought of myself as Gil Recaldo. I find it odd now that I didn't seem to have any idea what my real name was. I was just Gil. It might have been because of my hearing difficulty, who knows? It was a very long time before I realized that losing my birth name might have repercussions. Even so, I knew, deep down, that one day I'd be driven to seek an explanation.

It took ages to establish exactly where the estuary was because I'd only ever had two place names in my head – Coribeen and Trianach. I didn't remember them as sounds but as written words. I read much earlier than I talked so I might have seen them on signposts. I thought Coribeen was a village when, in fact, it was the name of our house as well as the hinterland on that side of the river. But it wasn't until I finally got to Passage South after I left school and saw an admiralty chart on the wall of Hussey's pub that it all fell into place.

Trianach was the real key. I first found it on an Ordnance Survey map of West Cork in my last year at school when I was doing a project on grain shipments from Ireland to England during the nineteenth-century famines. The name jumped out at me and I was enthralled. It appeared to be a small island on the river Glár, linked to the land by a causeway – a kind of near-island. Neither my mother nor Frank Recaldo had ever spoken to me of either place. Maybe they thought I didn't remember, or that if I did and it wasn't mentioned it would fade from my mind. They were wrong: the river was always in my head. The river and Tar. The more I learned about Trianach, the more I wanted to go home. Not that I knew where my original home was and when, in a roundabout way, I tried to question Frank, he clammed up. I knew better than to tackle my mother, who just got upset.

Halcyon appeared on the scene soon after we left the estuary. She was some sort of relation of Murray Magraw, a friend of my parents. She used to come and stay sometimes when I was a kid. I could never understand why my mother bothered with her because she was weird. A big galumphing girl who used to follow me around. I didn't mind at first but she seemed to become more peculiar with every visit, especially after Katie May was born. She was fixated on my mother and dead jealous of the baby, and was always trying to attack her until Frank said she couldn't come to the house any more. Sound man, Frank.

Halcyon is another bone of contention between Frank and Cressie, who insists on visiting her at the home in Tipperary whenever she's in Ireland – which isn't often. 'You spend more time with her than with me,' Frank used to moan, and I can see his point. I haven't seen Halcyon for years, but for some reason she always reminded me of my father. She had the same kind of swirling fury as him. Totally unpredictable. Thinking of either of them brings back that sinking feeling in my gut.

My mother never got over leaving Coribeen. Not really. She was deeply upset over the deaths of my father and Tar. Tar especially. Frank left with us. No, that's wrong, we left with him. He was always hanging around, even before my father died, so I assume he and my mother must have been having it off and, knowing Cressie, she would have been terrified of people knowing about it and turning against them. I suppose if it had come out things might have been awkward, him being the local copper and all.

Even before we left Coribeen the whole world turned upside down: Cressie bawling her head off, Frank looking fierce, people talking in whispers and no sign of John Spain or my father. I was staying with people I didn't know, my arm was broken and we seemed to be forever tearing along country roads in Frank's clapped-out jeep – which we had until four or five years ago.

I carried away one clear memory: the night they set fire to John Spain's boat. There were hundreds of people lined on the pier looking out to sea. I remember the red flames licking through the thick smoke and my mother telling me that all true sailors are buried at sea. Funny. My father was a sailor too, an Olympic yachtsman, but there was no funeral for him. I only remembered that a few weeks ago when I stood on that same pier at Passage South looking across the bay to the rocks where Tar used to take me to watch the seals.

After we left the estuary, we went to Kerry to stay with Frank's brother. We have a summer cottage there now. I was completely bewildered and kept asking for Tar. I'd ask and Cressie would burst out crying. Frank would tell me not to upset her. So, of course, I stopped asking. I suppose that's how the embargo on information thing started.

Email from Fiona Moore to Sean Brophy, Arts Editor,
Dublin Daily News
Hi. This comes with a proposal for a series of articles entitled 'Irish Artists in Profile' I thought might interest you. I've already started work and hope to have the first couple ready in the next few weeks. If you want more info, contact Jez Murphy at Jeu d'esprit *(the San Francisco art and literary review). I've been freelancing for him for the past few years. CV enclosed.*
Fiona Moore

Chapter 1

Of all the things Cressida Recaldo resented about her first husband, Valentine Sweeney – and there were many – his having deprived her of her beloved Coribeen was the worst. For that she never forgave him. Viewed dispassionately it might have seemed the least heinous of his crimes, because he was a violent, murderous brute. Yet somehow, in the aftermath of Val's death when Cressida and her lover Recaldo fled the estuary to avoid the scandal breaking around their heads, being cut adrift from her small, carefully constructed world affected her most.

That, and the death at sea – while in pursuit of her fleeing husband – of John Spain, the old man who had helped her lead Gil out of his silent world.

Born and brought up in a small village in Oxfordshire, she had lived in Ireland for eighteen years and it suited her, which was strange because she was dogged by one disaster after another right from the start when, as a young bride, she went to view the Georgian farmhouse she had inherited from her Anglo-Irish forebears. Coribeen was a ruin but it was situated on the glorious Glár river and she was bewitched by the country-side, the house and the estuary. She hardly registered that the property had no sur-rounding land, and only the most meagre access to the road.

It was fortunate that Val Sweeney – an Englishman, despite his name – was wealthy. A keen yachtsman as well as an astute businessman, he saw the possibilities of the land around Coribeen, with its long river frontage and private mooring. Before embarking on the house restoration, he bought the surrounding twenty-five acres. It was some years before Cressida discovered that, due to some fast footwork by persons unknown or at least unnamed, her title to the house included no land, not even the narrow track from the main road. Together, land and house were valuable; divided, less so. The land could be sold without the house, but the converse did not hold. With neither land nor access the house was worthless. In effect, Cressida could not sell her inheritance without her husband's agreement.

Ignorance was bliss for Cressida that first year. A few weeks after completing the purchase of the land, Sweeney's beloved yacht *Azurra* was moored at the bottom of the garden. The couple originally intended Coribeen to be a holiday home but Cressida was eager to get settled. She moved in, ostensibly to oversee the work, while it was still a building site. Her trips to London dwindled gradually and, once baby Gil was born, she took up permanent residence while her husband VJ – as he was universally known – returned at weekends. For him, Coribeen was an investment; he never intended to settle in Ireland. He didn't really like it. Soon weekly became monthly. The arrangement suited them both.

When Gil was two years old, he developed severe hearing difficulties. His parents reacted differently to this setback: VJ took it as a personal insult, while Cressida became focused on helping her little son. She learned sign language and how to lip-read, and taught Gil herself until a neighbour offered to help. There were those who thought it inadvisable to allow an elderly, solitary ex-priest near the child, even if he had once been a distinguished academic. But Cressida knew better: John Spain was more than a good friend, he was also her confidant and adviser. She regarded him as a kind of surrogate father and would have trusted him with her life.

With the discovery of Gil's deafness, the Sweeneys' relationship began to go seriously wrong. Overnight, VJ seemed to lose all sense of propriety: always something of a womanizer, now he openly flaunted his relationship with the American Evangeline Walter, who lived across the river. He also began to drink heavily, and with drink, he became violent and abusive towards his wife and child. His business failed and within a couple of years he was practically bankrupt. As money dried up, he determined to sell Coribeen, house and land together, and started a campaign to force Cressida to surrender her title to the house. For such a gentle girl she proved surprisingly resistant to even the most ferocious beatings. As she saw it, her marriage was in shreds and she had a handicapped child to look after: Coribeen was her only safeguard against the future. She refused to budge.

It was at this point that Francis Xavier Recaldo, a former detective inspector at Garda headquarters in Dublin, amateur musician and aspiring travel writer, entered the picture. After a premature heart attack he had retired to quiet, sleepy Passage South as its resident policeman. Tall, handsome and vulnerable, he was precisely the kind of man to appeal to a shy, neglected young woman. They fell in love, and conducted their affair with the utmost secrecy. Or so they thought.

Then disaster struck the estuary. Early one autumn morning old John Spain found Evangeline Walter murdered in her garden. VJ Sweeney went missing, suspected of killing her. As the lover of VJ's wife, Garda Recaldo found himself in an invidious position – the investigating detectives shipped in from the city certainly thought so. By the time incontrovertible evidence against Sweeney was found, both he and John Spain had drowned. Cressida and Gil fled, under Frank Recaldo's protection.

VJ Sweeney's name was not released to the press: he remained for ever 'suspect drowned at sea'. The police had their man and the case was closed. Against all expectation there wasn't a whisper in the papers of Recaldo and Cressida's involvement, although they were aware of the usual village gossip. And that, of course, was the reason they packed their bags and took off. There was also another reason: since VJ's liaison with Evangeline Walter was well known, his guilt would have been speculated widely.

Someone, some time, would blurt it out and the thought of her son being branded as the child of a murderer appalled Cressida.

Some months later, Coribeen was sold at a knockdown price; few were willing to live in the house associated with a recent murder. Deep in her heart Cressida knew that her old friend John Spain would have advised against the panic selling of her home. But Frank had urged it, and when she realized that he had no future in the Garda, especially in West Cork, she felt she had no choice but to leave. 'One day,' John Spain had once told her, 'you will have to learn to make your own decisions – for yourself and your son. Remember that. No one else, no matter how loving, will ever put Gil's interest first. You have to take responsibility, Cressida, for your life and his.'

Wisely or not, they packed their bags and took off. Just before the birth of their daughter, Katherine Mary – Katie May – they married quietly. Shortly afterwards, Frank adopted Gil and made his name-change official. Oddly, Gil never mentioned the estuary, except at the beginning when he kept asking for John Spain. Neither did he speak of his father. After an anxious year or so, Cressida and Frank concluded he had forgotten his previous life. He was a happy, charming child whose shyness diminished as his hearing improved.

They settled in Dublin, in a small semi-detached house in an outer city suburb within walking distance of the mountains. The Dublin house and a tiny holiday cottage in Kerry, near Frank's family, cost more than Cressida made from the sale of Coribeen. The balance ate up most of Frank's capital. He invested what remained to provide, however inadequately, for Gil's school fees. But at least they were clear of a mortgage. Frank's travel series – *Walking to Music around Ireland* – sold reasonably well and the occasional journalism and the rental income from the cottage, kept the wolf from the door.

Over time the Recaldos melted into their surroundings and convinced themselves that they were what they appeared: an unremarkable, ordinary family. Secretly, Cressida never stopped fearing that one day her and Gil's history would be discovered, but as the years went by it began to seem that nothing could intrude into their private cocoon. And perhaps that would have been so, had not Frank, tired of earning so little from travel writing, turned his hand to crime, under the name Frank Ventry. His first detective novel achieved a modest success but his second hit the jackpot. Fame beckoned, and the Recaldos were unprepared for it.

Duncreagh Listening Post *(archive)*
Body of woman found in the river by fisherman.
Name withheld until relatives informed. Foul
play suspected.

Regression 2

Just after my fourteenth birthday my
grandfather fell ill and my mother was
called upon to play Florence Nightingale.
She thought it would only be for a few
weeks, but it took the old bugger four years
to pop his clogs. Frank and I stayed in
Dublin: I didn't want to change schools and
Frank was tramping the length and breadth
of Ireland for his *Walking* series. There were
other reasons too: not much spare cash, the
Oxford house was too small, and neither of
us got on with Grandfather. But the real
clincher was that during the second year
Frank went back to work, part-time, for the
Irish police. His mate Chief Inspector Phil
McBride – Bridie to the family – fixed it.

After my Leaving Cert I took a year off
and spent a few months in Oxford working
as a waiter to please Cressie. It was not a
great success. She was stressed out all the
time, and my grandfather was always

grumbling about poor little Katie May. It was like a madhouse, so I went off to Germany with a couple of mates from school. After a few months we moved on to France where I got a job at a boatyard in La Rochelle. At first I was just a general dogsbody, cleaning charter yachts and doing general maintenance, but I knew how to handle a boat – I'd been sailing with Frank in Dublin Bay since I was a kid – and I was angling for a crewing job when my grandfather died. I intended to return to France after the funeral because I had been promised work with the biggest charter company in the Port de Plaisance.

A strange thing happened at my grandfather's funeral. In the church I found myself wondering why I couldn't remember there being a memorial service for my father. I was told he had drowned when his yacht ran aground during a ferocious storm and that John Spain had died trying to save him. But somehow the story didn't hold together. Was he really dead? I sneaked a glance at Frank and my mother, who were both looking tense and miserable as sin, and realized how little I knew about my origins. It was as if I'd arrived, fully formed, aged eight, as Gil Recaldo. How ridiculous is that?

As the vicar warbled on about Grandfather's supposed virtues, a great turbine was whirring in my head. That was my real moment of decision, although unconsciously I must have been travelling towards it for some time because my plan to return to France suddenly opened up all sorts of possibilities. What if I worked in the boatyard for a month or so, then sloped off to West Cork? I mean, if I was crewing it would be hard to keep track of whether I was in port or at sea so it wouldn't be too noticeable if I didn't keep in regular touch.

I made up my mind to crew for a few weeks then go walkabout. But when I got back to La Rochelle someone else had taken my place with the charter company and I was back to odd jobs, which meant I didn't earn much – at least, not enough to save anything. Then, one day, while I was cleaning one of the charter boats a gang of Irish guys had trashed, I came across a discarded copy of *Cara*, the Aer Lingus in-flight magazine. I was flicking through it idly when I spotted an article on my estuary. The minute I saw the photographs, I felt as if I was being sucked in. One shot must have been taken from our garden. It was like travelling back in time, because it was exactly what I had seen when as a child I sat on the dock, looking across the water. On the opposite bank was *that house* – where the American woman had lived. Something exploded in my brain and I knew the time had come. A week later I hitched to Beauvais and got a cheap stand-by flight to Dublin. I told nobody where I was headed. As far as my folks were concerned I was still in La Rochelle. Mobile phones are great that way.

Email from Arts Editor, **Dublin Daily News,** *to Fiona Moore*
Ms Moore, I like your outline and am pleased you offered me the project. I'd like a few days to think about it – we're a bit snowed under at the moment but I'll get back to you for a chat within the next week or two. Sean Brophy

Chapter 2

When Cressida moved back to Oxford, after eighteen years in Ireland, she changed her name for the fourth time. Born Hollingsworth, she had taken the names of both her husbands, first Sweeney, then Recaldo, but when she went home to look after her father the medical and Social Services people called her by his name. She realized it had something to do with the way the old man treated her, the way she acted the dutiful daughter. There was nothing in their relationship to suggest that, in another place and another time, she had had a life – or, more accurately, two lives, two husbands, two children. Even, for a while, something of a career. Within a few months of having stepped into the open jaws of the paternal trap, in a despairing gesture that she only half understood, Cressida was calling herself Hollings – the 'worth' was deleted. It was an accurate reflection of her state of mind.

Since his second marriage over twenty years before, Colonel Piers Roland Hollingsworth had virtually ignored his only child. He attended neither of her weddings and never indicated the slightest wish to engage with his grandchildren. Shortly after he and his second wife retired from Corfu to his native Oxfordshire, Cressida and Frank brought nine-year-old Gil and six-month-old Katie May to meet their grandfather for the first time. It was a dreadful weekend. The baby, sensing her mother's tension, howled throughout and the colonel seemed perplexed by his daughter's association with a man he treated either as an illiterate Spaniard or an Irish peasant, which didn't go down well with ex-Detective Inspector Francis Xavier Recaldo, a highly accomplished Kerryman with a deadly line in sardonic wit that, mercifully, passed over his father-in-law's head. The visit was not repeated, until the colonel's second wife died three or four years later and he took to writing and phoning Cressida with alarming frequency. Having had the devoted attention of women for all of his four score and two, boyhood to dotage, when his health broke down he was determined to haul his daughter back to where she belonged.

With Katie May about to start school, Cressida had found a job at a Dublin art gallery. However, while professing delight at her success, Frank drew her attention to the difficulties that might ensue. How would she manage when he was away researching his books? When either of the children was ill? During the holidays? The meagre pay would certainly not cover regular child-minding. 'You know I'm pleased for you, Cress, it'll be wonderful for you to get back to work...' The 'but' was unspoken. They were both miserable: Frank because he couldn't rejoice wholeheartedly in his wife's success, and Cressida because she'd brought to the surface the strains of the life they lived. In effect, they recognized that their relationship was too fragile to sustain change, and it had a profound effect on them both.

Cressida gave up the idea of returning to work and things settled back to normal until Grandfather Hollingsworth fell ill. 'Don't answer it,' Frank said, when the first letter arrived from Social Services. It was followed by an urgent summons from the Oxford hospital where her father was recovering from a stroke that had left his mobility impaired. Deemed too old and frail for further treatment, there was little to be done medically. He was confused, though not incapacitated to any great degree, but he needed constant care. He was coherent enough to refuse to consider a hospice, even if there was a bed available. There wasn't; he would have to be nursed at home.

'They're trying it on, and so is he. Keep cool, lovey, please. Don't rush over there. Once they get hold of you they won't let go. What about the children?' And then the real problem: 'For God's sake, darlin', we can't afford to have you traipsing back and forth to Oxford all the time.'

The words were no sooner out of Frank's mouth than they were faced with real crisis. The hospital needed Piers' bed: he was about to be discharged. The following day Cressida flew to Oxford and took her father home. What else could she have done? But Frank had been right; it had been a mistake to respond too eagerly. When Cressida looked at the Elsfield house through the eyes of the social worker, she understood at once why it was thought that her father could afford round-the-clock nursing care. Small it might have been, but it was well appointed, cosy and stuffed with valuable antiques. It was no use telling the authorities that the house and most of the contents had belonged to his deceased second wife and would, when Piers died, revert to her son – who lived in what the estate agents described as a compact artisan's dwelling in Jericho, in the centre of Oxford. He was, not unnaturally, resentful of his stepfather's continued presence in his mother's house.

The couple of weeks that Cressida had originally envisaged she would need to sort out her father stretched. For the first month Frank took the children to the cottage in Kerry where they ran wild and he finished the fourth of his *Walking to Music around Ireland* books. It was the first time the couple had been parted.

Trapped in Oxford, Cressida felt let down by Frank, who in turn felt she'd turned her back on him. They were running two households when Frank's income from his writing was stretched beyond its limit to maintain one. Eventually he succumbed to the blandishments of his friend Chief Inspector Phil McBride and, without consulting his wife, agreed to return to work, albeit on a part-time and flexible basis, at the Irish police headquarters in Dublin. Perhaps he hoped that returning to his old job might force Cressida to look at the reality of the situation into which she had plunged them, but she was too preoccupied to think about it. She was more concerned with what to do about five-year-old Katie May: September, and the start of the school year, was looming.

Frank and Cressida discussed the situation

endlessly by phone and letter, but as there was no easy way out, they resolved to make the best of it. The idea that they might sell the cottage in Kerry was rejected. They assured themselves that if they pulled together they could manage. They consoled themselves that it wouldn't be for long: the medical prognosis indicated that Piers would survive a few months, a year or so at most. At fourteen, Gil was settled in his Dublin school, and Frank's work meant that he needed to be in Ireland. Insidiously, the temporary split took on a kind of permanence. Frank and Gil remained in Dublin; Cressie and Katie May were in Oxfordshire, where the little girl was enrolled at the village school.

For the first year or so, Frank and Gil squeezed into Piers' house every holiday and half-term, but the arrangement never worked. The bedrooms were too few and too small – Katie May had a tiny attic room but Gil had to make do with a put-you-up in the living room; Cressida's bedroom barely held a small double bed and the space shrank further when Frank was in residence. As time went by the strain showed – especially between Frank and his father-in-law. A veteran of the Second World War, the old colonel had disliked Ireland's neutrality and its architect, Éamon de Valera, with whom he confused Recaldo. It wasn't that Frank disagreed with the sentiment: he just couldn't stand the condescension.

In the second year, Gil preferred to spend his vacations with friends, and Frank's visits gradually became fewer and shorter. Sometimes he took Katie May back to Dublin with him or else she was dispatched home by air as 'an unaccompanied minor'. It felt like *déjà vu* to Cressida, who watched helplessly as her family fell apart and the vacuum was filled by her father.

Email from Fiona Moore to Sean Brophy
Hi, Sorry to press you but I've only just returned to this country and I need to start working pronto. I'd appreciate it if you could let me have a decision asap? The Independent *is very interested but I have old loyalties to the* News. *I worked for the legendary Philpott for four years. I'll hold the* Indie *off till Wednesday.*
Fiona Moore

Chapter 3

Colonel Piers Hollingsworth was buried on a hot late-June day, in the Oxfordshire village of Elsfield, a week after his death. As Frank Recaldo followed his family into the half-empty church, he realized how little thought he'd given to this much-desired reunion. Little thought and absolutely no planning. Taking his place in the pew beside his wife, he squeezed her hand, and she gave him the shy, diffident smile he loved. But he felt a dispiriting sense of loss. Where had love fled? He knew he would find it very hard indeed to adjust to family life again.

From the moment he had arrived, tension had bubbled to the surface and he had soon upset Cressida by suggesting that they move their bed into his late father-in-law's room. You'd have thought the corpse was still *in situ* from the way Cressie reacted. She refused point-blank and they argued about it in whispers into the early hours, until she padded off to the kitchen to make tea, leaving Frank to fall into a fitful sleep. They had hardly exchanged a word all morning and were still not talking when they set out for the service.

In some ways, Frank thought, it was like meeting his wife for the first time all over again. She was like a stranger. She had always been slim, but she'd lost a lot of weight and was looking pale and ethereal. There were dark circles under her light brown eyes and her faded honey-blonde hair, grown half-way down her back, was tied in a loose bunch at her neck. She looked in need of love, yet Frank suppressed an urge to fold her in his arms. She was dressed in a dull navy blue suit with a string of pearls at the neck, and black court shoes. Eighteen-year-old Gil looked athletic and vibrant in black jeans and a white shirt, no tie. He was just over six foot tall, broad-shouldered, and tawny-eyed like his mother; he kept his blond hair unfashionably long to hide a tiny hearing-aid. At not quite ten Katie May was lean and leggy like her father, with his intense blue eyes, pale skin and a mass of blue-black curls. She was dressed in a navy and white striped Breton shift.

Frank himself wore a dark grey suit and black shirt; he was six foot four and as spare as he'd always been. His dark hair was now steely grey but the blue eyes were still electrifying. They made a handsome group. Cressie shifted along the pew and stroked her daughter's hair. Katie May had always been a daddy's girl but in their enforced exile mother and child had become unusually close. Cressie wondered how she was ever going to be able to share her.

The funeral service was short and perfunctory, the locum vicar incompetent. An almost visible barrier had erected itself, splitting the family neatly down the middle, men to one side, Cressida and the little girl to the other. Alliances formed during their enforced separation had taken, alarmingly, only a few hours to surface. Frank looked at his wife: she was lost in thought. The vicar announced the hymn, and he stood up. It was only when his rich baritone was raised in 'Onward Christian Soldiers' that she stood with the rest of the congregation. He noticed that Gil's shoulders were shaking. 'The colonel to the last,' the young man mouthed at him. Frank stopped singing, caught Cressida's eye and suddenly the four were giggling helplessly. We could start from here, Frank thought, and relief surged through him. He leaned across his daughter and whispered in Cressie's ear, 'Why don't we all go out to lunch?' He only just stopped himself adding 'to celebrate'.

'Good idea.' Then Cressida bit her lip. 'But what about this lot? They'll expect to come back to the house, won't they?' She had whispered too loudly, not noticing that the singing had stopped. The vicar looked at her over his half-moon spectacles, cleared his throat and began to intone a prayer for the dead. 'I've prepared sandwiches, just in case, and Grace brought some wine around yesterday. We can't just do nothing, can we?'

'Of course you can,' Frank murmured. 'How many of these people do you know?'

Cressida shrugged. 'Some are relations ... I think. Must be.' She gave a nervous giggle.

'Come on, Cress, you don't know a single one of them. Where were they when you needed help? You don't owe them anything.'

'But Grace–'

'Grace won't mind. Anyway, she can come too.'

Grace Hartfield was a close family friend who could be relied on to calm things down. Frank glanced around, but couldn't see her or her husband Murray Magraw.

'Oh, what the hell?' Cressie muttered. 'Why not? Let's go in to Oxford.'

Frank squeezed her elbow and put his arm around Katie May, who grinned up at him.

'Pizza Express?' she asked. Frank nodded.

'Thank God for that,' Gil murmured. And, for those brief moments, with the prayers for the dead as backdrop, the Recaldos relaxed.

After the service some people slipped away but the rest of the congregation followed the vicar to the graveyard for the interment, which he conducted with almost unholy haste. Afterwards they stood around with an expectant air, until Cressie apparently lost her nerve and invited them back to the house for tea.

'God, give me strength!' Frank said crossly. 'Why are you doing this?'

'Oh, Mummy,' Katie May moaned. 'We're going out for a pizza.'

'Shush,' Cressida hissed. 'It's OK. There's plenty of time. It's only half past eleven and they'll be gone in an hour.'

'Want to bet?' Frank snapped. 'I believe there's an excellent lunch to be had at the...'

'The Abingdon Arms in Beckley.' Gil came to his rescue briskly. 'It's only a couple of miles away. Cheap too. Real ale.'

Cressida stepped on his foot. 'You all know where the house is?' she said politely, looking around at the mourners. 'We'll go ahead. See you there in a few minutes,' she added, and was appalled when, almost without exception, they took her at her word.

Email from Sean Brophy to Fiona Moore
I like your style. OK, I'll have a contract drawn up in the next few days. I talked to Jez Murphy who's very enthusiastic about taking a selection for Jeu, *and Suzanne Philpott of* New England Review *also wants in on the act. I suggested she contact you direct since you'll probably do a better deal for yourself. I disinterred some of the stuff you wrote for this paper ten, twelve years ago. What took you to the States? Look forward to hearing from you. Sean Brophy.*

Chapter 4

The wake was not going well. A reluctant gathering however you looked at it, Frank concluded, being more used to the Irish variety, which usually contrived to be rather cheerful. In Oxford, though, the hastily assembled guests were uniformly subdued and formal. Frank, made irritable from recurring angina, was in sore need of diversion. But none was forthcoming. No amusing anecdotes, no awkward belly laughs. Nobody falling down drunk. A heated argument might have livened things up, but the robust intake of wine had had no obvious effect; the subdued remained impassively subdued. He'd vaguely hoped someone might at least remark on Cressida's years of filial devotion, but no one did. Instead they seemed to regard *dear Piers'* daughter and her family as an alien species. It was plain to Frank that few of the mourners had a clue who he was and none asked.

An hour had gone by and none of the guests showed any inclination to leave. What had seemed a sparse enough gathering in the churchyard filled the small house to overflowing. In need of allies he looked around for Grace and Murray, but couldn't see them. The only light relief was provided by Katie May who, every few minutes, passed the sitting-room window, pulling mournful faces and making pleading gestures with her hands. When this had no effect she stood on her head and waved her skinny legs in the air. These familiar antics usually made her father laugh but somehow he couldn't rise to it on this occasion.

Gil was no help either. He slouched in the most comfortable armchair in the room with his nose buried in a book, generating waves of resentment. 'Why don't you help your mother?' Frank said to him irritably.

'Why don't you?' he muttered back sullenly.

'Don't–' Frank began.

Gil uncoiled himself and stood up. 'Speak

to you like that?' he growled. 'That's what you were going to say, isn't it? For God's sake, Dad, get off my case.'

'No, it isn't,' lied Frank, and hated himself for being conciliatory when he wanted to tell Gil not to be so effing disagreeable.

Gil glared at him. 'I'm off,' he said, and shrugged away his stepfather's restraining hand.

'Hang on, Gil, I want–'

'Look, I don't give a toss what you want. Or think. Or do. I traipsed all the way back from La Rochelle and got here two days ago. *You* couldn't manage to turn up till last night. Why don't *you* go and help my mother instead of standing there looking superior? She's shattered.' He clenched his fists and stuck them into his jeans pockets. 'Look, I don't suppose Mum wanted this – this...' he looked around wildly '...excuse of a wake. I bet she wanted to have lunch with the rest of us. But he was her father, no matter whether we liked him or not. If he'd been yours, you wouldn't behave– Oh, what the f– hell.'

His face was scarlet and he reminded Frank painfully of the damaged and vulnerable child he'd been when they first met. He felt thoroughly ashamed of himself. 'Gil, please,' he began, but Gil ignored him.

'Why don't you bloody well look after her, Frank? What is it with you two?' He rubbed the back of his hand across his forehead.

'You're never around when you're needed.'
He twisted away and made for the door.

Two elderly women stepped apart to let
him pass then turned to glare accusingly at
Frank. 'Some kind of policeman,' he heard
one mutter, as he brushed past her on his
way to the kitchen. 'God give me patience,'
he said to himself, under his breath. 'Can't
these feckin' people get anything right?'

I'm a shit, he thought, as he pushed open
the kitchen door and saw Cressida standing
by the stove, staring into space, waiting for
the kettle to boil. As she turned to greet him
a shaft of sunlight caught her face. My
sunflower, Frank thought. He put his arm
around her and drew her to him, surprised
by a surge of desire.

She went rigid. 'Sorry, love, have to get
on,' she said, and pulled away.

'Let me know if there's anything I can do,
Cressida.'

Frank swivelled to face a young man he
hadn't noticed when he'd come into the
room – he was standing almost behind the
door, leaning against the kitchen counter.

'Who are you?' Frank said rudely, caught
by surprise.

'This is Dr Ford, Frank.' Cressie sounded
flustered. 'He's been wonderful with Daddy.'

'Just doing my job.' The man came
towards Frank with his hand outstretched.
Frank took it reluctantly. 'Paul Ford, I'm

the local GP,' he said confidently.

'Been here long?' Frank asked.

'In Elsfield?' It wasn't what Frank had meant but he nodded. 'About five years. I cover several of the villages around.' An awkward silence followed. Then the doctor added, 'I have to get on, I'm afraid.' He smiled charmingly. 'Cressida, bag up the surplus drugs and drop them off at the surgery. I've told Mrs Jones to expect you. Anything else, just give me a call. Nice to meet you at last.' He nodded at Frank and left.

'Did I interrupt something?' Frank asked.

Cressida stared at him coldly. 'Don't be ridiculous,' she said.

At that moment the kettle let out a shrill whistle. Cressida rinsed out the teapot while Frank watched her. She seemed unreachable. Passive, but definitely out of range.

The doctor's 'at last' stung him. He and Cressida needed to talk before it was too late, he thought, before they forgot what had drawn them together. Once, they couldn't bear to be apart but now, whenever he wanted to make love, Cressida shied away.

Katie May was standing by the open window, watching them. Listening too, he told himself, with a sinking heart. Damn, damn, damn. Was it his imagination or had his adored daughter grown distant with him? He registered, painfully, how she skirted him when he came on his flying visits, which were too short for the ice to begin to crack, much less break. When had this state of affairs become the norm? At first it had only amounted to a brief awkwardness as the little girl felt her way back into his affections, but recently he had sensed her consciously trying to get used to him. It was even more humiliating watching her struggle to shoehorn him into her world. Rage surged through him, but he was at a loss on whom, beside himself, to focus it. Usually he diverted it to his late father-in-law but now it settled into misery as he confronted his wife and watched her turn away. Her first husband had battered her, mentally and physically, and in that instant, to his horror and everlasting shame, Frank thought he understood why.

'When do you have to get back?' Cressida asked.

'Why?'

'For God's sake, Frank, what the hell's the matter with you? I only want to know when you've to get back to the film set.'

You? It was supposed to be *we*. 'Tomorrow or the day after. They're trying to get as much done as possible while the weather's good.'

Frank's second novel was being filmed for television when word came of his father-in-law's death. His immediate relief was replaced rapidly with anxiety that his ordered routine was about to be shattered. For a wild, dizzying moment he was tempted to stay in Ireland and get on with his work – he brushed aside the nasty thought that his late flowering had happened during Cressida's absence in Oxfordshire. It wasn't that he didn't recognize she would need his help in the aftermath of her father's death, and he wanted to give it, but he couldn't bear the thought of being away from the action. He'd waited a long time for success. Why shouldn't he savour it?

'So soon?' she murmured.

He folded his arms. 'Cressie, what ails you? You *are* coming, aren't you? You need a break, after what you've been through. We can come back and clear this place when the filming's over.'

She gave him an odd look, her mind elsewhere. She bit her lip. 'When will it be finished? The film, I mean. Do they need you there all the time?'

Frank's temperature began to edge up, his heart raced. 'Well, they would, wouldn't they? It's my book, my script. Yeah, they need me.'

'Stop patronizing me.' Cressie's eyes held his until he was forced to look away.

'I'm sorry, sunflower.' He hadn't called her that for years. 'Please come. Waterford's beautiful and for once the weather's marvellous. It'll be a bit of light relief and we could use some of that, couldn't we? There's only a week or so left. Afterwards we could have a few days to ourselves – on the company. Just you, me and Katie May. I found a great hotel near Ballyhack.'

'Where's that?'

'On the coast, Wexford–Waterford boundary. It's lovely. Or, if you prefer, we could go down to the cottage – it's free now until the last week in August. Come on, darlin', how about it?'

The name Frank Ventry was on everyone's lips. The production company making the film had bought the rights to his third and latest book, which was due to go into production early the following year. There was talk, too, of an option on his first. Business was booming and for the first time the Recaldos were in a seriously comfortable financial situation. Frank was disappointed that in the bosom of his family there was so little jumping for joy.

'I don't think I can,' Cressida said softly, not meeting his gaze.

He was distressed at how expert she'd become at avoiding confrontation. She looked now as she had when he'd first met her – a dozen years before when she was being knocked about by her bastard husband and desperate to break free – except older. 'Please, Cress. It would be like old times. I haven't had you to myself for so long.'

'I have to get this place sorted,' Cressida mumbled.

'It can wait,' Frank reiterated angrily.

'I don't think it can. I promised Tim – Marjorie's son – that we'd be out–'

'Promised?' he exploded. 'Christ, it's always somebody else, isn't it?' He counted to ten silently and tried to calm down. 'Tell you what, Cressida,' he said stiffly, 'I'll take Katie May back to Waterford with me. That'll stop her mooning around the garden.'

'What do you mean?'

'Look at her. The child is always on her own. She doesn't seem to have made a single friend since she came to this place. She's lonely.'

'You think you can do better? Is that what you're saying?'

'Yes, Cressie, that's exactly what I'm saying.' Though not, perhaps, what he had intended to say.

'So who'll take care of her while you're working?'

'Oh, she'll be fine,' he said loftily. 'Two or three of the crew have their families with them.'

'So the wives can look after her? Right?'

'That's not what I meant. I *can* look after my own daughter. And there'll be other kids so she'll have company. Though I'm sure she'd prefer you to come. And so would I.'

When she didn't respond, Frank picked up the newly filled teapot, turned on his heel and returned to the living room. He refilled a few cups, then plonked the teapot on the table, noting, *en passant*, that the vicar was as inept a guest as he had been in church. The young man was stuffing sandwiches into his mouth, demolishing the smoked salmon Frank had picked up the previous day in Dublin airport. He felt a furious antipathy to the man and not just for his greed. Had it been through stupidity or laziness that he had failed to remember either Cressida's name or her relationship to the deceased? During the service he had reduced her almost four years of devoted care to a mumbled, 'Mrs ... em ... er...'

Oddly, Cressida had found it unaccountably funny.

'Frank, darling?' Cressie had come up behind him, unnoticed, and murmured in his ear. 'Let's talk about it later.'

Frank didn't trust himself to speak. He felt like kneeling down and banging his head on the floor. He touched his wife's arm fleetingly, and went to open the window – the west-facing room was stifling in the early-afternoon sun. When he turned, Cressida was plying the clergyman with yet more food. Frank embraced the shame of his own neglect of his small family. As his eyes followed his wife around the room he felt as miserable as she looked. Her isolation was almost palpable. He was moved almost to tears at how withdrawn she'd become. Lost.

Not knowing how to make amends for his jealousy at Cressida's regard for the old man's GP, he slouched against the wall and willed the wake to end. Long-distance relationships were always hard to sustain, the thread binding even the closest of couples pathetically flimsy. Frank wondered sadly if there was anything left to save.

Email from Fiona Moore to Sean Brophy
Hi, Sean (or should I say Ed?), Second thoughts. I've slightly broadened the range to include film-makers as well as artists (as in painters/sculptors) and writers (including drama). One thing's for sure, there's a hell of a lot of talent around. I've completed the first four, have done the interviews for the following three and have drawn up a shortlist of eight from which to draw the remaining five. Could we meet for a chat? Fi

Chapter 5

Whoever invented wakes? Gil wondered sourly. He lowered the book he was pretending to read and stared at a couple of old army types who were blocking his view of the room while they ground on and on about the inadequacies of the Labour government. Gil worked the armchair forward, the better to observe his stepfather while he flirted with Grace Hartfield on the other side of the cramped sitting room. Frank was looking a bit more cheerful but, then, Grace always had that effect on him. Normally Gil admired and liked them both, but today he wasn't so sure. They had a lot in common, he knew, the same reserved manner, the same way of not rushing to fill silences, but Grace was easier to be around: she was less confrontational, didn't challenge every damn thing you said. Which Frank did all the time, these days.

Old habits die hard: Gil watched their lips. He couldn't catch everything because they kept turning their heads away, but they were talking about Halcyon sure enough. He raised his book in front of his face. It was better not to know some things. Every time he thought about Halcyon, his heart sank and his head filled with questions to which there seemed no answers. He had been asking them ever since he discovered she wasn't just stupid but deaf, like him. Had she been bashed up the same way he had? And, if so, how did that leave him? A genetic psychopath? The more he thought about it the more terrified he became, but he kept it to himself. Festering.

His eyes moved from one conversation to another. It amused him to collect a word here, a word there, making a patchwork of the talk. With a bit of practice it was possible to 'hear' what people were saying before they opened their mouths. Deafness was both a barrier and a label. As soon as people noticed the device he wore in his ear they signalled that they 'understood' by raising their voices. To everyone except his mother it was what he was. While for Gil it was simply another factor in who he was – part of his personality. Cressida and old John Spain had taught him how to handle it, but later, when he had to accommodate himself to the improvements that technology and, eventually, surgery brought him, he had to figure his own way through what seemed at the time thunderous changes to his perception of the world around him. For Gil, progress was often intrusive and exhausting. Sometimes it appeared that the better he heard, the less he could understand the nuances of what people meant. Every step towards clearer sound seemed to erode his confidence until the day he decided he'd had enough and switched off his hearing-aid. He still wore it most of the time because he couldn't stand being nagged if he didn't. And it had its uses; it created a kind of protective no-go area. It amused him that many people couldn't deal with his disability at all. Maybe they thought it was catching.

Gil let his book drop to his lap as the old men who'd been standing in front of him moved away, leaving his view of the room unimpeded. He liked being the quiet observer; his ability to be on the sideline yet in the thick of things gave him a sense of power. It was an excellent way to find out what was *really* going on. There were better ways of hearing than with the ears – lips, eyes, body language. He had absorbed it all when he was a child and his hearing was almost non-existent. As a child he had unconsciously used his disability to shut out the unacceptable and had never lost the knack. As he grew older he had become aware that he could switch off sound at will. His use of sight and instinct was deft, so he missed little, and he was bright, his grasp of what went on around him acute.

At school he'd been nicknamed Cluedo. It had started with a chance remark in his second year. One day a new guy asked him a question and Mullins said, 'What are you asking that thicko for? He hasn't a clue what you're saying – he's stone deaf.' Gil's mate Baz Phillips had butted in: 'Don't you believe it, he lip-reads faster than you can think.' Cluedo/Thicko? What was there to choose between them? But fortunately 'Cluedo' stuck and made his so-called disability acceptable to those who found it embarrassing. The silly name wasn't used anywhere else and after a while it was forgotten, but it had one lasting effect: none of his schoolmates ever again equated deaf with stupid. It was OK to be bright.

Katie May stuck her head through the window. 'Gilly? Why don't you come out in the garden? Please?'

'In a minute, Twink. I'll come in a minute.

Promise,' he said. His little sister turned away and ran off. Gil watched her. She didn't look like him, but somehow she awoke in him a memory of things that had happened when he was her age. It was if there was a volcano inside him, waiting to erupt. On the outside he acted just like every other adolescent, grumpy, withdrawn and charmless, but this successfully masked his inner confusion.

He went back to his book and turned the pages listlessly, with one eye on the clock. At last people were beginning to leave. Gil snapped the book shut, edged towards the door and slipped quietly out of the house. He went round to the side to collect his bike: when things got on top of him, he cycled – in Dublin to the sea or the mountains, in Oxford usually towards Otmoor. It was not far, at most three miles by the winding country roads, but enough on a hot day to work up a good sweat.

Katie May was lying in wait for him – literally: she was stretched full length on the grass. She was making two straggly plaits of her fringe incorporating coloured glass beads, which dangled over her eyes. It was something she did while she watched television or when she was fed up. When she saw him she jumped up. 'Where are we going?' she asked, and he remembered his promise. 'Please, Gil?' Her clear blue eyes looked suspiciously watery.

'I heard Dad say he was taking you into Oxford for an ice cream?'

'Yeah, he did. But where is he? I'm fed up waiting.'

'He'll be out in a sec. The party's breaking up.'

'That's what he's been saying for hours and hours. Anyway, it's not my idea of a party.'

'Nor mine. What a shower.'

'I'll get my bike.'

'No.'

'Please?' She pouted. Gil suppressed a laugh. She looked ridiculously like Frank – slim to the point of emaciation with legs that seemed to start at her armpits. Gil, who adored her, reckoned that she was going to be a stunner – she already was. She could normally twist him around her little finger, but not today.

'Sorry, Twink,' he murmured. 'I just need to be on my own for a bit.' He jerked his head at the house. 'Ghastly, eh?'

Katie May shrugged. 'I can keep up with you. Why won't you take me with you?'

'I'm going to see Jackman in the Radcliffe,' he said. 'Jackman' was Gil's version of Oscar Wilde's Bunbury – invented as a means to escape from his grandfather. He forgot momentarily that Katie May had worked out the ruse long since. 'He's broken his arm.'

His sister played along. 'When?' she asked.
'Now.'
'No. When did he break his arm?'
'A few days ago.'
'How do you know? You were in France.'
'He rang me,' he added hurriedly. 'In France.'
'Liar,' she hissed. 'I saw Jackman yesterday and he looked OK to me.' And with that surreal remark she stuck out her tongue. 'You think I'm stupid or what? There is no Jackman. Didn't you tell me so yourself?' She wrinkled her nose at him. 'You just don't want me to come, do you?'

'Not today, Twink. Sorry,' he said. 'What are you doing out here, anyway?'

'Keeping out of the way. What do you think?' She sighed dramatically. 'Why is everyone so cross? You, Dad – and Mum keeps blubbing. You'd think she'd be happy now we can go home, but she's not, is she?'

Gil shook his head. 'I expect she's upset about Grandfather dying and that–'

'Why? He wasn't very nice, was he?' Katie May cut clean through her brother's piousness. 'He was always grumbling, telling me to shush.' She wrinkled her nose. 'I shouldn't say that, should I? Sometimes he wasn't so awful, he told me stories. Still and all, most of the time he was a grump. Know something? Funerals make me sick. So do you, Gil Recaldo, you're really mean.

You've been away for months and months and now you just keep running off by yourself. Bet you're after some girl.'

'No, I'm not.'

'Well, then, why can't I come?'

'I'll be back soon. We could go swimming or something.'

Katie May thought about this for a moment. 'Don't feel like it. Anyway the Stephenses are away so we can't use their pool.' Her face brightened. 'Grace invited us to a barbecue in her garden. We *could* go to the Ferry Hinksey pool and then to her house after swimming, couldn't we?'

'We'll see,' he said.

Katie May yelped. 'I hate that. Why are *you* so grown up and boring? Dad always says that when he doesn't want to do something.'

Gil turned his bike and checked the tyres. 'You're right. Sorry.' He gave one of her plaits a playful tug. 'I'm a brute – sorry, Twink – but I'll be back soon. Promise. Word of honour, trust me. I'll be back in an hour or so.' He went a few yards and looked back at her. 'Could you do something for me?'

'What?'

'Tell Dad I've booked Ryanair back to France tomorrow. I'll need a lift to Stansted. See you in an hour.'

'An hour or you're dead,' she shouted. And with that she stumped off down the garden, kicking the turf furiously as she went.

Gil wheeled his bike out on to the road. The cottage was on the Oxford side of Elsfield, half-way up the hill to the village. John Buchan's house, complete with the blue plaque, was about thirty-nine steps away from the church. Grandfather Hollingsworth had a whole shelf of his novels, which Gil had repeatedly tried and failed to read. As far as Gil could see, the whole of Oxfordshire was littered with the houses of living and dead writers. R.D. Blackmore, the author of *Lorna Doone*, had once lived in the next village of Beckley, where he was headed.

Shortly after passing the church, Gil ran slap into the first of four recently installed traffic-calmers and careered into the ditch. He lay there, winded, for a few minutes, then pulled his bike upright and looked over the plain to where the city was spread out below. The dreaming spires were shrouded in the shimmering heat, a fairytale panorama. Oxford *was* beautiful – Gil didn't often allow himself to think any good of the place that had robbed him of his mother. He remounted his bike and proceeded more cautiously over the succeeding sleeping policemen.

About ten minutes later he arrived in Beckley, which looked out on to Otmoor.

The first time Gil had visited his grandfather, an old neighbour had told him that in ancient times the Roman army had marched across the moor. The image had struck him and fired his imagination. Thereafter, whenever he went to Otmoor he laid his head on the ground and was certain he could feel the tramp, tramp of marching feet. But today was too hot and sunny for illusion: on chill damp days the moor had a frail whiff of the sea, which helped him project himself back to his mythical estuary – with the tide full out, of course. Otmoor had been drained for half a century or more, but because of the unusual volume of rain over the previous few weeks there were still traces of surface water. When he made his eyes into slits, he could imagine it ebbing and flowing. A small flock of inland gulls completed the picture.

He sat hunched against a low stone wall edging a pasture, his arms crossed on his knees. He wondered when the straggle of guests would leave, when it would be safe to go home without having to talk to one or other of his mother's distant relatives. They looked old and dusty to a man. Just like Grandfather Hollingsworth who, in Gil's experience, had never taken the trouble to disguise his dislike of the young. Katie May had come in for special disdain. The miracle was that she somehow retained her *joie de vivre*, which was more than he could say of himself.

The amount of grief their mother had taken from the old man was something else. As far as he could see, his grandfather had always treated her like that, ever since she was a child. Yet the minute the old fascist announced that he needed looking after, she went running, poor little Twink in tow. Had Frank not put his foot down, they too would both have been transported. Surely there must have been a way for Cressida to care for her father without pulling apart her own family?

Gil had to admit that he was grateful to Frank for digging in his heels about remaining in Dublin. He chuckled. Frank had probably been thinking of himself – not that you'd know it, he played his cards close to his chest – but at least it had meant Gil hadn't lost all his friends and, most of all, that they hadn't had to squeeze into the Elsfield house and tiptoe around the bastard sickroom all the time. It was full of old-man smells and fussy chintzy furniture, built for cats.

The funeral had been as grim as everything else. The cold, damp church, the vicar barely mentioning the corpse – he couldn't even get Cressida's name right. Then she'd had to go and invite him back to the house. Gil wondered if the sandwiches were his mother's idea of a joke. He threw himself back on the grass and sniggered at the memory of Frank's face when he saw Cressida piling his expensive smoked salmon on to Mother's Pride. 'That'll teach him to come when he's needed,' he muttered. But the satisfaction of shifting blame to his stepfather was lost as he contemplated the Recaldo family's future. When he considered it, Cressida, in Grandfather Hollingsworth's immortal words, 'had gone native'. The old man had meant what had happened to her in Ireland, but as Gil saw it, she had changed when she returned to Oxfordshire. And, in the process, he had lost his mother. He closed his eyes, the better to contemplate his grievances and only incidentally to plan the last leg of his gap year.

As he got to his feet to start his return journey, the idea of going back to the estuary hardened. He didn't know it yet, because his head was too full of his return to France, but the seed had been sown. The article in the magazine would do the rest.

Email from Sean Brophy to Fiona Moore
I do like your style. Sean will do fine. For now.
What about Monday or do you insist on a day
of rest? We could have a lunchtime pint in the
Liffey on Batchelor's Walk? Half-one suit? If
you're free. Sean

Chapter 6

In Elsfield, the few remaining guests showed no sign of leaving.

'We just don't have the talent for it.' Grace Hartfield came up behind Frank, startling him.

'What?'

'For wakes. The English just don't *do* wakes.'

'Oh, is that it? And there was I thinking it had something to do with the corpse,' Frank said, irreverently. 'Piers Hollingsworth had a rare talent for putting the kybosh on enjoyment.'

'In death as in life, then,' she intoned, with a grin, and handed him a glass of red wine. 'Have a drink. It might help.'

'I'm not sure it will, I've already had a couple,' he said, but took it anyway. 'Excellent wine, Grace. Don't we have you to

74

thank for it? Cress said you brought it round yesterday.'

'Glad it came in handy,' she said, 'but it was intended for you two. Thought you might both need cheering up.' She smiled.

Grace Hartfield was a general favourite with the Recaldo family. She and her American husband Murray Magraw were antiquarian booksellers of some repute, who ran the business from their vast Victorian pile in North Oxford. The two couples had met in Ireland, more than a decade before, when Frank had been investigating the murder of Murray's cousin, Evangeline Walter. Not an ideal start to a friendship, yet they had maintained contact over the years, mainly through Evangeline's daughter Halcyon, but they had become much closer during Cressida's years in Oxford.

Although she was in her late fifties Grace was still striking, with an air of serenity that little seemed to disturb. She had strangely pale grey eyes that Frank always felt could see into his soul, which he sometimes found uncomfortable. Her hair was white-grey, cut in a stylish bob, and her skin was pale and faintly lined – like parchment that had been crumpled and then inefficiently smoothed out by hand. One of the things he admired about Grace was her stillness. She also had a talent for observation – little passed her by. Most of all he loved her for her irreverence.

'I'm very glad to see you, Grace. Did you just get here? I missed you in the church.'

'I was late, I slipped in at the back and half-way through got so irritated with his reverence' – she glanced over at the hapless clergyman who was propping up the sideboard – 'that I left, and went home to sort a few things. We sent out our latest catalogue a week ago and if I don't keep up with the calls we'll be swamped.' She smiled ruefully. 'Lousy timing, one way and another. I've only just got here. I thought the party would be over. I was hoping to persuade you all to come back to our place for a barbecue or something. Katie May's already agreed – I saw her on my way in.'

'Poor kid's bored rigid,' he said. 'A barbecue would be lovely. Anyone ever tell you what an angel you are?' He put his arm round her shoulder and gave her a hug.

'Not much of an angel – I should have been here to help but I didn't realize there was to be a wake.'

'Not sure any of us did. It just happened. Cressie felt she had to offer but we didn't really expect them all to take her up on it. Is Murray around?'

'He's in Ireland.' She grimaced. 'Tipperary.'

'Halcyon?' He raised his eyebrows.

'Halcyon,' Grace replied, with feeling. Halcyon Walter was Murray's brain-damaged ward, left to his care by his dead cousin. The girl, now in her late twenties, had been in institutions since childhood. It was a spectacular mess, which Grace had stepped into with innocence and trust that even now enraged her. The plan to make Murray, and thereby Grace, the girl's legal guardian had been hatched shortly before his cousin's murder, without Murray – an impractical man – having consulted his wife. She could not recall without shuddering how she and Murray had turned up, at Evangeline's invitation, to be introduced to her daughter only to find that Evangeline had died a couple of days before. During the murder investigation, when it emerged that Cressida's then husband, VJ Sweeney, was allegedly Halcyon's father, Cressida had offered to help care for the girl. But for that, Grace knew she and Murray would never have managed. By mutual if unstated agreement, the girl's putative relationship to Gil was kept from him; he knew her only as Halcyon Walter, Murray's ward.

'I suppose Cressie filled you in on what's been going on?'

'No, she hasn't said anything.'

Grace sighed. 'Sometimes I wonder if it will ever end, Frank.'

'What's happened?'

'What hasn't? Since Sister Angela died, Halcyon's been distraught. Violent.' She drew a deep breath. 'I simply don't know how that good woman managed. A few hours of Halcyon and I'm tearing my hair out. Now the convent we moved her to in Clonmel is closing. And she's only been in it six months. Poor girl hasn't a clue what's happening to her. She's got completely out of hand. If only she could talk.'

'How long has Murray been over there?'

'Ten days. She ran away. Now she's in hospital with pneumonia.' She held up her hand. 'Don't say it, Frank, don't even think it...'

'I'm sorry, Grace.' Frank touched her hand. 'It's what you always feared, isn't it?'

'Yup. Murray's bringing her back with him,' she said bleakly. 'What else can we do?'

'To live with you? My God, how–'

'Will we manage? I've no idea. Murray assures me that it's only until she recovers. Heaven only knows what we'd have done if Cressie hadn't found a private home in Witney who promised us the next available place. So let's hope. Meantime Murray's stuck in Ireland until she's well enough to travel.'

'Ever feel tempted to say I told you so?'

'Often, but most of the time I desist,' she said. 'Anyway, what's the point? You can't blame Halcyon. It's terrible for her. Mind you, she's been luckier than most with her condition. She's had the same devoted carer most of her life – the only constant while one convent after another closes down. First in New York and then in Tipperary.' She drew closer to him and lowered her voice. 'Sister Angela was always anxious about what would happen when she could no longer manage. She once told me that she'd hoped Evangeline would gradually take charge after they brought the girl to Ireland. Fat chance.' She snorted. 'Old Morticia only had her home twice. Did you know that? Twice – in the six or seven years she lived in Ireland. That woman was something else.'

'Morticia? Is that what you called her?' Frank chortled, then shuddered as an image of the dead woman's white face appeared in his mind, her chiffon scarf floating in the wind. 'I guess she had no real idea of the problems...'

'That's putting it charitably. It's one hell of a legacy. For us all, Murray and me, you and Cressie. I hope we can survive it,' Grace said, grimly.

Evangeline's Legacy?' Frank murmured. Good title. He pictured it across a book jacket. Could he? 'Evangeline's legacy,' he repeated.

'You've an unhealthy gleam in your eye, Frank Recaldo. I've often wondered when you'd get round to it.'

'I couldn't,' he protested. 'Wouldn't.'

Grace wasn't fooled. 'No, I suppose not,' she said. 'Too Gothic, even for fiction. You'd be hard put to it to make Evangeline believable. And it'd be impossible to make her likeable.'

Frank shook his head. 'Too close, too involved.' He changed the subject. 'When does Murray expect to get back?'

Grace shrugged. 'A few days? Who knows? Poor man. Mind you, I'm not sure I don't envy him, looking at this lot. Cheerful, aren't they?'

'As a roomful of undertakers. Have they no homes to go to?'

'I'm sure they'll be off soon,' she murmured, 'if we can persuade Cressie to stop doling out the sandwiches.'

'Maybe you should try – she listens to you.'

Grace looked at him sideways. 'And not to you? Since when, Frank?'

He passed his hand over his eyes wearily. 'We had a bit of a barney last night.'

'Cressie's worn out, Frank.' Grace spoke urgently. 'She's grieving. Don't look at me like that, it's true. She tried so hard. For heaven's sake, she only wanted what everyone wants – for her parent to love her. And, as we know, Piers was pretty miserly with his affection. I don't honestly know how she kept going. You should take her away for a holiday, just the two of you.'

'I've already asked her and she's refused.' He ran his fingers through his hair. 'At least, I think so,' he added dubiously.

'Try again, Frank. Katie May can come and stay with us – Gil, too, of course, if he likes.'

Frank guffawed. 'If he likes? Hard to know what Gil does like at the moment. He seems to think I was put on earth specifically to blight his life. He's furious at having to come back from France. I'm not sure which of us is the baddie – me or his mother – but either way he's being a royal pain in the arse.'

'Oh, come on, Frank, he's a nice boy.'

'Indeed he is – if you don't have to put up with his moods.'

'But he's been away for months,' she said.

'OK. There's a pair of us in it.' Frank held up his hands in mock submission. 'He's heading back to La Rochelle tomorrow. Cressie's a bit upset – she thought he'd come home with us for a bit of a family holiday, but he's having none of it. He's so far up his own arse there's no talking to him.'

'What's gone wrong, Frank? You two used to get on really well.'

'Before the testosterone kicked in,' he said wearily. 'Not so much adolescence as obsolescence – mine, I mean. For the past

81

couple of years everything's been a battle.' He felt the familiar but almost forgotten pang of parental outrage, just as he had first time round, when his two sons from his first marriage had reached the same state of sullen inertia. It had affected his marriage then, and he was alarmed to find himself again in a similar position. Or was he using Gil to shield other problems?

'That bad, huh?' Grace asked lightly. 'Anything I can do?'

'It'll pass, I hope.' He turned his face to the window. He and Cressida had been so close before the upheaval. Lately Frank had found himself wishing that neither he nor she had the baggage of previous marriages to spoil their joy in what they'd found together. Would Katie May also crystallize into another fly in their ointment? It seemed hard to believe. He watched her clowning around in the garden.

When she saw him she waved and made faces at him. 'Daddy, when are we GOING?' she mouthed.

'Hang on there, I'll be out in five minutes,' he called to her out of the window then shut it with a bang. He debated whether or not to tell his wife where he was going but decided against it. He looked around the half-empty room. Gil had disappeared and Grace was heading for the kitchen. He strode purposefully to the door. His sudden movement must have signalled that the party was over because the stragglers began to work their way, crabwise, towards the hall. Frank almost galloped out of the house and into the back garden where Katie May was waiting impatiently.

'Seen Gil?' he asked.

'Yeah,' she replied. 'He's gone to the Radcliffe to see Jackman. He told me to tell you he's booked a flight tomorrow morning and wants a lift to Stansted airport.'

'Did he now?'

'Yeah. He said the wake was too much for him.'

Frank grinned down at her. 'For me too, baby,' he said, with feeling.

Email from Fiona Moore to Sean Brophy
Sean, Thanks for the (unexpected) lunch as well as the compliments – I didn't know where to put myself but I'm really pleased you like the first three profiles. I've certainly developed a taste for it. As the man said, you meet such interesting people. I was thinking over what you said about including a few newcomers and I like the idea. I'll dig around and see what I come up with. Fi

Chapter 7

While Frank was in the garden with his daughter, Grace went to look for Cressida. She found her sitting on the floor just inside the kitchen, her head cradled in her arms. 'Cressie, for heaven's sake what are you doing?'

Cressida looked up and made a *moue*. 'Keeping out of the way. Have they gone yet?'

'Almost. Stay here for a few minutes, and then we'll catch them in the hall to say goodbye.' Grace sat down beside her friend and put her arm round her. 'I'm sorry, Cress, was it awful for you?'

Cressida bit her lip. 'Much worse than I expected. Somehow I thought I'd be relieved, you know, start my life over ... but now...'

'Cressida?' One of the guests put his head around the door. He was a small, plump, middle-aged man, with bushy eyebrows and bad teeth. He looked at the two women on the floor. 'We're off now. I'll see you tomorrow morning at eleven o'clock.' Not a word of thanks, Grace noticed.

Cressie struggled to her feet. Her skirt was crumpled and there was a grease stain down the side. 'Tomorrow? Can't you leave it for a few days, Tim? I haven't been able to talk to my solicitor yet. She's been away,' she added lamely.

'That's most inconvenient – we'll have to manage without her,' he said rudely.

But it seemed that Cressida wasn't about to be pushed around. 'Tomorrow isn't possible,' she said, then spoiled it by adding, 'Sorry.' Grace, who hadn't a clue who he was or what was being discussed, wondered if Tim would have apoplexy on the spot or if he'd have manners enough to wait until he got outside.

After a moment's pause he pulled his diary from his jacket pocket and leafed through it irritably. 'Saturday?'

'I'm not sure solicitors work on Saturdays, do they? In any case mine won't be back till next Tuesday, I'm afraid.'

'This is a damn nuisance. Don't you realize–'

Cressie drew herself up and pushed her hair out of her eyes. 'I don't want to discuss this,' she said, 'at my father's funeral.'

'A week tomorrow, then,' he said, with finality. 'Ten o'clock. It's time for closure.' He spoke loftily, and withdrew.

'Time for what?' Grace stifled a laugh and raised her eyebrows. 'Who dat?' she mouthed.

Cressida peered out into the hall before replying. 'That's the Blessed Marjorie's son. You know, my late stepmother.' She wrinkled her nose. 'He's a terrible fusspot – and,' she added, with a surprising show of spirit, 'he has dreadful breath. He can't wait to get rid of us.'

'Rid of you?'

'Well, it's his house and he wasn't best pleased that his mama left it to Daddy for his lifetime. Yesterday he served notice on me to quit.'

'Yesterday? That's obscene. And he had the gall to come back here and stuff himself with your food? Cheek.'

'Yeah, well, I guess he was checking up on us. He's probably afraid I'll run off with the contents,' she giggled, 'which he seems to think belong to him.'

'And do they?'

'Most, but not the few important bits and pieces. That reminds me, Grace, there are some prints I want you to look at. Could you? Lovely watercolours too.' Her eyes filled with tears.

'Of course, any time. I may not be any use but I can put you–'

'–in touch with a man?' Cressie finished, and managed a wan smile. 'Thanks.'

'So when *are* you moving out?' Grace asked.

Instead of replying Cressida said she'd better check on the guests. 'Back in a tick, Grace, don't go.'

Grace had almost finished tidying up the kitchen by the time Cressida returned. 'All gone, thank goodness,' she said. She poured them each a glass of wine and they sat down at the table. 'Gil seems to have disappeared.'

'He's gone out for a spin on his bike. Oh, and Frank's taken Katie May into Oxford for ice cream or something.'

'I caught them as they left.' Cressida picked up her glass and took a long draught of wine. 'Well, thank God that's over. I've no idea who half of those people were. What did you think of the vicar?' She giggled. 'Wasn't he something else?'

'Lazy sod. He might have got your name right.' Grace glanced at the clock. It was nearly five. She was expecting a call from a customer in New York and she couldn't remember if she'd diverted her calls to her mobile. If not, he'd just have to ring back. Cressida finished her wine and Grace refilled her friend's glass, then topped up her own. 'Cress? Do you want to come and stay for a few days?' she asked, and looked around the cramped kitchen. 'Frank can't stand upright in this place, or Gil, for that matter. They both look bloody miserable.' She added quietly, 'And so do you. D'you want to talk about it?'

Cressida looked away and changed the subject. 'Murray isn't back, is he? What's happening with Halcyon?'

Grace sighed. 'She's still in hospital in Clonmel. He's staying nearby, visiting every day.'

'He's very good,' Cressida said.

Grace looked as if she might not agree, but held her tongue.

'They managed to keep her in bed, then?' Cressida sniffed. 'That'll be a first.'

'Oh, yes. She's not at all well, Cress. I didn't want to say anything until all this was over. Both lungs are affected and she doesn't seem to be responding to the antibiotics.'

'Will she ... will she be OK?'

'Murray seems to think so. At least, if she's in immediate danger, he hasn't said so to me. But then...'

'He would say, wouldn't he? D'you think Gil should see her?' Cressida asked. 'He's going to go back to France. We could go over to see Halcyon together and he could get a flight from Dublin – or Cork. Couldn't he?'

'I suppose so, but I think I'd be a bit careful, honey. For one thing Frank would have a fit. Gil hasn't seen her for years, has he? You said yourself it was better that way.'

'He should see her now.'

Grace wondered if her friend was having a breakdown. She had never figured out why Cressida had persisted in visiting the girl much more frequently than Murray did. But all those years before she had said, 'Val abandoned her, so I have to take some responsibility.' She'd been as good as her word. Even while she had been in Oxford, she had made time on her rare visits home to see the girl.

'But Gil doesn't know she's his sister, does he?' Grace said impatiently. Half-sister, she corrected herself silently. 'So what's the point?' In her view Cressida was acting very strangely. Halcyon could neither talk nor hear, and was locked in a strange half-world of her own. She rarely recognized even her most frequent visitors and when she did she was often aggressive and violent.

Until Grace had known Frank well enough to ask him, she'd always wondered how he coped with Halcyon. 'Visiting's one thing,' he'd burst out, 'but trying to integrate her into a family with more than enough emotional turmoil already to cope with is a step too far.' And so it had proved. When Katie May was a toddler they had stopped having Halcyon to stay, and from then on Cressida had visited the girl alone. Grace didn't know what straw had broken Frank's back, or even if there had been one, since neither he nor Cressida had offered an explanation. But why should they? The girl was Murray's ward, after all.

At that point Grace didn't admit to Cressida that she and Murray were having their own communication problems. They rarely discussed what Grace called the Halcyon situation, but the girl had become a bone of contention between them. Its latest manifestation was that Murray, who had slipped over to Ireland only for a few days, seemed curiously unwilling now to return. Something peculiar had happened to him: when he rang he talked non-stop about how beautiful and peaceful Halcyon was – 'She looks just like Evangeline did at the same age. She's so pleased I'm here. Do you know, Grace? She won't let go of my hand, poor baby.'

Grace shivered. 'Why not just let Gil go off for the rest of the summer, Cress? He'll be home in September. He can see her then, can't he? By the way,' she asked, keen to get off the subject, 'what's he going to read at university?'

Cressida hunched her shoulders. 'You tell

me. One moment it's marine engineering, next languages. He either wants to build boats or become a writer – take your pick.'

Grace laughed. 'He could easily do either. Or both. At that age they can conquer the world, do anything they want.' She smiled at her friend. 'Gil's a lovely boy, Cress. And don't worry about Halcyon. She's very strong, she'll recover.'

'You're right,' Cressida said slowly. 'I'll go and see her as soon as we get back to Dublin. Did I tell you Frank's all for leaving at the weekend? He wants to drive to Fishguard on Saturday or Sunday.' She pursed her lips.

'And is that what you want?'

'I don't know what I want.' Cressida ran her fingers through her hair. 'I thought it would all be so simple once Daddy died. I thought... Oh, Christ, Grace, I'm in a terrible muddle, I don't know what to do.'

Grace topped up Cressida's glass, which she'd emptied twice to no noticeable effect. 'It might help to get it off your chest.'

'Frank seems to think I'm too cosy with Paul Ford. He came into the kitchen while we were talking and was so rude. I was furious.'

'Paul does hang around a bit...' Grace began. It had been obvious to her for months that the GP was making a play for Cressida.

'Oh, for heaven's sake, Grace, don't you start. I like Paul, and I don't know how I'd have managed Daddy without him, but I've never fancied him. Never,' she added emphatically. 'He's easy to talk to, though.' She made a face. 'I'm making a frightful mess of everything.'

'Oh, for God's sake, Cressie, why do you always take the blame on yourself? You've had a hell of a few months – few years, when you think about it. Your father was very demanding.' The minute she said it Grace knew she'd made a mistake: her friend's expression was a mixture of hurt and anger.

Cressida clasped her hands and leaned across the table. 'We got on all right. Well, better and better, in fact. He was quite sweet to me towards the end. Which is something of a first. Every other relationship I've ever had started all right then went steadily downhill.'

Grace could hardly believe her ears. That Piers Hollingsworth had charm she could not deny, but he had also been completely self-centred and made a slave and skivvy of his only child. Not even little Katie May had been allowed to take precedence over the old man's demands. Grace, as Cressida's only real friend in Oxford, had observed the household on a daily basis and she was an unsentimental woman: she didn't understand how Piers Hollingsworth had been able so easily to bewitch the daughter he had neglected into devoting herself to him. No wonder Frank was fed up.

'Is Frank well, Cressie? He seems lethargic and he looks awfully pale.'

Cressida seemed not to hear her. 'I don't want to leave,' she whispered. 'I don't want to leave Oxford.'

'But I thought you hated living here, that you couldn't wait to get back to Ireland.'

'That's what I thought too. But now I can I'm suddenly terrified.'

'Are things that bad between you and Frank? Is that the problem?'

'No. Yes. Well, only partly.' Cressida leaned closer to Grace, but didn't meet her eye. She licked her forefinger and began to trace circles on the table. Then it all came out in a rush. 'Once Frank started hassling me to go back with him, I realized that I feel safe here. It's where I grew up, near enough. Cressida Hollings. Not Cressida Sweeney or Cressie Recaldo. I can pretend there is no past. Nobody knows about the murder or Val or any of that. I'm not perpetually looking over my shoulder, wondering when someone will blurt it out to Gil or Katie May.' She bit her lip. 'It wasn't Ireland I was so struck on; you know? It was Coribeen – Gil and me together in Coribeen. I can hardly remember what Val looked like any more. Anyway, he didn't matter. I was happy in Coribeen.'

Happy with a murderer who had abused her and her child? Some happy. Grace took Cressida's hands in hers. 'But, my dear, when I first met you, your poor face was covered in bruises, one eye was closed, little Gil's arm was broken. Cress, Val was being hunted for murder. He abused you, darling. Knocked you and Gil about. Frank looked after you both. He was there for you. He's a good, kind man. Cressie?'

Cressida dropped her head but her finger continued to move frantically in an endless circle. 'Yeah, a bloody saint. Don't you see?' she cried. 'That's the whole damn problem. With Frank I can't get away from the past, can't forget. I hate being an object of pity. Someone to be kind to. It's pathetic.' She began to weep softly. 'Oh, Grace. I think I was happiest when it was just Gil and me, when we were on our own, not being told what to do all the time. I should never have left the estuary.'

Grace sat quite still. And now, God help us, it's you and Katie May, she thought sadly. You don't want to share her. She almost gagged with the pity welling up in her. And the disquiet. 'Will I see you later, Cressie?' she asked gently. 'For supper?'

Cressida got up and hugged her. 'Thanks for letting me get all that stuff off my chest, Grace. Thanks for listening. Thanks for everything. I'd love to come.' She smiled. 'Matter of fact, I told Frank I'd meet him there. I'll just wait for Gil, then we'll come straight away.'

Gil put his head round the door. 'Hi. Where's everybody?'

Cressida turned to him with a smile. 'Dad's taken Katie May into Oxford. They're meeting us later at Grace's house for supper.'

'When?'

'In an hour or so.'

'Are we coming back here tonight?'

Grace looked at Cressida, who said, 'Afraid so.'

'Right. Did Dad tell you I got a flight for tomorrow?' he asked, then bolted.

Cressida threw up her arms. 'Nobody tells me anything,' she said, but she didn't seem too put out. 'Give me five minutes, Grace?'

'That was a bit of a thunderbolt. Will you be all right, Cress, with Gil going so soon?'

Cressida looked thoughtful. 'Yes,' she said, in a surprised voice. 'I think what I need is a bit of time. Funny how you don't realize what you're feeling till you say it out loud, isn't it?'

'What do you mean?'

'I don't want to go back to the way things were – with me and Frank, I mean, me the dependent one, him the tower of strength. I'd prefer something a bit more grown-up.

More equal. Frank's just going to have to hold on until I work out a way of achieving that.'

'Good for you,' said Grace.

Somehow or other her chat with Grace seemed to clear the air for Cressida, and things began to improve between her and Frank. This was partly, though inadvertently, due also to Tim Wallace, who rang the next morning just before Frank left for Stansted with Gil to try to renegotiate the deal he'd made with Cressida the previous day. Now he insisted she vacate the house over the weekend: his builder, he said, was free to start the renovations the following week. Cressida was unwilling to give in to his bullying but Frank suggested mildly that, since Tim's urgency matched their own, they could cut a deal. She responded by listing what had to be done: appointments with the bank, the solicitor, her father's clothes to be sorted and sent to Oxfam, NHS equipment returned to the hospital, furniture to be put into storage, papers gone through, the house cleaned. The list grew and grew. 'Bugger the cleaning,' Frank said robustly. 'If Wallace is so damned impatient, I don't see why we should bother about any cleaning – especially with builders coming in.'

'I don't believe there is a builder,' said

Cressida, and was about to add that whether there was or not she couldn't leave the house like a tip, when Gil took her by the shoulders. 'Look, Mum, stop being such a martyr. Haven't you done the slave bit long enough? Leave it. The house looks fine.'

'Why don't we just divide what's to be done between us?' Frank suggested. 'I'll sort out the wardrobe, then ring Mallam's and ask when they can collect the furniture.' He put his arm around Cressida's shoulders. 'The sooner it's done, angel, the sooner we can get home.'

Still Cressida demurred. 'I don't think we can sell anything until the will's gone through probate.'

'No, but surely the auctioneer has storage space. There's only a few items.'

'But his papers are stored in that tallboy.'

'Mum, we can box them up and you can go through them at Grace's house,' Gil interjected impatiently. 'Or at home. I bet most of it's junk anyway.'

Cressida smiled. 'No,' she said triumphantly. 'One of the drawers is full of watercolours. I haven't been through them but there's a few good names and Grace has promised to look them over with me.'

'Sure they're your father's?' Frank asked. 'Wasn't Marjorie an art dealer? They might have belonged to her.'

'No,' Cressida said firmly. 'They were my mother's. I remember them from when I was a child. They've always lived in that chest. Anyway, my father left them to me.'

'You've seen the will?'

'No, but he mentioned them a few months ago and I rang the solicitor when Tim started agitating, just to check. I wanted to be sure what belonged to me. Daddy lodged a list with Stephanie – the solicitor – when they moved back from Corfu.'

'Bit of luck, that,' Frank said. 'Careful, wasn't he?' Somehow he made it sound like an insult. It occurred to him that the contents of the drawer might have been sold to help pay for nursing care, but he held his tongue. The situation was already fraught enough.

'We've got to get out of here, Dad,' Gil said, 'or I'm going to miss my flight.' He hugged his mother. 'Stop fretting about everything, Mum. And don't worry about me. I'll be back in a couple of months.'

'Let's talk it over when I get back, Cress,' Frank shouted, out of the car window, as they drove away.

Duncreagh Listening Post *(archive)*
Local Gardai investigating the mysterious river death have been joined by detectives Superintendent Peter Coffey and Inspector Phil McBride. Supt Coffey leads the investigation.

Regression 3

After I left France I didn't go home or contact my parents. I worked in a Dublin city hotel for a couple of weeks to top up funds, then hitched south early one bright Monday morning. That was the easy bit. Cork to Duncreagh was trickier. The bus was a real old bone-shaker that stopped at every village *en route*. My plan was to go straight to Trianach but when I got off at Duncreagh and asked a passer-by the way, he said it was a good six miles off but I was sure to pick up a lift along the road. The extra bit of information was nice, but somehow I didn't fancy hitching and it was rather late in the day for such a long walk. I hadn't intended to work – time was too short – but I suddenly lost courage and wondered what on earth I was doing. My quest seemed silly and pointless. I wasn't sure what to do.

I was wandering around the town aimlessly when I spotted a card – advertising for a temporary waiter – in the window of a jazzy-looking restaurant called Provender. A woman standing at the bar waved at me when I peered in. The tables were set for dinner but it was too early for customers. I went inside, applied for the job and showed her the references from my various gap-year jobs that I carried around with me. 'You're well prepared, anyway.' She laughed. She looked a bit like my mother, but smaller and jollier. She made me do a practice run with plates and glasses. It was a doddle, but then it would be, after the months I'd spent doing silver-service. 'The lad working for me had to go home to Cork – to train for some athletic event, if you please,' she said. 'He won't be back for a fortnight so if you promise to stay that long the job's yours.'

Twenty minutes later I was being shown a small room, painted lurid pink, at the top of the house, which seemed to be part of the deal. 'If I've learned one thing it's that we can't keep staff unless we provide accommodation and three meals a day,' Mrs Cronin told me cheerily. 'The condition is that you stay for the whole two weeks, mind. If you don't I'll charge you rent for the room. Deal? We close on Mondays but otherwise it's a split shift every day. Sorry, but there it is.' She was nice but firm about what she would and would not tolerate. She talked a mile a minute but, apart from a cursory look at my references, didn't ask for any personal information. Suited me.

The restaurant was consistently busy: about forty covers at lunchtime and the same in the evenings. The menu wasn't vast but the grub was good – nothing special but plenty of it. On Fridays and Saturdays a jazz trio played in the evening. I'm not musical, like Frank and Katie May, but it seemed to be quite a draw because the place was packed on those evenings. Duncreagh people were friendly and great tippers: I earned much more than I had in either Germany or France. Trouble was, I worked so hard that I was completely knackered and spent most of my free time sleeping. During the whole fortnight I never once made it to Trianach. I don't think I was ready somehow. Sad.

There was one advantage to my fortnight in Duncreagh and one disadvantage, neither of which I realized until later: I could come and go in the town without comment, but I had no idea who among Provender's customers might be from Trianach. I suppose, in my innocence, I assumed that being a waiter made me kind of anonymous. The first thing you learn in the job is how to avoid looking at the customer directly.

You're the guy taking the order and nobody really notices you. Unless you spill the soup in their lap, of course. But I'm a bit better than that.

I had one definite bit of luck. The office of the local weekly newspaper, circulation around three thousand, was two doors down from the restaurant. It was called the *Duncreagh Listening Post* and took itself very seriously. My mind must have been working at half speed because it was a couple of days before I remembered that the newspaper was likely to have archives. The woman at the front desk was gullible enough to believe me when I told her I was doing a project for my English course at Oxford – she must have been impressed because she couldn't do enough for me. She was really nice and I felt mean for lying – or nearly lying.

In the following days I popped into the *Listening Post* for a browse whenever I could. I had assumed that the back numbers would be on microfilm or microfiche, but in fact they were all loosely bound in huge folders, month by month, year by year. That, of course, slowed my search. It was easy to get sidetracked, reading about local antics. Nothing remotely interesting turned up until I stopped messing about, retired to my pink bedroom and worked out a plan of attack. I stopped going through back issues randomly and became rigidly systematic.

First, I tried to work out when we had left the estuary. Using my birthday, in March, as a reference point, I thought I could make a stab at an approximate date. It took several visits for me to find a little article about a yacht going aground on the Baltiboys Rocks. The only reason I knew it must have been about Spain and my father was because it mentioned that 'A fisherman who went to the rescue was drowned.' Neither man was named. That was odd in itself because elsewhere in the paper names and vital statistics were scattered all over the place. I sat very still and felt a draught of freezing air swirl around my head. No names. No clues to guide me, except the improbability of the same sort of accident that had killed my father occurring twice in the same year, much less the same month.

I began to trawl through the two weeks on either side of the drowning, but anything remotely relevant was confined to just three issues: one before and two after the accident. I know it was only a local rag, a weekly one at that, with more interest in agricultural shows and local dignitaries than anything else, but I'd say that something fishy happened around Duncreagh in late September ten years before. Then I checked the old reports against some more recent ones and realized that the *Listening Post* was a far cry from national tabloids: no sensationalism, not even vague excitement. It seemed to worry about people's reputations. I suppose that if you lived all your life in a small place that would be important, since everyone knows everyone else. According to Mrs Cronin, 'Around here they know what you're having for breakfast before you open the fridge.' If that was true then it probably wasn't necessary to print names or lurid details. Still, a report about a woman found dead in her garden that gave neither name nor location struck me as pushing respectability a bit too far. But I was intrigued. During that week, and once or twice later on, I photocopied a series of articles I thought might be relevant and took them away to mull over later. Amazingly, most of them turned out to be like little pieces of a jigsaw and gave me plenty to worry about.

Before I knew it my two weeks at Provender were up. Before I said goodbye to Mrs Cronin and while there was still juice in my mobile-phone battery I left a flurry of carefully phrased messages for my parents and my little sister. Fortunately they didn't answer the phone personally – but that might have been because I rang at five a.m. I felt guilty that I hadn't sent Katie May any postcards and hoped that Thierry, one of the guys at the Port de Plaisance, had kept his promise to send one every few days from a bundle I'd written. I didn't hold out much hope. He was a nice guy and all, but generally spaced.

While I was at it I checked my text messages. There were two from Katie May, the first saying I was a dead loss for not writing (thumbs down for Thierry or maybe he didn't understand my franglais?), the second telling me that Dad had caved in and promised to buy her a puppy. Dear little Twink. There were none from my mother but she'd never managed to get to grips with texting: she left messages on my voicemail – the usual stuff about the weather, eating properly, getting enough rest, when was I coming home? I ran through the others, but paid little attention to them. I felt cut off from home and family. Drifting away without a thought of how I might ever get back.

Duncreagh had one more shock for me. I picked up a few bits and pieces before I set out, but only what would fit into my overstuffed backpack. As I wandered from shop to shop I passed an estate agent and in the window was a picture of a heart-stoppingly familiar house with a FOR SALE sign plastered over it. Monday closing seemed to apply to estate agents as well as restaurants: they were shut. I felt sick. I didn't know whether to go on or throw myself on Mrs Cronin's mercy and ask for my pink room back. When I left she told me I could have a job in her restaurant any time and I promised I'd return the following summer. Now I felt like running to her and saying, 'Take me back. Now, now, now.'

I had done little to prepare for the next bit of the adventure – if you could call it that. In the cold damp light of day I decided there was no point in the whole mad escapade. Tar was dead. Who would know me after so long? I was a stranger in my own birthplace, yet I hadn't really taken that on board until my first Saturday night in Provender when the band struck up and people began to dance. They didn't slouch around the way guys my age do, they really went for it – holding each other, laughing, singing, having fun. I was dead jealous, they looked so carefree and happy. An illusion? Maybe, but one I'd never experienced. I thought it unlikely that any of them would give a second thought to the grim stuff that preoccupied me. I made up my mind to go and take one good look at the estuary then give up.

It was a fine afternoon when I set out on the six-mile tramp, with a fresh breeze that smelt faintly of seaweed. One of the first things I noticed in that part of the world was how quickly your skin tasted of salt. I suppose it got carried in on the rain – and it rained a lot, which made my hair crinkle up in a tangled mop. Weird. I looked like a Sixties hippie.

One or two cars stopped to offer me a lift but I preferred to walk. Every step of the way seemed to carry me further and further from reality. I felt detached from the past, but I pressed on like a robot. I'd gone about three miles when the sea mist rolled in and everything disappeared. I was marooned in space until a passing delivery van almost ran me down. 'For God's sake, you put the heart across me,' the driver shouted. 'D'you want a lift?' This time I hopped in gratefully.

Ten minutes later I was in Passage South, simply because I didn't want to tell the driver where I was headed. While I was there something happened to make me revert to my original plan.

Passage South was crawling with foreign students. The man in the pub spoke to me in German. The fair hair, I suppose. I answered before I even thought about it. I'd done German at school for a few years, so we were about even, language-wise. I mumbled something about waiting for a ferry to the islands. It made things less complicated if they thought I was a stranger passing through. When I asked – *auf Deutsch, natürlich* – for a pint, I thought the barman was going to challenge me about my age but in the end he pushed the brimming glass across the counter with just enough hesitation to make sure I knew that he doubted I was old enough. I just grinned and said, 'Cheers.'

An old codger in sunglasses and a tweed cap was sitting further along the bar, chatting up a woman wearing leather trousers (fat bum) and a dark grey sweater with loads of silver jewellery. I nearly burst out laughing. She was all over him and he was gagging for it, which surprised me a bit because, with his get-up, I'd have put him down as gay. They didn't take any notice of me.

The walls were covered with framed sea charts. One even had tiny flashing lights that came on in rotation along the coast, marking the lighthouses. As my eye moved inland I found myself staring at Trianach and I realized I must have passed the causeway without noticing it before the van picked me up. For some reason that excited me. I finished my drink and checked the name over the door as I left. M & J Hussey didn't ring any bells. As I set off back up the road the mist lifted and I was spooked by how familiar the fuchsia hedgerows seemed. Or was it the scent of the wild woodbine? Something vaguely remembered twitched in my nostrils. I half expected to see the nameless faces that crowded my memory, but I recognized no one and I might have been invisible for all the attention passers-by paid me. I suppose I looked like all the other scruffs about the place. Another anonymous backpacker drifting through. I really thought I was invisible.

All over Trianach, newly built houses spread like a rash across the landscape. Plenty of cars passed me, most of them new and flash, but it was eerie how few pedestrians there were. Tar's tumbledown cottage stood apart from the other houses in the settlement – still, miraculously, not overlooked. It took me a while to locate it: I couldn't find anything that matched the picture in my head until I went down to the shore and found the inlet where he had kept his boat. I stood at the water's edge and it all came flooding back, as if someone had switched on a zillion-watt bulb. We'd trudged up that little path so many times, lugging the fish basket behind us, that my feet seemed to know the way and I found the garden without any difficulty. It was completely overgrown in front but the area behind the house was exactly as I remembered: mostly bare rock and natural sandstone paving. The track to the rotting back door was clear.

The sour smell of mice hit me as I entered. They had eaten most of the curtains and the stuffing spilled out of Tar's battered old sofa. I could hear them scuttle away when I sat down – a hungry cat would have been useful. There were bits of old boat engine on the table. I had to laugh when I saw that. It threw me right back. Poor old Tar. He was forever tinkering, but he could never get anything going again: if it was bust, it stayed bust.

I wondered why none of the neighbours had cleaned the place up. Had it lain empty since John Spain died? Besides mouse, it smelt of mould and damp, and something else I thought I recognized. There were large stains on the ceiling where the rain had leaked in. There was no electricity, and I'd brought no matches, but although there was plenty of turf in the outside shed I didn't want to attract attention by lighting a fire. I downed a can of beer and ate the squashed sandwiches I'd picked up in Duncreagh. By now it was growing dark and the cottage was chilly so I went into the little bedroom at the back and stretched out on the remains of John Spain's bed.

That was when the events of that last night on the estuary began to roll through my head like a faded film, and my memory returned with a vengeance. Because, you see, I had slept on that bed before.

Email from Sean Brophy to Fiona Moore
Fiona, New faces would be good. Very good in
fact. I'll brood on the suggestions you sent for a
day or so. Meantime I have a bit of good news
for you. Think it calls for another lunch. Next
Monday? Same time, same place? Sean

Chapter 8

After Gil left, the rest of the family went to stay with Grace in North Oxford, where, after a little nagging from her husband, Cressida at last agreed to go back to Ireland with Frank. She scribbled a note to Tim Wallace, promising to return at the end of the following week. Then she would also go through the watercolours and tie up whatever loose ends remained. Three days later, the Recaldos flew to Dublin, collected Frank's car from home and drove down to Waterford for the last day of filming. After it was over and the crew had dispersed, they went to a country-house hotel near Ballyhack, on the Wexford side of the Barrow river, for the weekend.

The glorious weather held up and with it their spirits. 'Why don't we live here?' Katie May asked one afternoon, as the three strolled by the river.

As she ran ahead, Cressida and Frank looked at each other enquiringly. 'You know, I was just thinking that myself,' Frank remarked. 'Here, or somewhere like it. We don't need to stay in Dublin now that Gil's finished school, do we? If we sold the house we could afford quite a nice place in the country.

Cressida's response disappointed him. 'You really think we'd get that much for the house?'

'At least. And my income is only going to improve, surely.'

'Oh, Frank, of course it will.' She smiled at last. 'It would be wonderful – I've been dreading going back to the house. Let's do it. As long as there's a school nearby for Katie May.'

'We could start looking now, if you like,' Frank said tentatively. He hoped it was just the house she was dreading. 'List your preferences.'

'You first.'

'Somewhere on a river.'

'Estuary,' Cressida cut in. 'It has to be near the sea too.'

Frank raised her hand to his lips. 'Nothing I'd like better, love.' He hugged her to him and, for the first time in ages, she responded warmly.

'Garden. Big garden. I could grow herbs.'

'Big kitchen.'

'Big dog,' Katie May shouted. 'Like Finnegan.' Finnegan, their red setter, had lived to a great age and died just before Cressida went to Oxford. 'And a massive bedroom with yellow curtains.' Yellow was her favourite colour.

Cressida brushed back her hair. Her eyes sparkled. 'Oh, Frank, oh, darling, wouldn't it be fine? Let's do it.'

He grinned down at her. 'Right, we'll decide exactly what we want and then start the search. If we aren't too particular which county, we should have a good choice. It'll have to be near enough a town for shopping, library, bookshop. A train link with Dublin would be good. Anything else?' He linked Cressida's arm. 'As long as we're all together again, my own darling, I don't give a damn where it is. Wicklow, Wexford, Waterford, Kerry, Clare, Galway, Donegal.' He skipped around the Irish coast with agility but neatly missed out Cork, although it was in both their minds. 'Of course, we could always extend the cottage,' he added thoughtfully.

'Oh, no. I like it as it is,' Cressida demurred. 'Anyway, it's too remote for all year round.' This was true: the cottage, near Castlebrion, was seven or eight miles from the nearest school. They'd originally bought it to be near Frank's family. 'I think I'd like to get a job if I can,' she said, 'now that Katie's in school.'

'That would be great,' he said, and meant it. He cupped Cressida's face in his hands. 'I feel a right pig for being so mealy-mouthed that time you were after the gallery job. I'm very sorry about that. Ashamed. I wake up sometimes and feel sick at how stupid I was.'

'It was the wrong time, love.' She smiled ruefully. 'No, I mean it. It really was the wrong time, when you think what the next year brought, with my father and every-thing. I'm glad it's over,' she added quietly, 'but I'm also glad I did it. Looked after him.'

'You're a kind and thoughtful woman, Cress. I hope...' he trod carefully, knowing how touchy she could be on the subject of her father '...I just hope he showed some appreciation.'

Cressida shrugged. 'Appreciation wasn't his forte. I did it for me as well, you know.'

'Yes, I know. Have you anything in mind, jobwise?' he asked lightly.

Cressida laughed. 'Well, not nursing, I can tell you that much. I've had it up to here with bedpans. I'll just keep an eye open. But if we're going to move from Dublin–' She stopped suddenly. 'Frank? What about Phil McBride? Won't he be upset if you jack in your work at the Phoenix Park?'

114

Frank gave her hair a little tug. 'Or is it my plots you're thinking of? Would inspiration dry up if I didn't keep my detecting hand in?' he teased. 'I've hardly done anything for Phil this past year,' he added carelessly, and could have kicked himself. One of the fictions he had maintained after Gil finished school was that his part-time job at Garda headquarters kept him in Dublin.

It might have been a passing cloud that cast a shadow over Cressida's face but the atmosphere chilled a little. She glanced at him sideways, but said nothing. They caught up with their daughter and found a small secluded beach at the mouth of the river where they went for a cold, swift, silent swim. There was no more talk of moving house.

The following day Murray Magraw drove over from Tipperary and joined them for lunch. Afterwards Cressida went with him to visit Halcyon, who was still in Clonmel hospital. From there, she planned to travel by train to Dublin and then on to Oxford while Frank and Katie May went to the cottage for a few days. She promised to be back home in Dublin by the end of the following week.

As soon as she had left the atmosphere lightened but Frank felt guilty and disloyal for even thinking it. He and his daughter drove across country to Kerry for the weekend. Frank was feeling unwell but Katie May was in her element. The heatwave continued, she swam and played with her cousins who lived a couple of miles away, while Frank tried and failed to come up with a schema for his next book. Usually he never lacked good ideas but this time inspiration eluded him. He half wondered if this was divine intervention, chastising him for the hubris of his claim that he could devise plots independently of his police work. Or, more likely, for fibbing. Either way, coming up with a worthwhile plot proved unaccountably difficult.

Having Katie May to himself was compensation, and he had time at last to become easy with the little girl – or, rather, her slave. She'd had a solitary time of it in Oxford and she adored having her father to boss around. The Castlebrion cottage was in the township of Dunquin, in beautiful rugged country where he'd set the first of his travel series. On a good day it was possible to get a boat to the Great Blasket island, but although it was warm and sunny there were also gusting winds so the ferry wasn't running. Katie May had been promised a trip but didn't seem unduly bothered when it fell through. Soon it was as if they had never been apart and he found himself wishing that the hiatus would last for ever. He had always been at his best one to one.

Cressida phoned each morning and promised she'd soon join them. When? When everything was sorted. The list of hitches lengthened: the solicitor had been delayed coming back from holiday, the insurance company questioned the cost of the funeral, Grace had advised her to have some of the watercolours valued at Sotheby's, Marjorie's son Tim was being stroppy about everything – the inventory, the state of the house, the neglected garden. 'He's threatening to get it all put in order professionally and bill us, Frank. It'll cost a bomb.'

'Tell him to go to hell,' Frank said dourly. 'If you don't, I will.'

'I already did. I completely lost it yesterday. We had a screaming match in the garden in full view of the neighbours.'

'That must have livened things up for you.'

'He wouldn't let me into the house. Said I'd taken stuff that belonged to his mother. Fortunately I'd arranged for Stephanie to come. She sorted Tim out, pronto.'

'So what good are you doing over there? Why don't you leave the pair of them to it and come home? We miss you.'

'Well, I would, except the car broke down. The bloody clutch cable needs replacing. I've booked it in for Monday. I should be all set for Wednesday – Friday at the latest.' For once she didn't apologize, Frank noted. He didn't believe a word of it. Whatever was keeping his wife in Oxford, he doubted it was the clutch cable of a three-year-old Volkswagen Beetle, the one thing her father had provided for her. He felt resentful and confused, wondering if the good-looking, healthy doctor had something to do with her reluctance to leave Elsfield – then squashed the idea. Cressida was too disengaged to be open to falling in love. Wasn't she? Heigh-ho, he thought, one step forward and two back. His emotions had been in turmoil since his father-in-law's death. The brief, happy rapprochement in Waterford rapidly faded into confusion. Had the idea of moving released her old demons, made her think of the Glár estuary again? He knew her heart was still there. Yet somehow, on that glorious day in Ballyhack, she'd been able to voice her preference for an estuary – any estuary – without strain. Or had he imagined it? The increasing angina attacks terrified him. He desperately needed his wife. She has to come of her own accord, he kept telling himself. She has to want to be with me.

Poor Frank was too busy feeling martyred to realize how irrational he was being. Had that chance remark about giving up his police work rekindled her resentment at his refusal to move to Oxford? Once upon a time they had discussed everything, but separation had encouraged their natural inclination to withdraw into themselves. They were both very private people with a fragile hold on trust.

Why was marriage such a roller-coaster? he asked himself angrily, feeling aggrieved and not a little hard-done-by.

Duncreagh Listening Post *(archive)*
Murdered woman was international art expert. She was recovering from recent surgery when she was felled. A number of people are helping Gardai with their inquiries. No one has yet been charged.

Regression 4

I slept for almost sixteen hours, until the sunshine woke me around six the next morning. I lay on the bed, trying to ignore the smell of decay, and willed myself back into the mindset that had led me so far. I decided I wouldn't give up. I had enough provisions to last me a few days, if I was careful. My time was my own. I got up and began to explore. That was when my problems really started.

The landscape was nothing like the version in my head. The real thing was a distortion of my childhood dream, which was uncluttered: bright green grass, grey rocks, brown and purple hills. I had a clear picture of individual houses because there had been so few. Now there were buildings scattered all over the place, obscuring my landmarks. What I remembered was simple, almost abstract beauty, *empty* except for three or four buildings that had seemed so monumental I hadn't even thought of the possibility of missing them. Now either they didn't exist or were lost among the bright new houses, scattered randomly like pebbles.

I wondered if it was because I'd approached Trianach from the land. Even after tramping every inch of it, endlessly retracing my footsteps up and down the waterline and the lanes in search of familiar sights, nothing seemed to fit. Fences had been thrown up, hedges planted and bog-roll trees marked out the boundaries. The contours of the land were not so crisp or clearly defined but, then, maybe they never had been. The mountain backdrop, when it was visible through the mist or the lashing rain, was smaller in scale, not nearly as impressive as I recalled. I was looking for something huge and I didn't find it. In my dreams I saw myself wandering through familiar haunts with Tar, but when I woke the sense of belonging evaporated and I felt like a stranger, alien in what I'd hoped would be my refuge.

The river was different too. I'd pictured myself gliding over it so many times, face down on the glassy surface. There was no glassy surface now – had there ever been? Each day brought a change of weather; strong sea breezes freshening to downright gales were the only constant as I tramped up and down the roads and the riverbank until I was completely confused. And lost.

I couldn't bring myself to go into Passage South and there was no way I was going to walk to Duncreagh. I got more and more depressed. The squalid business of surviving seemed to take up most of my time. I slept later and later in the musty old bed, only getting up when my growling stomach woke me. Hunger was ever-present; that, and a deep chill that settled into my clothes until I wondered if I was carting the dank cottage around on my back like a snail. The smell of mould stuck in my nostrils like rotting cheese. My brain became so sluggish that the idea of shifting my landmark search *from the river* evaded me for four days. But once the idea struck, I knew it was the only way that any of it would make sense.

When I was a child, I was always in some boat or other, crossing and recrossing the estuary. Occasionally it was my father's yacht, *Azurra*, but more usually I was with Tar. Cressie was never keen on boats or being on the water. What she liked was looking at the river, living and walking alongside it. But, like a true countrywoman, she kept her distance. She never swam and she loathed the yacht. Somehow I was aware that it wasn't just fear of the sea that guided her, more fear of my father. I didn't like being on the yacht either. It had been only in the hours and days when he was at sea – and out of the way – that we were truly happy and relaxed. Did I contribute to this state of affairs? Apart from kneeling by my bed each night and praying that my horrible father would leave us in peace? For ever and ever. Amen.

Alone in Spain's cottage this uncomfortable thought disturbed my fixed sense of things. Until now I was certain that my unhappiness was a result of my parents not getting on. They had avoided each other, and it bothered me that I couldn't recall ever seeing them smiling and happy together. I had only a hazy memory of when the violence had started because nothing much then had penetrated my silent little world – but, sure as hell, once it did, Coribeen was filled with fear, which I was certain I could see and feel, even touch. Cressie must have felt it too because, towards the end, whenever we went into the house the two of us would stand in the hall, holding hands and sniffing the air in the way our dog Finnegan did. Holding our breath, waiting for the next explosion. If my mother knew how much I remembered and how much I've discovered about us, the Sweeneys, she would die. *Gil Sweeney, murderer's son.*

Why or how did the marriage become

such a nightmare? I'll tell you something for nothing: all my life I held Sweeney responsible and blamed him and him alone. Now that I was back where it all started, that seemed too neat. Too juvenile. Did couples turn savage for no reason? Was Cressie only a victim? Helpless, as our family fell apart? That was certainly how I had seen it as a little boy when I gave her my total, unquestioning devotion. But in the couple of days around Grandfather's funeral, as I watched Cressie and Frank circling each other, saying one thing and looking another, I wasn't sure of anything any more.

When I was small, Cressie was my heroine. I thought she was a goddess. She was, without a doubt, the most important person in my life. My father was a marginal figure and, until he turned vicious, hardly impinged at all. In the glory days when the business in London was booming, there were parties in the house all the time. Sometimes I'd wander downstairs to find the dining room filled with big red-faced men and women who puffed at cigarettes while Cressie danced attendance. I remembered them as legs: long corduroy legs, brown brogues, shiny black stockings on slim calves, the women's high heels dangling in my face when I hid under the table. An occasional face would bend to smile or pinch my cheek – playfully – but, taking my cue from Cressie, I ignored these tentative overtures, fearful of entering the enemy camp. Once Sweeney and the gang were safely aboard the yacht, Cressie and I would take off, sometimes to see John Spain or else to a town, to a gallery of some sort, with big bright pictures on white walls and a huge piano in the centre of the polished floor. In retrospect, those times were coloured with a rosy glow of safety and contentment. Although I searched I didn't find anything like the gallery around Duncreagh. Maybe it was in Daingean, about ten miles further on. Not that it mattered: there were other places I was more anxious to find.

I haven't a clue why I didn't think of a boat first. Except for money – or lack of it. I'd recently worked at a marina so I knew how expensive they were to hire and then, of course, there'd be all that identification stuff to go through. There were a few aluminium tubs lying face down at the cove that I thought of borrowing – and probably would have done, had I been able to find a decent pair of oars. I remembered seeing a boat-yard as I tramped from Duncreagh to Passage South – at least, I was sure I had, although it wasn't marked on the faded old map I'd found in the cottage. I had a vague idea it might be near the old bridge where the river comes closest to the road, but that was a fair step away, three or four miles from the Trianach causeway along the Duncreagh road. It would be easier to investigate nearer possibilities before traipsing all that way. There was certainly a yard near the marina in Passage South but somehow that was a bit public, too full of people. I didn't want to explain myself at this stage. Not at any stage, for that matter. I couldn't bear the thought of people rattling my family skeletons or knowing my story before I knew it myself. I suppose I was scared of what I might discover about my background. There's some advantage in anonymity. I kind of relished the sense of freedom. Anyway, it was teeming with rain for the first three days. Unbelievable. It just poured down, hour after hour. I suppose it must have rained like this when I was a kid but, funny thing, I only remember the sun.

It was hunger rather than curiosity that eventually got to me. Tramping across the causeway from Trianach one late evening in search of something to eat, I noticed the lights of a wayside pub I had missed when I first searched for John Spain's cottage. There was a black Mercedes parked outside. Inside, there were only a few people but it was so small and dim that it looked full. There was a guy at the bar and two men at a side table, deep in conversation. A chalked blackboard offered fresh mussels and chips. I asked for a double order and a pint of lager, and sat by the fire to wait. The man at the bar left, and as he passed me I thought I recognized him as the guy who'd been in Hussey's bar the first day. I ignored him. No sign of the girlfriend but he was still in the cap and glasses. Bit of a dresser. He had a leather coat draped around his shoulders. *Ve haf veys of making you talk.* Posy git. The two tough-looking men at the table continued their conversation, which, as far as I could make out, consisted of a series of amiable grunts. They had about six teeth between the pair of them.

I was half-way through my plate of mussels when one left and the other man, the wirier of the two, pulled his chair nearer to my table. 'Do ye enjoy them things?' he asked, pointing at the mussels.

'Yeah,' I said. 'Don't you?'

He gave a loud guffaw. 'Wouldn't touch them – well, apart from handling them. Myself and the brother,' he nodded at the door, 'own the mussel beds at the mouth of the estuary. Those are some of ours. Are they all right, then?'

'They're good. Great,' I said, and he looked pleased. I suddenly had a brilliant idea. 'D'you have any work going? Casual? Part-time?'

'There might be, then. For how long were

you thinkin' of?'

'Couple of weeks? I'm staying with friends, I like to pay my way,' I said, not sure he believed me. In fact, I'm certain he didn't. He looked like an inquisitive ferret.

'Not permanent and pensionable, then? By gor, that's a relief. Would you be up at the university?'

I was going to say something snippy, like 'In a manner of speaking,' or 'Mind your own business,' but he had something I wanted the use of, so I told him the truth: 'Not till October.'

'Ye look like a strong lad. Can ye handle a boat? It gets rough out there.'

'Yeah. I sculled at school and I can sail a dinghy. My dad taught me,' I added winsomely, to add credibility.

He took my hand and turned it over. 'You'd find it hard on those soft hands,' he said. 'The old shells'd cut the fingers off of ye. What do you think?' he asked, his sharp little eyes twinkling furiously. Test question.

'I could wear gloves, couldn't I?'

He threw back his head and laughed. 'Well, now, young fella, you could indeed. I'll find something for you. You're in luck. My nephew that was helping out for the summer walked off the job this morning. The ungrateful scut,' he added, and I wondered what I was letting myself in for. Too late.

'I could give a week's work, that's all. Four hours every morning. That OK? One week certain, after that the tourist trade begins to fall off and me and the brother can manage on our own. Six quid an hour old money – you'll have to work out what that is in euros yourself. I've as little as possible to do with those things. So, if you want to try it, meet me tomorrow morning and we'll see how you get on. The old slipway at six o'clock sharp. You know where that is?'

'I can find it,' I said, a bit dubiously.

'Fine so. See you then.' He pushed back his chair and stood up, his face wrinkled in an impish grin. 'What's your name, young fella?' he asked, not quite catching me by surprise.

'Hollings.'

'Oh? Hollings? Right so.' He held out his hand. 'Mick Sullivan – the brother is called George. By the way, the slipway's up beyond the Old Corn Store, and that's about a mile down-river from Spain's Cove.' He chuckled. 'You can walk it in low tide, otherwise you'll have to go by the road. You know where it is, don't you?'

I hoped he didn't notice my jaw drop.

Chapter 9

'How ill is she?' Cressida asked Murray, as she settled into the car.

'Bad. Both lungs are affected now.' His soft American drawl betrayed no sign of his years in Oxford. In normal times, when they saw each other regularly, Murray was affability itself, but on the cross-country drive from Ballyhack to the Clonmel hospital, with Halcyon's future in the balance, they were preoccupied with much the same thoughts. If the girl lived, there would be the continued strain of ensuring proper residential care for her. If she died, relief would be tempered with guilt, but, even so, it would be easier to live with. Cressida wanted desperately to talk it over, but Murray wasn't his usual garrulous self: she could hardly drag a word out of him. She stopped trying and they fell into gloomy, uncomfortable silence.

Something had changed in Murray. He had no wish to discuss or analyse his feelings – he had enough of that from Grace. He blamed VJ Sweeney for the plight he was in and, by default, Cressida. He knew it wasn't fair but he couldn't help it. The fact that she tried to atone for her late husband's cruelty to and neglect of his natural daughter didn't wash with Murray. Never had. 'Cressie's not to blame,' Grace always protested. 'You can't lump her with Sweeney. Think how it must have been for her.'

From the beginning Cressida had made Murray feel unworthy. He resented the way, without any prompting, she had willingly visited Halcyon while he only did so because of the vow his murdered cousin had wheedled out of him. Over the years he had begun to admit, grudgingly, how much of the burden Cressida had lifted from his shoulders. His present irritability was petty: while he had failed to find suitable care for his young cousin, Cressida had found a vacancy in a home right on their Oxford doorstep – just as she was bowing out and returning to Dublin. 'And you think that was deliberate, do you?' Grace had asked tersely. 'For God's sake, Murray, get real. You've been trying to find care for her in Ireland for months. You said yourself it was hopeless. Look at you, you're worn out flying backwards and forwards.' Mercifully, Grace stopped short of asking him why, if he was so fond of Halcyon, he'd kept her in her mountain eyrie for so long. Out of the way and out of sight.

'What happens if it doesn't work? I really couldn't bear to have her living with us,' he said, plaintively. 'I think I'd have a nervous breakdown.'

Grace gave him one of her clear-eyed stares. 'Just you?' she asked quietly. 'I think you're forgetting, Murray, that we will *both* have to deal with her.' They did not refer to Grace's long anticipation of such a crisis then or at any other time, though it hovered like a sword between them. Grace, who had never had a good word for Evangeline, had always claimed that Murray's cousin had taken unfair advantage of his good nature, but what she meant was that neither of them had had the courtesy to ask *her* opinion of the arrangement.

Evangeline hadn't liked Grace but, then, she'd not liked his first wife or any of his girlfriends. In dark moments Murray allowed himself to wonder if his cousin had intended the strain she'd placed on his marriage when she reclaimed him as her slave by bequeathing him the child she could not cope with herself. Perhaps she was re-enacting the relationship they'd had as adolescents when she had always dominated him. The worst thing of all was that, as time went by, he was less and less inclined to discuss his disquiet with Grace.

Murray looked at Cressida out of the corner of his eye, marvelling that he had never before noticed how beautiful she was. But remote: she was miles away, in a world of her own. He wondered what dark thoughts were passing through her head. Though she and Frank had appeared to be in reasonable form over lunch, he had sensed an underlying tension between them, particularly when Frank mentioned that they were considering moving out of Dublin. 'Now that our boat has come in,' was how he had put it. 'We prefer the country, preferably near the coast somewhere,' he added, then went on to describe the sort of house they were looking for and the location. It sounded exactly like the Glár estuary to Murray, but as he could see Cressida growing agitated he didn't remark on it. And the same disquiet stopped him mentioning that he had met Rose O'Faolain, an old friend of hers, at an auction near Thurles the previous week.

Halcyon had had a bad night, and he'd only gone to the auction because Grace had phoned to say that she'd received the catalogue and it might be worth while taking a look at a small number of books of Irish interest included in the sale. Murray couldn't resist: the late Alex Mure Robertson was known chiefly for his art collection so it was safe to assume that few would consider the sale worth the detour. And thus it proved: there were only a handful of book people among the stampede of art dealers. But, as it happened, Murray had been there barely five minutes when he recognized a face from the past.

Some months after Evangeline's death Rose O'Faolain had arranged a simple memorial service in Daingean where she had an art gallery. 'Evangeline did a lot of catalogue notes for me over the years and I feel I'd like to do a little something in return,' she said. Murray was touched but, apart from a letter of thanks, he had not kept in touch. However, the art dealer was not easily forgotten.

The passing years had done nothing to subdue Rose O'Faolain – if anything, she was even larger and more flamboyant. Murray didn't think she'd recognize him and was shy of coming forward, but he didn't have to. 'Well, if it isn't Mr Magraw. You *are* the bookseller, aren't you? Evangeline Walter's cousin?' She held out her hand. 'What a very nice surprise. Mure was a great admirer of Evangeline,' she gushed. 'A great admirer.' She looked around. 'Is your wife with you? No? That's a pity.' She held her face to his conspiratorially. 'I suppose it's the books you're after.' She laughed merrily. 'How is Grace? I remember her well – lovely woman. I'm delighted to see you after all this time,' she said breathlessly, then patted her capacious bosom. 'I'll have to give up the old smoking,' she wheezed, 'or it'll be the death of me. How *are* you?'

Murray smiled. 'I'm well. And pleased to see a familiar face, Mrs O'Faolain.'

'Oh dear me, that's much too formal. Rose, remember?' They shook hands.

'Murray,' he mumbled, a little overwhelmed, and even more so when she said, 'Still in Oxford?' But he hadn't realized that Grace and Rose had kept in touch.

'Yes, although we don't have the shop any more, we work from home,' he said. 'I guess we've down-sized.'

'Aha, same as myself. It's easier on the nerves, isn't it? As well as more economical.'

'Sure is. And you don't have to get up so early in the morning.'

'Isn't it true for you?' She had another coughing fit. 'What about a spot of lunch? I've got more or less everything I earmarked, and the books don't come up till about three o'clock so we've a bit of time for a chat.

135

There's a buffet downstairs.' This was news to Murray, and he followed meekly in her footsteps.

'Buffet' was stretching it, but there were heaped plates of sandwiches and open bottles of wine on a long refectory table in the medieval dining room. Rose and Murray settled themselves at a small table by the roaring fire, a glass of cheap burgundy apiece. They chatted about the collection, their businesses, this and that, and Murray only gradually became aware that Rose was steering the conversation round to Cressida.

'Do you have anyone working for you, or do you and Grace manage the business on your own these days?' she asked.

'We have secretarial help and a book-keeper, the rest we manage. Or did. For the past few years a friend has been giving us a hand, mostly Grace's end of things – you know that she's interested in ephemera with a regional slant. These days, she likes good illustrations – chapbooks, pamphlets, prints, that kind of thing – which often turn up in lousy condition. Grace used to do her own conservation and was able to ... er ... train her up.' He looked up and gave his goofy, rather charming smile. 'Turned out very well, but she's leaving Oxford soon so I guess we're back to square one. We'll miss her.'

'That wouldn't be Cressida Recaldo, by any chance?' Rose asked.

Murray gave a loud guffaw. 'The very same. You knew she was in Oxford, I take it?'

Rose covered her face with her hand. 'Sorry, I'm not very subtle, am I? Yes, I'd heard on the grapevine. She used to work for me, you know. I was very fond of that girl. Such a dreadful business. I think it's great you've become friends. I congratulate you. It can't have been easy for you, one way and another. Or for Cressie and Frank.' And for the next half-hour Rose pumped Murray for news of her 'young friends'. It was only as they were about to part that she mentioned Cressida's old home was on the market again. 'And considering house prices these days, it's a bargain. Though, mind you, it's been empty since Cressie left, and allowed to moulder, and what with the damp and everything...'

'You've seen it?'

'Well, yes,' Rose admitted, with a faint blush. 'I drove over last week, as a matter of fact. Curiosity got the better of me.' She grinned. 'To be honest it wasn't just curiosity. Marcus Brady's an old friend.' She half pointed at the auctioneer, who was deep in conversation at the other end of the room. 'He told me he'd sent you the sale catalogue so I hoped either you or Grace would be here...' She shrugged. 'Oh, all right, I'll come clean. I asked him to send it to you, so I was looking out for you. Amn't I the terrible old meddler altogether?' she said archly.

Murray raised his eyebrows. 'Well, Rose, I wouldn't say that, but I'm not sure why you're telling me all this,' he said. '*I* quite liked the estuary but Grace didn't. It spooked her. But that's another story.

'Hmm,' murmured Rose. 'You have me all figured out, haven't you, Murray Magraw? As it happens, I was really thinking about Cressie. Is her father still to the good?'

'You're remarkably well informed, Rose.' He chuckled then put on a solemn face. 'No. As a matter of fact he passed away a coupla days ago. Cressie was with him to the bitter end. Four years she's been waiting on the old tyrant, hand and foot. Frank's pretty browned off with the situation.'

'They *are* still together, aren't they?' she asked, in some alarm.

Murray shifted uncomfortably in his seat. 'Grace thinks they'll work it out,' he mumbled, 'but I wouldn't want to bet on it.' He looked up. 'Frank's doing very well – as I'm sure you know. One of his novels is being filmed.'

But Rose wasn't to be sidetracked. 'Look,' she said gently, 'I'm not just being nosy. I know – knew – Cressie better than most.

She worked for me for years and I became very attached to her and the little boy. After the murder...' Rose put her hand to her lips. 'Oh dear me, my big mouth. I keep forgetting Evangeline is ... was... I'm sorry. How is her daughter? Halcyon, isn't it?'

'Yes.' Murray nodded slowly. 'Poor kid's in hospital in Clonmel. That's one of the reasons I'm over here right now. You knew she was in a home, cared for by the nuns, not far from here? Near Twomileboris? Well, it was closed down. They haven't had any vocations for years. Halcyon and Sister Angela, the nun who cared for her, moved on to a smaller convent in Clonmel but then the poor old nun died a few months ago. Hally fell apart. Refused to eat, cried all the time. Poor kid's pretty ill.'

'That's terrible,' Rose said. 'I don't believe I ever saw her.'

'You may have, without realizing it,' Murray said. 'She was at John Spain's ... er ... funeral.'

'Oh? Was she?' Rose frowned. 'That wasn't the girl Cressie was minding? I thought at the time she looked a bit like Gil.'

'Oh? I don't think so.' Murray's tone was sour. 'Hally has a habit of tagging on to the youngest in any company – I guess it was that. In fact, she looks remarkably like Evangeline did at her age,' he said. Had he looked up he would have seen Rose gazing at him pityingly. 'I've grown very fond of her – we have no kids of our own, y'know, Grace and me. Hally is the nearest we ... *I* got to family. I see her as much as I can. She used to be hard to manage but now, just in the last little while, she's been really sweet. Cute, too. Grace and I talked about having her at home with us, but Grace doesn't care for the idea.' He looked at Rose for sympathy but received a vague stare.

Rose was feeling a bit of a fraud, cheap, and didn't quite know what to do about it. Should she come clean? Murray obviously hadn't a clue that his wife had met her on a couple of occasions when she had been over *alone* to see Halcyon Walter. Rose knew all about the circumstances of Grace's first meeting with the girl, two days after Evangeline was murdered. Halcyon had been seventeen or so at the time but with a mental age of three or four. Murray had not told Grace that he had agreed to become her legal guardian – in fairness, he had probably thought Evangeline would outlive him, but she had omitted to tell him she had cancer: she had been dying when she was murdered. So the Magraws had arrived to find Evangeline dead and responsibility for the girl dumped on them. As Grace herself had said, 'I was flabbergasted. I had no idea how to manage her and Murray hadn't a clue either. God knows what we'd have done if Cressie hadn't stepped in.'

'Cressida helped out with the girl, didn't she?' said Rose softly.

'Yeah, for a while, until she had her own daughter. Hally used to go to them weekends sometimes, that kinda thing, but it all stopped when she came to Oxford to nurse her dad. I guess it was down to me after that.'

'Oh?' said Rose. The story was turning into a nifty little three-decker with Murray self-cast as hero. Worse, a repetitious, self-congratulatory hero. Rose was disappointed: she'd had him down as the easy–going, humorous type.

'Everything was hunky-dory until Sister Angela passed on. Hally just turned her face to the wall. I've been back and forth almost every week for the past four months or so. Now she caught pneumonia and she's not responding to antibiotics, poor lamb.'

'Oh, I somehow thought...' But Rose didn't disclose what she was thinking. 'I hope she'll be better soon,' she said kindly, and out of habit added, 'Is there anything I can do?'

Murray looked at her. 'Thank you, Rose,' he said. 'I'll never forget how you managed that memorial service for Evangeline.' He leaned towards her. 'Nobody else did a thing, y'know. Even her great pal O'Dowd walked away. I hope you know how much I appreciate your efforts. Perhaps...' He hesitated. 'If anything ... if poor Hally...' He ran his fingers through his thinning hair. 'If Halcyon... You seem to know how these things – funerals ... work.'

'What about the nuns? They would–'

'Like I said, the original home's closed down. The nuns in Clonmel, the few who are left, hardly know her. I think we'd have to do it ourselves.'

'Oh, well, in that case, Murray, just give me a call.' She passed him her business card. 'Any time. You can count on me.' She got up slowly and fetched herself another glass of wine.

When she got back Murray was in contrite mode. 'Rose? I'm sorry for sounding off. Stress, I guess. Cressie's done a lot for Hally and I'm really grateful. It's just that since her dad's illness...' He trailed off. 'You know how it is. We're very close to Cress and Frank.' He gave her a shamefaced grin. 'Some friend I am, huh?'

'That's OK, Murray. It happens to us all from time to time. You're looking worn out, if you don't mind my saying so.'

'I *feel* worn out.' He grinned again. 'So, you think Frank and Cress would be interested in the house on the estuary?' he asked.

'I'm not sure, but Coribeen was more than

a house to Cressie. She adored the place. I used to wonder how a young woman could live in such isolation – but, then, being alone never bothered Cressie.' Rose leaned closer. 'Val Sweeney was brutal to her, you know, and the child as well. I always had the feeling that Gil's disability... VJ was a big man, athletic and strong.' Rose drew herself up. 'I'm sorry, I shouldn't be gossiping like this.'

'So why would she go back? The place must be full of bad memories.'

'It's all a long time ago. Very few people would remember anything about it.'

'I understood Jer O'Dowd bought the house. Wasn't there to be a golf course or a marina or something?' He scratched his head. 'Funny guy. Never could quite figure him.'

'It seems he couldn't get planning permission – that's what I was told, anyway. If it's true, it would have been a first.' She gave a derisive little snort. 'They say the life went out of him after Evangeline was killed.' She didn't add her informant's other remarks: that he and Evangeline were like a pair of old queens, the one as camp as the other. That Smiler had never managed to come out of the closet and continued to make a right eejit of himself chasing after married women, usually blow-ins. 'Poor old sod,' she murmured, half to herself.

'You know him well?'

'Not directly, but a couple I know live on Trianach. Matter of fact, they bought Evangeline's house from O'Dowd a few years ago and run it as a guest-house. Cressie knows them – Marilyn used to char for her.'

'Ah. The Donovans. They bought Evangeline's furniture too.' He raised his eyebrows. 'Not so much bought, as obliged me by taking the stuff off my hands. Real sharp, they were,' he murmured, suddenly repelled. At the same time, pity for Cressida stirred in him. So much was known about her, all her misfortunes gossiped and gloated over. Rose had only just stopped short of blaming Sweeney for Gil's disability and, by implication, Halcyon's – about which Murray had agonized for years. He didn't wonder that Cressie had done a runner. How could she have protected Gil if she had stayed? Or lived down the rumours about her husband? Or that the investigating policeman was her lover – which he and Grace had assumed to be the case from the first moment they saw the pair together, three days after poor Vangie was killed? Rose claimed that after all those years people would have forgotten the scandal. Not so you'd notice, Murray thought wryly, as he listened to her prattle.

He stood up. 'Time to go, I guess. Look,

I'm sorry, Rose, you're going to have to tell Cressida all this yourself. I really don't want to get involved. I wouldn't like them to know I was, er, discussing their business. I'd be ashamed. But say, I sure as hell wouldn't go back, if I were her.'

'No? Perhaps you're right. But she and Frank were well liked. Everyone knew that Cressie wouldn't harm anyone. Nor Frank. He's a decent man. I've heard it said many times.' And with that the two fell silent.

Afterwards Murray had wondered what Rose had meant when she claimed that Cressie and Frank wouldn't harm anyone. He wondered about it again now, as he and Cressie pulled into the hospital forecourt, but he kept his troublesome thoughts to himself.

Email from Fiona Moore to Sean Brophy
Sean, I owe you one. No, scratch that, a hundred and one. You've changed my life. It's been a lean few years. Getting stuck into this series is brilliant. I'm back down to Cork tomorrow to talk to that young installation artist, God help me. I'll strut my stuff with Slimer – oops, Smiler – at the same time. Like I told you, he can't get the bile out fast enough so I'd better keep on the right side of him. He bangs on and on about Spain. Have you managed to dig up anything on the sainted Evangeline? I'm on the track of her alleged husband – he was an art historian with the Courtauld but popped his clogs years ago. The bookseller in Oxford is next on my list. Lunch on me? Same place or would you like a change? I suppose a late dinner isn't on the cards? Fi

Chapter 10

St Bridget's was a fine modern hospital just outside Clonmel. Cressida and Murray climbed the newly painted staircase to the first floor then walked down a long corridor to the ward, which was divided into a series of four-bedded rooms. Halcyon was in a small room – hardly more than a cubicle –

right in the middle, opposite the nurses' station. One of the beds in it was empty; the other two held elderly women, both either asleep or comatose.

Cressida had last seen Halcyon about five months before and was shocked to see her so frail. She, too, was asleep, lying perfectly still. Tendrils of white-blonde hair curled damply on her forehead and over her ears. As Murray approached, her eyes fluttered open but they looked through him and beyond to where Cressida stood at the foot of the bed. 'Halcyon?' she whispered. The dull eyes held hers for a moment then drooped.

Murray took the girl's hand. 'Hi, honey,' he said. To Cressida's surprise Halcyon eased away her hand and she thought she caught a flicker of annoyance on the blank face. Either Murray didn't notice or chose to ignore it. He sat down at the side of the bed and lifted the lifeless hand again. This time Halcyon let him hold it, or she'd drifted off to sleep again. Murray turned to Cressida. 'She's beautiful, isn't she? She's grown so like Evangeline.' Cressida fetched a chair from the corridor and placed it on the opposite side of the bed. She tried to shut out the sound of Murray's whispered endearments.

She couldn't get over the change in Halcyon. Now nearly thirty, she looked more like an anorexic teenager. The scene was reminiscent of a Victorian illustration of a deathbed. But if that was disturbing, Murray's behaviour was more so. He clucked around the cramped space like an old hen, tut-tutting over the stale flowers and the empty water-jug when anyone with half a brain could see that the poor girl was way past drinking or looking at dreary chrysanthemums.

'Anything I can do?' whispered Cressida, exasperated. He said no, went to the nurses' station, came back with a damp cloth and began to wipe the patient's brow. At first she remained passive, then she tried and failed to push him away, her arms too weak to do more than flail helplessly.

'I don't think she wants you to do that,' Cressida said gently.

Murray ignored her and continued his ministrations until a nurse came in and asked him to stop. 'Let the poor creature be,' she said, quietly but firmly. 'You'll get her all agitated. Don't you know she hates being touched?'

'Busybody,' Murray muttered, when she'd gone. He sat back and looked at Cressida disconsolately. 'She liked having her hair brushed,' he said.

'Yes, I remember. Even when she was at her most manic, she liked it.'

'Do you think she'd like it now?'

'Yes, Murray, I do. I have a soft brush in my bag. It's the only thing I brought for her. The only thing I could think of that she might like.' She unwrapped a child's pink hairbrush, pushed it across the covers to him, and was so touched by his gentleness that she could have wept.

He started to run the brush gently over the fine hair. At first there was no response but after a little time Halcyon's mouth twitched in a faint smile. 'I never did enough for her,' Murray said. 'She's so adorable. I've been thinking about that home in Witney, y'know? But I reckon I'd like to have her come live with us. I think she's ready for it.'

He's mad, Cressida thought. 'Will she recover, Murray? It would be quite a journey for someone so ill, wouldn't it?' We're both mad, she thought.

'Oh, she's going to get better. She's much brighter today.' He touched Halcyon's forehead with the back of his hand. 'Her temperature is way down.' He continued stroking her hair for a while longer. 'I used to do this for Evangeline. I was wild about her, y'know. Ever since I can remember. She came to live with us when I was about ten. Her parents were divorced and her mother lit out for Watts County with some folk singer. My mom was her first cousin. Vangie had no one else. For years I wanted to marry her...' He hunched his shoulders. 'I

149

remember when this little one was born. Yeah, she'll be OK with us in Oxford. No point in her staying here, is there? I wish I'd thought of it sooner.'

He was still talking when Cressida tiptoed out. The nurse caught her half-way down the corridor. 'Are you related to Halcyon?' she asked.

Cressida hesitated. 'No,' she said. 'I'm just a friend. She's very ill, isn't she?'

'Yes, very. But Mr Magraw doesn't seem to understand, does he? I've tried my best to break it to him. She's not going to last very long and he keeps telling us he's going to take her home to Oxford. He's very attached to her, isn't he? And, God help us, he gets very little in return.'

'She can't talk, you know. And she's deaf. She's never been able to communicate – well, not in speech.'

'Oh, yes, I know all that. But...' Something was troubling the nurse. 'I was wondering why she was in the... I mean, him being so fond of her and all...' She brushed the air with her hand. 'It doesn't matter. It'll all be over soon enough,' she said abruptly, and turned away.

Duncreagh Listening Post *(archive)*
The body of a Trianach fisherman was recovered from Baltiboys Rocks early yesterday by the Passage South lifeboat. It is believed the man died while attempting to save the life of an unidentified yachtsman.

Regression 5

The Sullivan brothers were OK – a bit nosy at first, full of questions, but I can work the old deaf act pretty well. They soon got the message and backed off. When we were out at the mussel beds we worked flat out and didn't have much time for chat, even if you could have made yourself heard above the wind and the waves. The weather got worse and worse. You'd have thought the place would lose some of its appeal but somehow, without me realizing, it was growing on me. The best time of day was the early morning before the rain started. The light was spectacular and the colours extraordinary. Multicoloured sky at dawn, cotton-wool clouds and emerald green grass. The constant deluge seemed worth it – at least, until it started again.

I was at work at six each morning; on the

first day I finished around ten, but after that it was more variable and it was usually noon when I got away. The afternoons were my own. Mick let me use the boat whenever I wanted. 'Just leave it as you find it, son, and you're welcome.' I never met them except at work, mainly because their hours were much longer than mine. Also, they lived in Passage South and I seldom went there. Most of the time I kept myself to myself.

Apart from the occasional wave from passing cars, I hadn't come face to face with any of the neighbours, though that was in part because I only moved outside the cottage when I'd made sure no one else was about. I convinced myself– laughable, really – that if I didn't see the neighbours, they didn't know about me. I was a bit nervous about squatting: if anyone started asking questions there was no way I could justify myself. I made up imaginary confrontations where I was dead cool and the neighbours welcoming. In reality, I'd no idea what the local reaction would be and I wasn't ready to find out.

The nights were turning chilly, although it was only the beginning of September, and the leaves were losing their colour. On the odd day there were a few hours of brilliant, sometimes even warm sunshine, but the cottage had been lying derelict for too long and never warmed up. Still, I managed –

more or less. I'd found a small camping stove in the Sullivans' boat shed, which I borrowed for minimum cooking and even more minimum heat. Thank goodness I had a warm sleeping-bag. On really bad days I spent long hours huddled in the back bedroom. In a way I was behaving like a wounded animal nursing himself into strength, in solitude and silence, for whatever dragons lay in wait. Because there *were* dragons, I had no doubt about that. The urge for action ebbed away: I harvested mussels, made a few expeditions in the heavy old rowing-boat and that was that. It seemed enough that I was able to get through the days. Getting up at six every morning on a lousy diet was no joke. I was constantly hungry. I felt aimless, weightless, half dead. And completely pissed off.

I'd arrived all hot-fired to discover my past history, lay the ghosts. Somehow, away from the estuary, it had seemed that just making the journey would provide solutions spontaneously without any effort from me. I had this quaint theory that my story would be etched into the landscape for me to read. But the opposite was true: memories hovered just out of reach, impossible to grasp. At some level I recognized that the key to my past was in the hearts and minds of the people around me. Working this out was one thing; confronting the keepers of the information was something else. Much easier to skulk in my safe little corner.

Because of my childhood deafness, communicating had always required substantial effort and I'd never lost my mistrust of strangers. Thoughts of going home to prepare for university gradually slipped away. The future became vague. Since I'd got back to Ireland I'd not been directly in touch with home or spoken to my mother. As long as I was in Provender I kept my mobile charged, and I was able to leave my usual messages, carefully avoiding all mention of my whereabouts. When it went dead things became trickier. I stuffed it at the bottom of my backpack and made the odd call from the phone box in Passage South. I didn't want to give the game away by sending postcards with Irish stamps, and since I didn't have any other bright ideas, I did nothing. Something would turn up.

It did. I had been reading on the bed one night and had just dozed off when something disturbed me. I pulled myself upright and sniffed. And immediately identified the faint smell behind the other smells that had puzzled me for days. I took off my boots, padded to the door, eased it open and peeped into the living room. Here, the smell was stronger, although nothing seemed disturbed. The second time my eyes swept the room I saw the girl in the shadows. She was hunched on the old sofa with her legs tucked under her, staring into space. As she would.

I stood pressed against the bedroom door, silently watching her. She had already stubbed out the joint but its cloying scent lingered in the musty air. The faded jeans and sweater she was wearing blended well with the dingy grey blanket I'd found in a cupboard and thrown over the exposed springs of the sofa. She appeared so blissfully unaware of my presence that I thought she was completely stoned until she blinked. 'Howya,' she said nonchalantly, motionless.

I nearly burst out laughing. 'You comfortable, then?'

'Yeah, grand,' she said, calm as you like.

'Who are you?'

'I could ask you the same.'

'Why don't you?'

She stretched out one longish leg and examined a scruffy white track shoe. 'Don't need to,' she said casually. 'I know already.'

I did my best to keep a poker face. And failed. 'What are you doing here?'

'What are you doing here?' she mimicked, and tittered. 'D'ya always talk like that?'

'Like what?'

'Like you've a plum in your mouth.'

'Yeah. I always talk like that. D'you mind?'

She lowered her leg and sat up a bit

straighter, but not much. 'Doesn't bother me. One way or the other. Sounds a bit weird, though, but then, I suppose you would.'

'Why's that?'

'No why.' She shrugged, bored. 'By the way, I finished your beer. It was warm. Disgusting. Made me feel sick.'

'Really? Am I supposed to feel sorry for you?'

'You can if you like.' Her shoulders began to shake, almost imperceptibly at first but eventually she threw back her head and laughed outright. I could barely stop myself joining in. And while she was still whooping away I stayed cool and edged nearer. Not easy to get a good look at her until my eyes got used to the dim light. But then ... well, she was all right. My age, or maybe a bit younger. Good-looking. Or would be if she cleaned herself up a bit. Short black curly hair with orange or red stripes, kept straight with a phalanx of hairgrips on either side of her high forehead. She had a glinting stud in one nostril and both ears had rows of silver rings, climbing from the neat lobes till they disappeared into the hairline. Her skin was amazing: either it was unnaturally white or she was wearing some kind of luminous makeup.

'Björk, I presume?'

She wrinkled her nose in disgust. 'Get off.

No way, Sweeney.' I almost jumped out of my skin.

'Aha,' she crowed, and sat up straight. 'That got ya.'

'That's not my name.'

'No? Why did you jump, then?'

'Jump? Who jumped? What you doing here anyway, besides spliffing and nicking my beer?'

She threw herself back against the armrest, releasing a cloud of dust. 'Checking you out, Sweeney,' she said defiantly, and when I didn't flinch, she looked uncertain.

'Why Sweeney?'

'Why not? I like the sound of it. Kinda cool, isn't it?' She sat up. 'Matter of fact, I was thinkin' of it for myself but then I had a better idea.'

'And you are?' I plonked myself on the arm of the sofa, which groaned ominously.

'*Shay* Donovan.'

'Shay? As in Seamus? Bit butch, isn't it? You look like a girl to me. Well, almost.' My mind was racing. Donovan. Donovan?

'Feck off,' she replied, but I hardly heard. Why had the name some sort of resonance? More to the point, how the hell did she know who I was? I could feel the shivers running up and down my spine. Her hand brushed mine, then immediately withdrew. 'I was thinking of Sweeney but it doesn't go with Donovan, does it? Sweeney Donovan?

157

Nah, you need something short, one syllable. Shay Donovan's got a real ring to it. Better than Noreen anyway.' She turned her head, and I saw that she was a lot younger than I'd thought. Fifteen or sixteen. A kid.

'Noreen? That your name?'

'Yeah. Called after my grandmother. Never even met her,' she added, with disgust. 'I just made up my mind. From now on I'm going to make everyone call me Shay.'

'And I'm the first? I'm honoured, but actually I prefer Noreen.'

'"Actually?"' she mimicked. 'Hmm, easy for you. Ever heard of anyone famous being called Noreen?' She made a face.

'And you're going to be famous?' I grinned. 'Pop idol?' I loved the way she talked: her clear, light voice lilted up and down, making it easy for me to hear what she said.

'Nah. An actress. A famous actress – like Fiona Shaw. She's from Cork, you know. Or I might be a film star.' She pronounced it fill-um, and star with a long flat A. Fill-um staar.

I did my best not to laugh. I didn't want her to go. 'Bet you will too.'

'Stop laughing at me, you. I'm dead serious.'

'Am I laughing? No, I'm not. Tell you

what, though, lose the hardware, Shay. The ears are OK but holey noses won't look too good, will they? In close-up, I mean.'

Noreen alias Shay peered up at me to see if I was having her on. Reassured, she delicately rubbed her nose. 'Holey noses. Ha ha. Holy Moses, very funny,' she said witheringly, but she couldn't suppress a grin. 'You could be right,' she said. 'To tell you the truth, I'd be glad to get rid of it, it's always getting infected. I only got it to wind the mammy up.' She giggled. 'God awful when you get a cold.'

'Shouldn't you be in school?'

'When? Now? I don't go to night school, do I?' she drawled. 'It's all day school around here – we're that ordinary, God help us.' She stood up, pulled open the curtains and looked out. She was shorter than I expected, about five five, fantastic shape with a six–inch expanse of pale flesh between her jeans and sweater. I tried not to stare. The girl was gorgeous. I could almost see the poster: *Shay Donovan, drop dead gorgeous*. Bit of attitude too.

'God,' she moaned suddenly, 'would you look at the feckin' rain? This place'd put years on you. Middle of feckin' nowhere.' She sighed. 'Are you from London?'

I nearly said yes, but somehow I couldn't lie to her. 'Nope.' I should have left it at that but didn't. I don't know why. 'I live in

Dublin. Oxford sometimes – my mother's English.'

'That where you got the accent?'

'What accent?'

She shrugged. 'Whatever. So what's the story?'

'About Oxford? None. My grandfather lives there – lived there. He just died. My mum was looking after him. I stayed with my dad in Dublin.' I sniffed to make the point that it was a pain. Hoping she'd get off the subject. Did she hell.

'Pain in the neck, parents. Did you mind your mam being away?'

'Not much,' I lied. I didn't want her to think I was a sad bastard.

'Same as me. My folks are away on holiday. Bit of a relief. Are you at college? In Dublin?' she asked.

Which put me in a quandary. If I admitted I wasn't yet in college she'd lose interest. I really wanted her to stay – for a while at least.

'I'm starting in October. I took a year out after school. I've been travelling around Europe.'

'I won't do that. I'm going straight to London. To RADA,' she said, and sniffed as if it were a foregone conclusion and she was bored. Then I noticed her fingers were crossed. She'd make an actress all right. 'But not till next year, worse luck. I can't wait to get the hell out of it but I've another year of school.'

Seventeen, then. Great. I felt like dancing a jig. 'Why? It's lovely here.'

'Oh, yeah? And you're the expert, I suppose? Right. Easy knowing you haven't your mother on your back the whole time. Nothing ever happens here. I'm bored stiff with it.'

'I know what you mean,' I said. 'But it's not the place, you know, it's the feeling that while you're in school you have to do what other people want all the time, isn't it? I felt like that the last couple of years. I hated–'

She swung round, and I saw that her mood had changed. I suppose she thought I was patronizing her. 'Fat lot you know. It's the place all right. The only bit of excitement that ever happened here was years ago. But, then, you'd know about that, wouldn't you, Sweeney?'

'Stop calling me Sweeney. My name's Hollings.'

'Yeah? I bet.' She cackled. 'Hollings what?' She mimicked me again and rolled her eyes. 'Rotten luck. This isn't your gaff, is it? You're trespassing, same as me.'

'What makes you say that?'

''Cos this place doesn't belong to you, does it? They say the old guy that owned this place left it to a kid called Sweeney – though he's probably not a kid any more. Spain, he

161

was called, the old guy.'

This was news to me and I didn't believe her. I mean, she might have believed it herself but it was probably just local gossip.

'You OK?' Shay asked. 'You look a bit peculiar.'

'It's the bad light. I'm fine. What were you saying about the old man?'

'The cove down the way is named after him – Spain's Cove. Some say he was a bit odd, but they're always hedging their bets around here so that probably means he was a downright old pervert. I mean, why would he leave the place to a *boy?*' she said innocently, but she had a sly look in her eye.

God, I nearly exploded. It all seemed so familiar somehow. That awful word and poor old Tar. His face flashed before my eyes. Old man dies, cottage lies abandoned. Of course the locals made up stories about it. But surely if, by the remotest chance, it was true Cressie would have known. And if Cressie knew, she would have told me, wouldn't she? Well, wouldn't she? As these thoughts were racing through my mind I was overtaken by something more sinister: *not if it was true.*

I stood up and went over to her. I was a good few inches taller than her but she stood firm, although she was clearly intimidated. 'You don't know what you're talking about,' I said angrily. My voice was shaking and so were my hands. I clenched them and stuffed them into my pockets so she wouldn't notice.

'Yes, I do – so there. People still talk about it.' She sniffed and made a face at me. 'OK, OK, I'm making it up. I never knew a thing about it until I asked my aunt Marilyn about this place when I noticed you coming in and out of it.'

'You saw me? Shit. You didn't tell anyone, did you?'

'Keep your hair on! Who would I tell?' She grinned cheekily. 'What they don't know won't kill them. I just happened to get talking to the aunt and said something like how sad it was that the place was going to rack and ruin. No mention of yourself, sorry to disappoint...'

'Thank you.'

'You're welcome. Wouldn't you do the same for me?'

I could see she was teasing but she waited for an answer all the same. I closed my eyes and tried to breathe evenly. 'Yes, Shay, I'd do the same for you. *I never saw the gear.* Now, tell me.'

Shay laughed. 'Right so. As I was saying, when rudely interrupted, Aunt Marilyn's great. 'Twas her told me about the old man and the boy and how the old man was driven to his death by the gossip,' she said, in a rush, then waved her hand in the air and made a deep bow. What a drama queen.

'And she said the old man left the cottage to the boy?'

She coloured. 'Well, not exactly. She just mentioned that there was some talk about Spain and the little boy.' She looked at me mutinously. 'Well, it *might* be the reason the place was abandoned, mightn't it? Anyway, I thought it was really romantic and all. I mean, it could be true, couldn't it? It's not impossible.'

'So she just made it up?'

'My aunt Marilyn?' She giggled. 'I wouldn't be too sure about that. I bet she knows more than she let on,' she said. 'Didn't she used to work for the boy's mother? That's how I know they were called Sweeney. Cleaned the house for her – before she got grand and started the B-and-B below.' She rolled her eyes.

'Where's below?'

'Where does she live, you mean? Near the old slipway. Huge barrack of a place, but it's always full. My mam says they've ruined the old place putting balconies all over it.' She whooped with laughter. '"Key West", she calls it, but she's only jealous, Marilyn's worth a fortune these days.'

'Did you tell her I'm here?'

'Ah, for God's sake, what do you take me for? I don't even let on I come here myself, or she'd tell my folks and then I'd be in for it. So will you, if you're found. Trespassing, it's called, in case you don't know.' She raised her eyebrows. 'Breaking and entering. They'll have Guard Ryan on to you, for sure. Unless, of course, you are the Sweeney boy?' she added sweetly.

I didn't answer. Why didn't I remember her aunt Marilyn if, as Shay claimed, she'd worked for us? 'Do you live on Trianach as well?'

'Yeah, the other side. The remote bit, wouldn't you know? Our nearest neighbours are a quarter-mile away. *Tranquillity*, the mammy calls it. It's so *embarrassing*. She has a B-and-B as well, but I often stay with Marilyn. That's how I know this place. I've been coming since I was a kid.' She gave a defiant little smile. 'I used to call it my secret den. Sad, eh?'

'Not sad,' I said. I wanted to put my arms round her so I changed the subject. 'Has John Spain been dead long?'

'Years and years. Ten, twelve. Maybe more. I didn't say his name was John,' she added sharply.

'Didn't you? Know what happened to him?'

'He drowned.'

'Anything else?'

'How d'you mean?'

'You said there was gossip, scandal.'

She shrugged. 'I suppose it was something

165

about the old fella being one for the boys...'

'Really? You know that for sure, or is something else you're making up?'

'What are you? The thought police? I suppose I took it for granted.' She shrugged. 'Scandal usually means sex, doesn't it? Gay sex, even better. You gay, Sweeney?'

'Neither gay nor Sweeney.'

'Ooo-ooo,' she mocked cheekily. 'Don't worry, it's dead cool being gay.'

'Yeah, I can see it turns you on, but sorry, no. How long have you been squatting here?'

'You've a bit of a cheek, haven't ya?' Her lilt became more pronounced as she got angrier. ''Tis you that's crashing, not me. I've been coming here for ever and no bother until you turned up, asking questions. Who d'you think you are, anyway?' She grabbed a knapsack from beside the sofa and staggered towards the door. When I put out a hand to stop her she slapped it away angrily.

'I'm sorry,' I said. 'Don't go. Until your head clears. You can trust me. I won't tell anyone you were here.'

'As long as I don't tell on you, is that it? That's a good one. Who do you know around here, anyway?'

That's when I decided I'd have to trust her. 'I don't know.'

She cocked her head to one side like an

inquisitive bird. 'Is that nobody? Or you don't know who you know?'

Sharp as a knife, she was. I think I might have fallen for her at that moment. I thought about it. 'The second. I don't know who I know. That's why I'm here. I might need a bit of help. Would you split another warm beer with me?'

It only took a second or two for her curiosity to get the better of her anger. 'Only if you tell me who you are. Your real name, not some old made-up thing.' She was priceless.

'Gil.'

'*Gil?*' She looked perplexed. 'Gil?' She dropped the knapsack on the floor. 'Are you having me on or what?'

'No. My name's Gil. It's not that unusual.'

'Gil Hollings?' she asked, and fortunately didn't wait for an answer. 'Do you know something? The Sweeney kid I was telling you about was called Gil as well. But you know that, don't you?'

I split the bottle of beer.

Email from Sean Brophy to Fiona Moore

Hi, good-looking. I've sent you the stuff I dug up on the late Mr Walter and your booksellers, etc., by messenger. You'll find it in your pigeonhole. Incidentally you may find when you've finished with the Walter case this new stuff has thrown up another. Magraw's wife was involved with some curious shenanigans about twenty years ago, all of which makes me realize what a clever little pussy you are. You've hit a gold mine, girl, it'll run and run. I had someone from RTE on the blower just now and I trailed your cloak, as it were. His reaction makes me think we could go global. What say you? S is going away to her mother's for a week from tonight. Holiday time? Sean

Chapter 11

Cressida was back in Oxford, staying with Grace for a couple of days, while Murray remained in Ireland with Halcyon. Grace was surprised and not a little upset when he rejected her offer to go over to Clonmel. 'I prefer to go it alone, honey, at least for the time being,' he said. Then, in an uncharacteristically maudlin way, he pleaded for time to get to grips with how he was

168

feeling. 'I don't think I ever really mourned Evangeline, y'know. Or my parents either. Hally's dying, honey. I never saw anyone, not even my mom, *dying*. I guess it's the big thing, isn't it? So I'd like to see it through.'

'He doesn't want me there,' Grace told Cressida. 'I feel he's punishing me for not liking Halcyon enough.'

'Oh, Grace, no,' Cressida said gently. 'I'm sure it's not like that. There are some roads you just have to go down alone. I felt that with my father. I always worried that he didn't think much of me, but what I really needed was to try and understand what *I* felt about him – if that makes sense?'

'Hmmm,' Grace murmured. 'I'm not sure if it applies to Murray. Maybe.' She gave a bitter little snort. 'I think our problem is more to do with us not having a family. Me not being able to. It doesn't half make you feel useless. Halcyon was never a substitute child for me,' she said starkly. Her voice rose. 'Murray has got so bloody pious about her all of a sudden. I don't know what's wrong with him. I can't stand all this sentimental getting–in–touch–with–your–feelings twaddle. To tell you the truth, the whole thing has been a bone of contention between us for years. Ever since Halcyon arrived on the scene, now I come to think of it. I'm sick to death of her.' She let out a long, pent-up breath. 'Not very charitable, am I? Oh, well.

How was he when you saw him?'

'In an odd mood. I didn't stay long in the hospital, felt I was in the way, so I got an earlier train to Dublin. He didn't mean to be unkind but I could see he didn't want me there. And, since we seem to be letting our hair down, I had the weirdest feeling he was playing – this is going to sound awful – happy families?' She wrinkled her nose.

'Tell me about it,' Grace said wearily.

Cressida took her literally. 'Well, you know how difficult it is to get Halcyon to keep quiet – stop her screaming, tearing around, fiddling with the blasted television? She's always on the go. You're so frantic trying to calm her down that you never really look at her. Well, I'll tell you something, Grace, she has a lovely face. I don't think I ever really noticed before. She was lying quite still in the hospital bed, her cheeks all flushed and her hair soft and blonde, as if it had just been washed. Murray was very gentle with her – he held her hand the whole time I was there. He kept talking to her too, as if she could hear, understand. And the strange thing was that she looked normal. Extraordinary. She's got very thin again and really quite beautiful. Murray said she was the image of her mother at the same age. I'd never heard Murray talk about Evangeline before.' Cressie bit her lip. 'I was kind of shocked. I'd never imagined anyone ever

170

liked her,' she whispered, 'but I could see Murray did.'

'Oh, yes, Murray *adored* Evangeline. He just idolized her,' Grace said softly. 'I couldn't stand her, nor she me, but that didn't change Murray's feelings one bit. He thought she was the cat's whiskers.'

'I see.' Cressida nodded slowly. 'Watching him with Halcyon was a bit surreal, all right. I didn't bring Evangeline into the equation until then. Somehow I had the feeling that maybe Murray felt guilty because he didn't help her with the child – after ... after ... Val ...' her lip trembled '...after the sod abandoned them.'

'Maybe,' Grace said thoughtfully. 'Murray and Evangeline... That whole relationship is ... well, I never really understood. Not sure I want to. He always said he didn't mind not having children. In fact, he was always quite positive about it. Until recently he regarded Halcyon as a real nuisance. I don't have to tell you how hopeless he was with her, especially when she first appeared on the scene. He couldn't have managed without your help. Even visiting her in the convent was a huge production – he'd never have gone at all without you showing him it was possible to make some sort of contact.'

'Either that or we made matters worse, gave her expectations none of us could fulfil. Maybe I shouldn't have interfered.'

'Who knows? You did your best. Murray did, too, but I really don't know where all this I'm-the-only-one-who-cares-for-her is coming from.' She looked up. 'I think I've lost him. He's been seeing someone else.'

'What? Are you sure?'

'No, not sure. He hasn't said anything, but haven't you noticed how often he goes to the States, these days? Between that and these trips to Halcyon he's hardly at home. It used to be just one lecture tour a year, now it's two, sometimes three.'

'But maybe that's all it is, lectures?' Cressida said.

Grace gave a little shrug. 'He's hankering after the fruit of his loins. He wants a child, even at this late stage.'

'You can't mean it? Aren't you upset?' Cressida asked curiously.

Grace thought about it for a moment. 'I don't know what I feel, to tell you the truth. Murray and I have a good life. We have a nice time together, and I like his sense of humour, though there's been precious little sign of it for a while.' She held her head on one side. 'It's all crept up on me very slowly, a hint here, a careless remark there, and then one day you realize your way of life has been decided without you being aware of it. I feel sad, that's all. And that's a pretty lame thing to say after almost twenty years.' She wrinkled her brow. 'You know, there's always been something missing. Children? I didn't think so but now I wonder. Maybe marriages need the cement of children. I just feel very, very tired.'

'Oh, Grace, I'm so sorry.'

'Don't look so tragic. It might be nothing. All in my head. Young Jamie stopped by yesterday with Reggie in tow, looking like the dear old lummox he is.' Grace laughed. Reggie was her first husband and Jamie one of his two children by his second marriage. 'He and Dee have finally divorced. I'm not sure I ever outgrew him, you know.' She shrugged. 'He treated me like shit but now ... well, I always enjoy his company.' She looked at Cressie. 'Sorry. This business of Halcyon's really got to me.' She drew in her breath. 'Evangeline's Legacy, I call her. Or, if I'm in a really foul mood, That Bitch's Legacy.' She smiled wryly. 'Always much easier to blame someone else, isn't it? I just don't know how I'll cope if we have to have her living with us, if the place in Witney doesn't work out.'

Cressida bit her lip. 'More of my meddling, eh?'

'Not at all. We'd be in one hell of a worse mess if you hadn't found it.'

'I don't think it's going to be necessary,' Cressida said. 'The nurse in the hospital more or less said she wouldn't survive.'

'Oh? She's very strong.'

'You haven't seen her lately. She's a shadow. Emaciated.'

Grace took a deep breath. 'Cress? I've always wanted to ask why you stopped having Halcyon home with you.'

'You must be reading my mind.' Cressida rubbed her eyes. 'Strangely enough, I've been thinking of little else since I saw her. She was looking so sweet and innocent, it was hard to remember what a terror she could be.' She put a hand to her mouth. 'She almost killed Katie May,' she said softly. 'Sometimes I wonder if I imagined it, but then the whole thing flashes through my mind, every detail, and I start to shake. Katie May was only eighteen months old. Halcyon was with us for the weekend. I remember it was a warm, sunny day, late afternoon. Frank was working upstairs. He had a desk at the window of our bedroom, overlooking the back garden, thank goodness. I was in the kitchen with Halcyon, trying to do the washing-up. She'd put on a lot of weight. She'd gone from child to woman suddenly and was very unpredictable, if you remember. I was keeping an eye on the children through the window. Gil was about twelve at the time and very nearly my height. He was holding Katie May by the hands, swinging her up and down between his legs.

'I didn't notice Halcyon leave the kitchen

until I saw her lumbering down the garden. I had a kind of premonition that something awful was going to happen but I couldn't move. She stopped a little away from the children and pointed her finger at Gil, jabbing it in the air. She regarded him as her private property and hated him paying attention to anyone else, especially the baby.

'There was a strange expression on her face. She began moving back and forth in time to Katie May, who was squealing with delight. Next thing, without any warning, she made a lunge at Gil, knocked him over and grabbed the baby. When Gil tried to get up, Halcyon gave him a vicious kick in the side. I screamed for Frank and ran into the garden. Gil was on his knees clutching his stomach. Halcyon didn't notice me – she was twirling Katie May round and round over her head. Faster and faster. At first Katie May was laughing but then she got frightened and began screeching.

'It all happened in a few seconds. Gil got to his feet, Halcyon turned round and saw me. She stopped, with Katie May suspended in mid-air, and looked from one of us to the other. Then she started shaking the baby. The more she shook, the more Katie May screamed. The nearer Gil and I got, the more furious the shaking. Then Katie May went quiet. It was shocking. More shocking than the noise. Behind me, Frank said,

"Don't move, don't move, Cress." It was uncanny. Though she couldn't hear, Halcyon turned towards him. She had a strange, terrifying expression on her face. Both her hands were around the baby's middle as she slowly raised her above her head. Katie May was all floppy, like a rag doll and all of a sudden I knew Halcyon was about to pitch her across the garden.

'"Keep clear, for God's sake move away from her," Frank yelled, and came barrelling past me. Halcyon let go and Katie May made a perfect arc in the air as Frank threw himself forward. She was almost on the ground when he caught her. He lay winded with Katie May spreadeagled on his chest, as if she was asleep. She was blue in the face. My legs went from under me. I crawled over to Frank and tried to breathe into Katie May's mouth. Halcyon was doing a lap of honour around the garden, whooping, her arms above her head like a footballer. Gil stood rooted to the spot, white as a sheet.

'Katie May wasn't moving. We carried her into the house and I ran next door for help. Our neighbour was a nurse and, thank goodness, she was at home. She drove Katie May and me to the hospital and insisted on staying with us. She knew they'd think I'd harmed my baby. She was right. They did. But Marie explained what happened. I don't know how I'd have convinced them otherwise.

'Poor Frank stayed at home with Halcyon. He was in a terrible state because he couldn't come with us. "She's going back," he said, as we left for the hospital. "Now. I'm driving her myself She's not staying in my house another second." I knew he couldn't bear to say her name. Gil said he'd go with him to keep her quiet. Poor little fellow. So brave. Terrified, but he went anyway.

'By the time we got to the hospital, Katie May was breathing properly. They kept her in for observation for a few hours. But she was fine, thank goodness. No lasting effects. "That's it," Frank said, when he and Gil got back that night. "She's never coming back here again." And she never did.

'He said a lot more when Gil went to bed – blamed me for being naïve, for thinking I could manage Halcyon when it was clear I couldn't. It was awful. "You're not responsible for that girl," he shouted. "Feeling guilty doesn't make you a good person. It's a waste of time. Our responsibility is to Katie May and Gil. They're the ones we have to protect. She damn near killed our baby." When I said she didn't realize what she was doing, he said he didn't understand why I had to be so fucking understanding, do my Mother Teresa act with every waif and stray that turned up, why I put Halcyon above my own children. "Get your bloody priorities straight, Cress," he kept saying.'

She fell silent.

Grace went off to the kitchen and came back with an open bottle of Meursault.

'That's pushing the boat out a bit,' Cressida said.

'Reggie brought it. We need cheering up,' Grace replied. 'What about Frank, Cress?'

'What about him?'

'Are you going back to him?'

'Back? I haven't left him, Grace,' she said.

'So why are you here?' Grace asked bluntly. Cressida began to list the things still to be done in Oxford, in much the same way she had with Frank. Grace listened until she ran out of steam. 'You know you're very welcome to stay, Cressie, as long as you like, darling, but I think you should be at home with your family. Don't let things slide. Frank is a lovely man. I know that's not what you want to hear at the moment because you're upset with him. All right, he can be a bit selfish, but you two are really good together – most of the time. And you're smashing parents. I'm a lot older than you, so take my advice – you need to be together, not apart. It's no good bottling things up, they'll just get worse. I know what I'm talking about. I'm in the same boat.'

'Oh, I'm going back, Grace. I love Frank, always have. But I bore him – I've become

178

such a wimp.'

'That's rubbish,' Grace said firmly, 'and you know it. For heaven's sake, just look what you've gone through in the past four years. No wonder you're feeling low.'

'I was really angry with him for not coming over after Gil finished school last year. He could have. We've drifted apart, Frank and me. I just need a bit of time to get my head sorted.'

'Like Murray, you mean?' Grace said laconically.

Cressida shrugged. 'We were getting on all right in Waterford until Frank admitted he hadn't done any police work for a couple of years. I mean, can you credit it? That was his reason for remaining in Dublin when Gil started his gap year. He lied to me, Grace.'

'Economical with the truth, I think it's called, Cress. Be fair. How on earth could you have squeezed Frank into Elsfield? There was no room. Besides, what would have been the point? Your father demanded every second of your time.'

Cressida made a brave attempt at a smile. 'Four years is a long time. A lot has changed, Grace. I've changed. I'm fed up playing the bloody doormat. I want to start again, but on my own terms – if that makes sense. Frank's been protecting me too long, kept me in a state of arrested development. Looking after my cantankerous old father taught me that.' She laughed at the expression on Grace's face. 'Yeah, well, I hadn't worked it out at the funeral.'

The atmosphere lightened.

'And now you have?' Grace grinned at her.

Cressida suddenly looked like a cat with a bowl of cream. 'I didn't come straight here after seeing Halcyon. I stopped over in the Isle of Man, for a few hours.'

'My goodness, Cress, you're full of surprises.'

'Not me, Grace, Daddy. He didn't die penniless, whatever fancy tale he told his in-laws. And Frank and me for that matter. He had a nice little stash in a bank over there. He came out with it about six months ago, when I threatened to go home and leave him to his own devices.'

'When he was giving you hell, you mean? Was this a bribe to make you stay?'

'You could put it like that, but of course I'd have stayed anyway. Seventy-five thousand. Crafty old sod didn't tell me it was in my name, did he?'

'Told Frank yet?'

'Not yet. Haven't had a chance,' she said sheepishly.

'He rang, you know, after you left Clonmel. And the next day, when you must have been in the Isle of Man.'

'Oh? What did you say?'

'I told him some porky or other. Said

you'd gone to see the lawyer,' Grace said drily. 'I prefer not to lie, Cress, if I can help it, not to Frank. I think you should talk to him.'

'It's OK, Grace, I already did, early this morning. I didn't say anything about the Isle of Man. I prefer to do that when I get home. He's agreed we can move out of Dublin. We talked about it in Waterford and again this morning.'

'He mentioned it vaguely at the wake. Any idea where you'll go?'

'The country. Somewhere near water. Other than that, not really,' Cressida said evasively. 'One thing's for sure, no matter how much Frank is earning right now, my father's wodge is going to make a hell of a difference to what we can afford. Whatever we buy, I'll have a stake in it.' She beamed.

Grace doubted Frank would be as pleased. Seventy-five thousand would have paid for nursing care, perhaps for as much as four years nursing care. It seemed a paltry price to put on a marriage.

Regression 6

After that Shay copped off school. She was in her final year so she had her own timetable, which was handy, but she went to a lot of trouble all the same. The school was in Duncreagh and the bus stopped at the causeway every morning to collect the kids who lived on Trianach. If she didn't catch it, questions would be asked. So she did, which meant she had to double back to Spain's Cove any way she could. Apart from saying it was a bit of a nuisance, she didn't complain. The first few days, she was usually waiting for me when I got back from the mussel beds, around lunch-time or, as she said, 'Dinner-time, Sweeney, don't be so feckin' posh.' She always called me Sweeney. I thought at first it was to annoy me until I realized that, under the histrionics, she was quite shy. So I let it be. I called her Shay; she called me Sweeney. Like characters in a play. I didn't have to tell her not to call me Sweeney outside the cottage: Shay was one smart woman – she loved conspiracies and I was dead popular for providing one.

So there I was, at the beginning of September, with a place to live, a boat, a pal and enough dosh to keep me going for a few weeks. I was feeling clever but, on the whole, not much wiser about my history. That was soon to change. Shay made all the difference: she was so clued in. 'First thing, we have to get you sorted,' she said. Bossy but practical. She took home my mobile and recharged the battery. She also came up with a good cover story for me. At first I was to be a new boy in her class but then she decided I looked too old. 'Bet you're dead sporty, Sweeney, with those shoulders,' she said, and whacked me on the back. When I didn't flinch, she said, 'Right on. You're the relief sports-person.' She put on a posh accent. 'The jocks are always leaving. Duncreagh hasn't got a sports centre so they soon drift off,' she said grandly.

'The school can't get good staff, these days.' I don't know who she was imitating that time, but she made me laugh. 'Let's see. You're between school and uni, so you're just taking the job for a few weeks till they get someone permanent.' She sniffed. 'Which they won't, of course. Whatever. We'll call you,' head on one side, 'Julian Wray.'

183

'No. That's a wanker's name.'

'Shut up. We will.'

'You know someone called Julian Wray?'

'Certainly do. He took a job in the school last term. English. Lasted exactly one feckin' week so if you didn't play tennis you never even got a squint at him.'

'And you play tennis?'

She laughed. 'Would have, if he'd lasted a bit longer. Hunky, he was. Like yourself, Sweeney.'

'I'll take that as a compliment, then?'

'Whatever, Julian.'

'OK, Noreen,' I said, and got another biff on the shoulders. For seventeen, she could be quite childish. Soon, some of the more useful contents of the Donovan house began to appear in Spain's cottage. As well as a steady supply of food, Shay 'borrowed' a couple of oilskin jackets, her father's old bike, a small paraffin heater, clean towels and a duvet. 'Won't your mum miss them?' I asked.

'No. She's got loads. Anyway, she's away. None of this stuff will be wanted until next year, if ever. Think you can make that old bike work?'

She slipped in and out of the cottage all the time. Several times I found her studying at the table when I got back from the mussel beds. When I worried that someone would see her, she reminded me she'd been going in and out of the cottage for years and no one was any the wiser. 'They will be eventually, though,' she said, 'if they aren't already. But you don't have to bother, Sweeney. They'll just think the "young Donovan one" is up to something. But nobody'll say anything straight out. Ever notice that old people are a bit afraid of young ones? Ever notice that, Sweeney? Let them worry. We're not doing any harm, are we?'

I wasn't sure if the Sullivan brothers knew where my gaff was but I suspected they did. Like Shay said, Trianach was a funny place: information oozed up from the wet grass. Or somewhere.

We explored the estuary in the afternoons. 'Evenings, Sweeney, evenings. We don't do afternoons around here.' But not every afternoon and not always at the same time, although we kept to the same routine. I'd describe the houses and places in my head and if she recognized what I was looking for, she'd take me there. The one place we avoided was her aunt's because Shay didn't want to be caught copping off school. The first few times I kept it fairly general, but on the third day, when I asked her where the woman was murdered, she nearly fell off the boat.

'What woman?'

'The woman in the garden,' I said, and

stopped – not because Shay's mouth was open in a surprised O but because of the pictures running haphazardly through my head. Dark but I could see a woman. Naked. Laughing. I swallowed. 'A woman died somewhere around here.'

'Murdered? You said murdered.' There was excitement in her eyes. 'When? Where?'

'I thought you'd know,' I said, and told her about the article in the *Duncreagh Listening Post*.

She shook her head slowly. 'Is that what this is all about?' She waved her hand at me, at the river, all about. 'Murder? Wow.'

'No – I told you, I don't know anything. It's something in my head.'

'Was she related to you?' she asked curiously.

'I don't think so.' Suddenly I was shaking so badly I couldn't pull the oars. Shay grabbed them and elbowed me aside. 'Let's go back to the cottage. We need to talk.'

When we got back, I lit the paraffin stove and started at the beginning. I told her I was born Gil Sweeney and that I had lived on the estuary until something terrible happened to my father and we had to go away. And that the house was somehow part of it.

'Which house?' she asked.

'The house where the woman died, I think.' She listened carefully and didn't make a single snippy comment. 'How do you know it was here? On Trianach?' she asked. 'How can you be sure?'

'I can't–' I started, and stopped. I closed my eyes and concentrated hard. 'It's near here. It's near this cottage.' It was like having the words pulled out of my mouth on a long string. I felt Shay's arms holding me and I dropped my head on her shoulder. 'I was there.'

'You were in the house?'

'No. In a car, high off the ground. It was dark.' I stopped.

'High off the ground? Do you mean a four-by-four or something? A jeep?'

Frank had had a jeep – we'd had it for years. 'No, not a jeep. Something like an Espace – maybe a Range Rover. I can't remember.'

'Tell me about the house? What was it like?'

'Big, isolated, with huge rocks around it. A tall building. I've looked all over for it but I couldn't find anything like it.' And then my jaw hit the floor. 'God, I forgot. I've got a picture of it.'

'You what? God, you're something else, you know that?'

'Hang on.' I hauled out my backpack and riffled through the pocket where I kept the newspaper cuttings and the page I'd torn from *Cara* magazine. It must have got wet at some stage because it had stuck together. By the time we'd unravelled it, it was crumpled and torn. Shay looked at it for a second, then said, very quietly, 'Get your mobile, Sweeney, and dial this number. If anyone answers, just switch off.' I did as I was told. After the fifth ring an answer-machine came on, so I passed it to Shay.

'Right on. I thought she might be out. She goes to the hairdresser in Duncreagh this time every Friday. Come on, Sweeney, I want to show you something.'

'What?'

'The house, stupid.' She grabbed my hand, we crept out of the cottage and shot across the lane to a gap in the hedge. We waded through two muddy fields, along a narrow track, then climbed a rocky outcrop and slithered down into a dense shrubbery. 'Wait here,' Shay hissed, and disappeared. 'Nobody home,' she said, when she got back. 'Let's go.'

It was a monster. It looked a bit like one of the buildings at my old school, except that it had wrought-iron balconies at every window, painted white and full of bright red geraniums. It was not the house. Shay waited for my reaction, all excitement, but I shook my head. 'No chance.'

'Oh, for crying out loud, Sweeney, use your imagination.' She pushed the magazine page under my nose and dragged me through the terraced garden down to the riverbank. 'Now,' she said, and pulled me down on the wet grass. We sat side by side in the lotus position. Nothing was the same. The house I remembered had huge rockeries at the side and a wide lawn sloping down to the river with fields on either side. A tree by the water's edge where the woman always stood – and, as I turned my head, she materialized for an instant. Her head is thrown back and she's laughing. I read her lips. 'Does your daddy know where you are?' the laughing face repeats and repeats. I faced Shay. 'No,' I said. 'It's nothing like.'

'Well, of course it isn't. Marilyn's made it over. She watches too much television. Scrunch up your eyes and look again,' she ordered.

She smoothed the magazine cutting on her lap. 'Where do you think the rocks for that awful terracing came from? Bulldozed. Marilyn thinks she's a feckin' film star. I told you what my ma said. Lose the balconies, Sweeney. Now what do you see?'

But all I heard was 'Marilyn'. 'Your aunt lives here? I don't understand.' My head was spinning.

'Yeah, my aunt. That's why we didn't come this way before. Is it the house or what?'

I couldn't answer for fear I'd cry. I felt so confused all of a sudden, disoriented. And afraid. But I still didn't recognize the house.

The tide was low, beginning to come in. I took off my shoes, then my jeans and waded into the icy water. I didn't look back until the water was up to my waist. I made slits of my eyes, and tried to make out the shape of the house without Marilyn's fancy balconies. The shrubbery was so dense at either side of the house that it was easy to pretend it was the rockeries I thought I remembered.

'Well?' Shay shouted.

I took a while to answer. 'Yes.' I nodded. 'Yes.'

'You'd better get out of there or you'll get your death of cold,' she cried.

Cressie used to say that. She'd take me by the hand and put her mouth to my ear, 'Come, little darling,' her butterfly lips shaping the words that floated into my head with her perfume. 'Come on, little darling.' I saw her running across the lawn, darting in and out of the reflection from a lighted window. I put my hands to my mouth then slowly sank into the cold, cold river.

When I surfaced a woman was walking down through the terraces towards Shay. She called, 'Noreen? What are you doing here?'

Shay waved, then ran off along the bank towards Spain's Cove. 'I'll be back in a few minutes, Marilyn,' she shouted, and disappeared into the hedge. Marilyn lit a cigarette and parked herself on the low stone terrace wall. I don't know if she could see me but she was looking in my direction as she blew out the smoke. Her hair was white-blonde and she was wearing an old-fashioned red dress with a wide belt. I half expected to see the wind catch up her skirts, like that famous photograph of Marilyn Monroe you see all over the place. Except this Marilyn wasn't laughing.

I struck out for the opposite shore.

Email from Fiona Moore to Sean Brophy
You'll never believe who I saw when I registered Lulu at the school today. Your man Recaldo. Couldn't miss him. Six foot four to five and still drop-dead handsome. OK, OK keep your hair on, I only fancy guys with red hair, these days. Sean, his kid's going to be in Lulus class. He's not in the directory, I checked, so I'm going to have to wait until school starts then follow him unless you can think of anything else. Thanks for all your info. The dossier is filling up nicely. Sean, a favour. Could you do the Ventry interview? Slimer gave me a couple of leads I need to follow up. Your woman Walter had a kid. Brain-damaged, stashed away somewhere. I'll fill you in tonight. My place? Fi

Chapter 12

Frank knew he was ill when they got back from Kerry. He felt utterly drained and exhausted after the long, tedious drive. He packed Katie May straight off to bed with a glass of milk, sat down at his piano for a half-hour to unwind and followed her shortly after, without checking the mail or telephone. He slept reasonably well and was over the immediate panic when he padded downstairs next morning. He listened to the telephone messages while the kettle was boiling. There were ten in all, including three from Gil that hardly varied. He continued to enjoy La Rochelle and the job. He sent love to them all and each time signed off, 'It's really hot here. Swimming's great. See you soon. Got your puppy yet, Twink?'

'Is this a conspiracy?' Frank asked over breakfast.

'No, I told you, Daddy, you just never listen. Gil wants a puppy too.'

'So do we all,' Frank said, resignedly. 'But why don't we wait until Mammy gets home? I need to do some work, so could you skedaddle for a while? Watch television or something. We'll go into town after lunch, if you like. OK?'

'OK,' Katie May said obligingly, and went back up to her room.

Frank sat down at his computer and stared aggressively at the blank screen. Grace Hartfield's chance remark at his father-in-law's dismal wake had lodged in his brain and wouldn't shift. He began to type.

Evangeline's Legacy

The fallout from Evangeline Walter's murder lasted a long time. Every family it touched was marked, though in different ways. Almost as if her languor and venom had leached into their lives, insidiously poisoning them. It seemed not to matter whether they had held her in any regard because Murray Magraw, her cousin as well as her true friend, was not immune, nor was Smiler O'Dowd who, in his own way, loved her. Others fared worse. Within a week of Evangeline's death, her ex-lover, VJ Sweeney, was in flight from the police for her murder. When overwhelming evidence of his guilt was found he was already dead, drowned when his yacht ran aground. Since he could not be charged, the case was quietly closed. Sweeney's widow and son left the estuary under the protection of Frank Recaldo.

Even for those who got away, happiness proved elusive in the long term. Evangeline Walter's life had been driven by hatred and a furious need for revenge on the family of VJ Sweeney, who had loved and abandoned her as a young woman, along with the severely brain-damaged daughter he denied. Perhaps if the unfortunately named Halcyon had died in childhood, as was expected, Evangeline's unhappiness might not have flourished until it was uncontainable.

Evangeline was not a woman to be trifled with. For almost two decades she stalked Val Sweeney. It was no coincidence that she eventually fetched up on the same remote estuary, their houses within sight of each other. Inspector Phil McBride, who investigated her murder, remarked more than once that her outlandish name was misapplied: 'Medea' might have been better suited to a woman with such a sublime sense of personal wrong. He didn't say whether or not this observation was prompted by the fact that her particular Jason – Valentine *Jason* Sweeney – was married to a much younger woman and the couple had a beautiful, intelligent little son.

The discovery that VJ Sweeney's second child was deaf – and, for a long time, mute as well – prompted Evangeline Walter to reassess her own child's condition, for which Sweeney had always held her accountable. She began to devise a means of revenge that would destroy not only her ex-lover but also his new family. Evangeline took it as a personal affront that Cressida Sweeney, whom she regarded, as she did most other women, as a silly little fool, didn't give up on her son, as Evangeline had on her daughter. She clearly doted on Gil, who was forever at her side. By contrast, Halcyon had been confined to one institution or another since childhood and had only infrequent contact with her mother.

The final straw for Evangeline was her discovery that old John Spain had taken a hand in the boy's education. Worse, it was clear even to the unobservant that Gil flourished under his tutelage. Up to now, she'd regarded Spain as just another of her casual conquests, a randy old man, easy and amusing to seduce and, as such, her private property. His defection to the opposition made her see him in a somewhat different light. He'd joined the ranks of her enemies; therefore his disloyalty had to be punished. It didn't take a woman of her flamboyant imagination long to work out how easily Spain's ambiguous position as a disgraced priest could be used to wreak her revenge on Sweeney.

At that time, in Ireland, there had been a series of child-abuse cases involving priests and religious institutions. Public outrage was running high and, naturally, there had been local speculation about Spain in this context. Nothing easier, then, for a mischief-maker to put it about that the old man had an unnatural interest in the eight-year-old boy. Evangeline, too devious to make a direct accusation, chose her words with care. Her pal Smiler O'Dowd could be counted upon to pass the word – if the word was neatly enough put – and in this case the serpent was highly persuasive. 'I worry,' Evangeline murmured in his ear, 'at that silly Sweeney girl letting her little boy near old *Father* Spain. Alone. On the old guy's boat. Up and down the estuary they are, all the livelong day. My, my, but someone ought to warn the child's father, don't you think? That poor kid is deaf and dumb. I mean...' Slim shoulders hunched, hands elegantly outstretched. 'I really, really worry about him. There's no way he could call for help or anything.'

The plot was laid, but it turned out to be something of an overkill. Literally. Did she guess that within a very short time those few vindictive words would lead to three deaths and ruin many more lives? Hardly. A good-looking woman, well past her prime, who was, in any case, dying of cancer, couldn't be expected to value her own, much less anyone else's life. Suffering rarely ennobles the soul. Evangeline regarded her disease as a personal insult: it disgusted and appalled her. Since she was doomed she became determined to take her enemies with her. The trouble was that her definition of 'enemy' blurred. Soon even those who professed to be her friends were sucked into her apocalyptic scheme.

She might not have been so triumphant had she realized how well she served VJ Sweeney by placing in his hands the means of forcing his wife into selling her beloved house. Sweeney's various business ventures had gone pear-shaped and he was virtually bankrupt. Coribeen was worth a small fortune, placed as it was in twenty-five acres, on the banks of the river Glár, close to the mouth of an estuary with some of the best sailing on the south coast of Ireland. A prime site, ripe for development, as Smiler O'Dowd often remarked, avariciously.

Sweeney wasn't too troubled about the fate of either his wife, whom he despised for a fool, or his deaf son, whom he regarded as an imbecile. But he knew that if his wife was forced to choose between Gil and Coribeen, there was no question but the child would come first. All he had to do was threaten to report his wife to the Social Services for allowing the old man unsupervised access to Gil.

The threat was enough. Once the accusation was made, Cressida knew it could not be unsaid. The sluice gates had been opened, they were all going to be swept away: herself, Gil and John Spain. When she started to protest, her husband attacked the child and knocked her out. When she came round VJ had disappeared and the nightmare had been set in train...

Frank scrolled back to the beginning and read through what he'd written, then tilted back his chair. He thought about it carefully, then decided not to show it to his editor until it was more developed. The names would have to be changed, as would the location. He always agonized over naming his principal characters, though minor ones usually popped into his head complete. Trouble was, the names in this particular story were locked into his brain and would not be easy to dislodge. 'Henrietta's Legacy', he scribbled, then crossed out 'Henrietta' and replaced it with 'Hester', which looked worse. He told himself to forget the names for the time being. He had a rough outline, and if he could disguise the characters he'd think about renaming them later.

He could hear Katie May moving around upstairs. He raised his eyes to the ceiling and followed the pitter–patter of her feet. After a while she began to play her clarinet. He listened to her practise scales, then switch effortlessly to a little passage from the Field nocturne he'd been trying to play the previous evening. She had real talent and, better still, clearly enjoyed her music. Frank swelled with fatherly pride. He turned off his computer, put his head into his hands and wept.

That afternoon he registered Katie May at her new school. When they got home the little girl returned to her 'Can we get a dog?' campaign. Finally, in exasperation, Frank handed her a copy of the *Yellow Pages* and challenged her to find the nearest kennels with Irish setters for sale. Mistake. Within a couple of hours he was driving down from the Dublin mountains with Katie May on the back seat nursing a tiny, yapping puppy for which Frank had just parted with an obscenely large cheque. He gave private thanks for TV windfalls and switched on Radio Three for *In Tune*, while his daughter downloaded her brain. Mercifully, most of her prattle didn't demand his attention until: 'What'll we call him, Dad?'

'Rafferty,' he replied absently, with half an ear on Brahms' *Alte Rhapsodie*.

'Sean Rafferty or just Rafferty?' Katie squeaked impishly. Frank laughed. 'Rafferty. I don't want to get sued.'

'What about Finnegan Two? Or Fudge? Or–'

'Whatever you like, Twink, you decide. Quietly.'

There was a nanosecond of silence before she piped up, 'I think I like Rafferty best, after all, Dad. It's kind of smiley.'

Frank turned off the radio resignedly. 'So it is. You're going to have to train him, Katie May, I don't want him peeing all over the house.' Or crapping, he added under his breath.

When he opened the front door the phone was ringing.

'Darling?' It was Cressida, and Frank's heart sank. He knew from her strained tone that something was wrong. 'It's Halcyon, Frank. She died last night. Passed away in her sleep. Murray's arranged the funeral for the day after tomorrow, at the convent in

Twomileboris. Grace and I will drive over in the VW, and I'll come home directly from there. Is that OK with you? You wouldn't like to come to the mass, would you, Frank?'

'No, Cressie. It would be hypocritical. You know how I feel about her.' He felt too full up to continue, too disappointed. 'I'll see you on Friday, then,' he said, and hung up. He leaned against the wall and closed his eyes, waiting for the angina attack to pass.

Duncreagh Listening Post *(archive)*
Spain, Father John Andrew, late of the Society of Jesus, deeply mourned by his twin, Sister Mary Philomena, of the Reparation Convent, Twomileboris.
Walter, Mrs Evangeline (of Minneapolis and New York), sadly missed by her companion and friend Jeremiah O'Dowd. Funeral private, no flowers by request.
American and Swiss papers please copy.

Regression 7

'You're mad, you know that, Sweeney? Nobody swims across this river – the currents are too strong,' Shay said, as I dragged myself aboard the boat.

She was right: the tide was coming in fast. Another five seconds and I'd have expired. I'd been in the water about twenty minutes and I was at the refrigerated but exhilarated stage. 'I was almost there,' I said grandly, 'but thanks for coming, anyway.'

'You were in your hat, Sweeney. You'd at least half a mile to go.' It was hard to keep the boat steady: it was bobbing about like a cork. I collapsed in a heap at her feet. 'You're full of it, you know that?' She was laughing, her face pink, the wind ruffling her hair. I wondered what she'd say if I dragged her down on top of me and snogged her. Probably push me back overboard. She took off her sweater and threw it over my face. 'Get yourself dry and put on your jeans, I don't know where to look.'

'Away, while I get off my wet knickers,' I said, and she fell backwards with laughing but she certainly didn't look away. Had we not been wedged in so uncomfortably, I might have jumped on her. She looked like a raspberry-ripple ice-cream, and there was only one thing to do about that, but the wet underpants were a turn-off, for me if not for her. We changed places, and as I took over the oars the boat turned into the wind and faced Aunt Marilyn's house again. She was still there, still smoking, still watching us.

Shay paid her no attention. 'So, where are we headed?' she asked.

We were not even half-way across the estuary. I pointed to the far bank, which was just emerging from the mist. 'Over the other side, if we can. We should soon see a house.'

'You mean Coribeen?'

I was just pulling up my zip and almost cut my balls off. 'You know it?'

'Are you soft or what? Of course I know it. Isn't it only the biggest estate around here?' Shay waved nonchalantly to two people who passed us on a sailing boat, heading upstream.

'Does anyone live there?'

She gave me a withering look. I couldn't tell what she was thinking. 'Why d'you want to go there?'

I shrugged. 'Not sure,' I mumbled.

'I thought you trusted me?' She was suddenly angry. 'You're full of shit, Sweeney. One minute on the level and the next...' She looked close to tears. 'I'm trying to help, in case you haven't noticed, and all you do is ration out the information when it suits you. I feel a right eejit bunking off school for you, d'you know that? Well, I'm in for it now.'

'You think your aunt's rumbled you?'

'Course. What d'you think she's standing there for? She's waiting for us, that's what. Feck.'

'Will she tell your parents?'

'No, that's one good thing. Marilyn's sound that way. But she'll have a go at me herself and that's just as bad.' She gave me the ghost of a grin. 'Didn't I tell you a few days ago that my folks went to Florida? Didn't I happen to mention I was supposed to be staying with the aunt? I told her I was sleeping over at my friend's house.'

'Me?' I leaned towards her.

'You wish. Don't try anything, Sweeney, I'm still mad at you. You feckin' lived in Coribeen, didn't you? Marilyn worked there. For a Mrs Sweeney.' She glared at me. 'And since she lived in Coribeen then you must have as well. So, stop messing me about. Either we're in this together or we're not.'

A sharp breeze had blown up and she was beginning to look as cold as I felt – more blackcurrant than raspberry. 'I'm sorry,' I said. I rested the oars in their rowlocks and put my hands out to her. 'Forgive me?'

Shay didn't answer: she just stared past me as if I didn't exist. I thought she was sulking but she wasn't: she was scheming again. 'You're over eighteen, aren't you? Have you passed your driving test?'

'Why do you ask?'

'Would you stop answering questions with questions, Sweeney? It drives me spare. Have you?'

'Yes. I haven't had a lot of practice but I can drive.'

'Right so. Look at us in this stupid tug – going nowhere fast. How much headway have we made? Square root of sod all. It takes hours trying to cross this feckin' river and how many hours have you got?'

'Not all that many, but it would take longer to cycle.'

'Who's saying anything about cycling? Look, it's six miles to Duncreagh and another six or eight by road to the Coribeen place.' She raised her eyebrows at me.

'We need a car,' I said, 'obviously. But who'd rent a car to an eighteen-year-old? Even if I could afford it. No one, that's who.'

'I wasn't thinking of renting, I was thinking more of, like, *borrowing*. The mammy's Fiat Punto is sitting in the garage and no one to use it.' She threw back her head and laughed. 'The keys are on the dresser at home. So, what d'you think?'

I looked at her dubiously. 'I don't know. I don't want to get you into more trouble. I mean, if it was you borrowing it that would be one thing, but me? Your mother would have your guts for garters.'

'God, you're full of yourself I wasn't thinking of you, I was thinking of me,' she said gleefully. 'I'm seventeen and a half, you know, I *have* a provisional licence. But I need a full licence holder with me. I'm always driving Mammy around. So? Are you up for it?'

I looked at her for ages. Her cheeks got redder and redder until I thought her face would burst into flames. I licked my lips and tasted salt. 'Shay? Why are you doing all this for me?'

She wouldn't look at me. 'Why not?' she mumbled. She seemed fascinated with her feet. 'I suppose I, er, must like you.'

'Like?'

'Fancy. I fancy you rotten, cretin,' she said, and covered her face with her hands.

I stretched out fingers and touched her damp hair. 'Oh, Shay,' I said, and beamed at her. 'You are one fantastic girl. I think about you all the time. You're lovely.' I leaned over and kissed the back of her hand. I was heading north when she pushed me off, but I could tell she didn't really want to. We looked back at the house and Marilyn waved. 'You want to call it a day?' I asked.

She nodded. 'Yeah. D'you mind? I'd better go and sort her out. Gil?' She looked at me shyly. 'I don't want to ... you know?'

'Make out?' I asked. Shay nodded. She was such a funny mixture. All that I'm-hard stuff and underneath she was gentle and sweet, and probably a bit afraid. Same as me, really. 'It would have to be the right time and it would have to matter. For the two of us,' I said.

Shay looked relieved. 'That's how I feel,' she said, and grinned. 'As my dad would say, "Game ball." So, start sculling, Gil.' I liked the way she suddenly switched to my name: it felt friendlier somehow, more intimate. A shared secret, same as 'Shay'. I knew, without her saying, that I was the only one who used her alias and she wouldn't want me to start calling her Noreen unless other people were around.

We headed straight for Aunt Marilyn's dock, or tried to. It couldn't have been more than a couple of hundred feet away but it took another half-hour. Even then the dock was rickety and we couldn't tie up. But in any case I had to get the Sullivans' boat back to its mooring, which was a couple of hundred yards downstream at the old slipway. I didn't mind, I was happy to be with her, and she didn't seem to mind either. We didn't talk much: the breeze was strong, the tide was pouring in and we kept being pulled off course by a ferocious undertow; it took all my strength to control the boat. When we'd tied it up and stowed the oars, she led me down an overgrown track through a couple of private gardens to her aunt's house. 'It's called the Old Corn Store, by the way,' she said, as we walked up the garden.

There wasn't time to ask her why, because Marilyn was waiting for us by the kitchen door. She put her hand on Shay's shoulder. 'Who's this?' she asked, looking at me.

'A friend,' Shay mumbled, wriggling free.

'Haven't I eyes in my head? What friend?' I must have looked a sight: my wet hair was plastered to my head and I was blue in the face with the cold. Close up, Marilyn looked older than my mother. Dark eyes, black eyebrows, heavy makeup and very red lips. Just like the geraniums. I could tell by looking at her that the feck-the-rain-balconies, as Shay called them, had been her idea. *Benidorm on Glár*. She looked like she might be fun but I didn't feel like crossing her. And when she said, 'Well, Noreen, I'm waiting,' I knew why. Tough bloody woman, no mistake.

'Julian,' Shay started.

Marilyn was eyeing me up and down. 'You're the boy that was working for Mary Cronin, aren't you?'

I was flabbergasted. I mean, she was hard to miss. If she'd been in the restaurant, I'd have noticed. 'Yes,' I said.

'How do you know that?' Shay squeaked.

Marilyn looked at us pityingly. 'Yirrah, for God's sake, Noreen Donovan, I'm not as green as I'm cabbage-looking. Doesn't the band play there every weekend?'

The jazz trio? I looked at Shay.

'Yeah, well, she's talking about my dad and Uncle Steve. And Johnny Moran. They've been jamming together for years.'

'You didn't say.'

'You didn't ask.' She blushed. 'Anyway, what does it matter?'

I don't suppose it did.

'You staying here tonight, Noreen?' Marilyn asked, in a way that didn't offer any choices.

'Yeah. And just in case you want to know, I wasn't at school today but I'll be there tomorrow, so don't start giving me a hard time. OK?' They were easy with each other, as if they were the same age, but I could see

Shay wanted to impress her, keep in her good books.

'Would I?' Marilyn laughed. 'You're fine so. Now, upstairs with you for a hot bath – use one of the guest rooms, you're frozen, girl.' She turned to me. 'You can use the downstairs shower room. I bet you haven't had a good wash for a while, have you? I'll shove your wet clothes in the washing-machine, if you like?' In other words, I know all about your comings and goings, young sir. Subtle or what? 'We might be able to find something for you to change into,' she said, 'while your kit is drying. Would you like something to eat? Julian?' She arched her eyebrows at me then casually touched the side of her right eye. 'Now, off with ye. Pair of drowned rats.' She hooted with laughter. 'The shower's over there.'

One thing for sure, I'd never been in that house before. Even ignoring the black leather furniture spread all over it, the room was so huge and oddly shaped it would have been impossible to forget. A boy of about twelve was slumped in one of the sofas watching television. He looked so much like Shay that I thought he might be her brother. 'Meet my cousin Liam,' she said, as we went past. 'Otherwise known as the Howler.' She ruffled his wiry black hair playfully.

'Aw, get off,' he grunted, and gave her a shove.

'Homework, Liam,' Marilyn shouted, from the stairs. 'Turn it off. Now.' She handed me a pair of worn jeans that were too big round the waist and a sweater that was a bit on the small side.

I had a scalding shower and shampooed the river out of my hair. There wasn't a brush or comb so I just ran my fingers through it. I needed a haircut. Shay was still upstairs when I took my wet clothes into the kitchen. Marilyn loaded them straight into the machine and switched it on. Then she turned and looked at me full in the face. There was a moment's silence. 'Gil? You're Gil Sweeney, aren't you?'

What could I say but 'Yes'? Subterfuge seemed pointless. I was in it up to my neck now. *Gil Sweeney, murderer's son.* I half expected Marilyn to throw me out. 'Gil Sweeney? Well, I'll be...'

This time she spoke much louder.

'Gil Recaldo,' I said.

'Ah, yes. Frank,' she said, looking a bit misty-eyed. I've noticed he has that effect on women, being the strong, silent type. 'Frank and your mother got married, then? I'd heard that all right. They were always mad about each other. This the first time you came back?'

'Why are you shouting?' Shay asked, from the doorway. 'He's not deaf.'

Marilyn looked at Shay and then,

pointedly, at me. I began to feel afraid of her. In the same instant I remembered her – not as a person but as a presence in my childhood. The look on her face was one I was used to, when people discovered I was deaf: the is-he-also-thick? expression, too easy to read. Marilyn was a bit nervous of me.

I went to Shay and took her hand. 'Yes, I am,' I said, 'but only a little. I couldn't hear at all when I was younger.'

She stared at me. 'God, but you're stingy with the info,' she said, and plonked herself down at the table.

I think it must have been the most uncomfortable meal of my life. I kept losing concentration, and when that happens my hearing goes to pot. I was tempted to throw myself at Marilyn's feet and beg her to keep my secrets but there were also things I wanted her to explain. I didn't much like her, though, but maybe that was because I suspected she'd turn Shay against me, if she could. Shay kept looking from one of us to the other, and I was sure that the minute I left her aunt would fill her in.

But what did she know? What did anyone know for certain? The article from the *Duncreagh Listening Post* was ambiguous: you could read it any way you liked. 'Man sought in connection with Trianach killing drowned'. It could have meant either of them, Spain or my father. Man sought for killing. But I knew which of them it was. Or thought I did. *Gil Sweeney, murderer's son.* The one important thing I hadn't told Shay, my friend, my champion.

Sitting at that table, with the light outside fading fast, things began to crowd in on me. Images kept flitting past but I was unable to grasp their meaning. I was more concerned with keeping the conversation at the table away from me and my family. Not a chance. 'How is your mother?' Marilyn asked blithely. 'You know I worked for her? Do you remember me?'

That at least I could answer truthfully. 'No.' But I remembered the feel of her in the room and when she brushed past me to make the tea I knew why. She still wore the same perfume.

I pushed back my chair. 'I should go,' I said.

Shay looked up. 'Ask me to show you the way,' she mouthed.

Awesome. She'd worked out that if I was deaf there was a good chance I could lip-read.

'Could you show me the way back, Noreen?' I asked.

Marilyn turned around. 'Your stuff should be dry,' she said, and I was afraid of her again.

'Thank you for everything, Mrs Donovan.

The tea was wonderful.'

She smiled and put out her hand as if she was saying goodbye for ever. 'Give my love to your mother, and Frank.' Then she surprised me. 'Tell them they're welcome here any time. We've plenty of room.' She looked as though she was about to add something else, but changed her mind. 'Hurry back, Noreen, it'll soon be dark.'

Email from Sean Brophy to Fiona Moore
Fi, I read the book and fixed up the interview
with Ventry for next week. You're right, he's good.
The TV company has apparently optioned all
his stuff so he must be pretty hot. There seems to
be very little info on him and no interviews. I'm
staggered at the way you go straight for the up-
and-comings. Precious little info on the jacket
but the name makes me wonder if he's Irish. I'll
leave the sleuthing to the expert. Did you notice
the death notices this morning? The one at the
bottom – Walter, Halcyon. Could this be the
daughter? If so, why is she living in Tipp? Sorry
about the hiatus. Family probs. In spades. I'll tell
you all when we meet. luv, Sean

Chapter 13

Nemesis caught up with him stealthily, unrecognized.

Early next morning Frank's editor rang to discuss publication dates. 'We want to get the timing right, Frank. Are you with me? This is what I'd like to do. A TV tie-in of the second book to coincide with its screening in October. They sent us some smashing stills. Then, hot on the heels of that, we do the hardback of your third in November, go all out with it for the Christmas market. Brass bands, banners, the whole razz-matazz. What do you say?'

'Sounds good,' he said, uncertain.

Rebecca refused to be discouraged. 'The really great news is that we've also got interest in radio serialization. The sales are going to be phenomenal. Did I tell you the initial hardback print run is going to be twenty-five thousand? Maybe more. I'm so excited. You're going places, Frank Ventry.'

The author and scriptwriter gave silent thanks that he'd had the foresight to use a pseudonym when he'd published his first novel. Ever since he had been punctilious in maintaining the fiction that it was his real name. Only his family, his few close friends and his bank knew different. He had written his travel books under his own name because he'd contracted the series before the Walter murder when anonymity wasn't such an issue. Even though Recaldo was a highly unusual name, few of the people he met associated the policeman or the ex-policeman with the author of the travel series. Not that it mattered: his readership was modest and the publicity minimal.

Happily he had realized that the same might not be true when he turned to crime writing. It was not that he expected his novels to hit the high spot so quickly but the same instinct that had kept his family private and safe for over a decade had prompted him to use a pen–name when he submitted his first manuscript. He had chosen 'Frank Ventry' simply because Ventry, Co. Kerry, was his birthplace and it had the right punchy sound for crime. 'I'll say this for you, Troilus, you've a powerful imagination, I don't think.' Phil McBride had snorted. 'Why didn't you go the whole hog and use a different Christian name while you were at it?' Frank replied that his own was common enough. He'd grown quite fond of it and would find it hard to get used to another. Much easier to cope with a change of surname. You didn't use it nearly so often.

'Did you hear what I said, Frank?' Rebecca cut in on his thoughts.

'I did. Will they sell? Seems a hell of a lot.'

'I'll say. But that's the power of television for you. When are you moving to the Bahamas?' she joked.

'Soon.' He laughed. 'After the screening. You'll be there?'

'Wild horses wouldn't keep me away. I got the invitation this morning. I hope you realize I just cancelled a week's holiday? Have you seen the rushes yet?' she asked.

'Only the first episode.'

'And?'

'And, yes, Michael Gambon is very good indeed. I think it's all right. But maybe I'm not the best judge.'

'Well, if you say it's OK,' she chortled, 'then I say it must be bloody marvellous. Congratulations. We're all delighted. Did I tell you we're putting on a dinner for you at the Criterion? Let us know who you'd like to invite,' she gushed. 'I'm really looking forward to meeting your wife – Cressida, isn't it? Will the children come?'

'Yes,' Frank said, crossing his fingers. His own invitation had been waiting for him when he got back from Kerry but he hadn't mentioned it to Cressida. 'If my son Gil gets home from France in time. There might be one or two others I'll want to invite. I'll send you the addresses.'

'We'll book a hotel and the airline tickets for the family, Frank. I'll get Ruth to phone you for the details. Two nights OK?'

'No, we'll just stay the one. Cressie won't want Katie May to miss school. Now, tell me, have you had time to look at the outline I faxed?'

She hesitated, just a fraction of a second. 'It's not a real-life case, by any chance?'

Frank's heart skipped a beat. 'Why do you ask?'

'Because it's something of a change for you. The story's all there in the outline, isn't it? And that's a first – you usually leave me guessing. Or are there other twists you haven't mentioned?'

'Something like that,' he said uncomfortably.

'Mystery man. Not giving anything away, huh? All I'm asking is how you're going to tackle it.'

'God knows.' He chuckled. 'I'll try inspiration – if you think it'll work.'

'It's extremely visual. Just wait till the film people see it! Geoff's been on the phone almost every day, he thinks you're the best thing since sliced bread.'

Frank panicked. 'I'd prefer you not to show it to anyone,' his voice rose, 'for the time being.' He kicked himself for sending it off. He hadn't meant to do so, but he'd been feeling sore with Cressida for haring off to the funeral and when he'd rung Phil McBride to sound him out, his partner, Mark, had said he was in the States and wasn't expected back for a couple of weeks. For reasons he now found spurious, Frank had sat down in a white-hot fury and changed the location and the names. With startling unoriginality he'd set the story in the very north of Donegal and retyped the outline. As he listened to Rebecca, he hoped he could make it unrecognizable to Cressida, but he knew in his heart that he was underestimating her. Still, it would all change in the writing. Or would it? 'I've been having second thoughts, Rebecca,' he said slowly.

His editor said nothing for so long that he thought she'd hung up. 'Whatever you say, Frank.' She spoke carefully. 'Are you telling me it's true crime?' she asked shrewdly. 'If so, I've two things to say. I want to know every detail, chapter by chapter. I'll need to get a legal on it. Frank? Take care. Being sued is hideously expensive. You do still work for the Irish police force, don't you?'

'Not any more. I jacked it in last year,' Frank said. 'And don't worry, I won't embarrass either of us. I think the plot needs more work, that's all. And I came up with a better idea last night,' he added mendaciously. 'I'd like to run with it, see how it works out. Maybe it's time to get away from the strict detective form. It's beginning to bore me.'

'What?' Rebecca spluttered. 'Don't be absurd! How many crime writers do you know with your police experience? For heaven's sake, Frank.' She went on with the usual flattery – his writing skills, his unique ability to open a window into the real world of police investigation, etc., etc., etc.

'I was only pulling your leg.'

'Oh? I'm a bit confused,' she said, after a pause. 'Let me get this straight. You're not withdrawing *Henrietta's Legacy?*' She giggled. 'I'll say one thing, the title will have to go. Not you at all. Sounds like an Aga saga.'

'Working title. I'll have a bash at the new

idea first.' He heard his voice grow tense with anxiety and touched the wood of his desk superstitiously. He asked himself what he thought he was doing – saying. There was no new idea. How could there be when he was preoccupied with his failing health and his marriage was going to pieces? Apart from her call about the funeral, he hadn't talked properly to Cressida for three days. Fuck Evangeline and her bloody legacy, he thought savagely, then edited it to: fucked by Evangeline's bloody legacy.

'Fine. As long as you don't change direction, Frank. Take your time.' Rebecca's mellow voice penetrated his train of thought. 'You've been working like a dog. End of October we'll need something for the spring catalogue. Just the usual little blurb – about a hundred and fifty words. Tell you what.' She became businesslike. 'Why don't I just return *Legacy?*' One of the things he liked most about his editor was that she let him make his mistakes in decent obscurity. She was giving him a chance to withdraw the outline, and if he did, she wouldn't refer to the wretched thing again. But if he chose to revise it and send it back, she would accept it as new, and make no more cracks about the title. Which he'd change, in any event.

'Do,' he said courteously. 'Thank you, Rebecca.'

'Anyone ever tell you you have beautiful manners, Frank? I'll put it in the post right away – I haven't made any copies, in case you're wondering. I'll Datapost it, shall I?' she asked.

That was the moment at which Nemesis tapped on his shoulder.

'Oh, one other thing, Frank,' she said casually. 'We'll want you to do some publicity – that OK?'

'We?'

'Me. The sales and publicity departments.'

'No, Rebecca. You know that's not part of the deal.'

'Ah, don't be like that, Frank. Things have changed. You knew when you sold the film rights that it would be expected – if not from us from the TV people.'

'I told you – and them – from the start what I will and won't do. No publicity stunts,' he said tightly. 'You know that.'

'But, darling, it's out of my hands–' She got no further.

'Don't darling me, Rebecca. You only do it when you've already committed yourself to something you know I'll hate. So, what is it? Spit it out.'

'God, Frank, you sound exactly like a policeman. Not me, guy – our publicity people got together with theirs. I promise you, it's nothing heavy, just a couple of radio interviews, newspapers, etc.'

'What does that mean?' he asked harshly.

Rebecca sounded annoyed. 'What I've said. A few miserable interviews. No telly, they're using a trailer for the telly so you'll probably be on the blower telling me they're not giving you enough credit. Radio. Any objection?'

'Radio OK, just no photographers. They can use the one from the book jacket.' Mystery man himself. A side view, sitting down, which disguised his height, a hat to obscure his features.

'What is it with you? You're a great-looking guy.'

'My privacy is important to me, as you know,' he said primly, then stifled a hoot of derision at his own pomposity. 'Your words, Rebecca: "If you want to keep your identity private, do so from the beginning,"' he quoted. 'Good advice, I'm very grateful.' He knew as well as she that, on the publishers' part as well as his, playing hard to get had been a deliberate publicity ploy that had paid dividends. There was, it seemed, nothing more desirable than a camera-shy author. 'What else?' he asked, in a more conciliatory tone.

'Couple of the heavies want interviews. *The Times*, *Telegraph*. Hang on, hang on. We agreed on condition you have approval on the interviewer. *You* have the right of veto. OK? And we'll limit it to, say, six altogether.'

'A few minutes ago you said two.' He felt too tired to argue.

Rebecca went all quiet. 'OK, then,' she agreed, after a long, pregnant pause. 'Two in London, two in Dublin. And the radio, of course.'

'Of course. Have I any choice?'

'Only on who interviews you – which took some doing, I can tell you. You want your books to sell, don't you?' *Otherwise why would you be writing them?* hung in the air.

Frank thought of the money he'd earned and was going to earn if he bent his self–imposed rules just this once. 'I suppose it could be worse,' he conceded. 'Just don't give out my address, OK?'

'As if,' she said briskly. 'You'd better buy a new hat. They insist on a photographer.'

Oh, help. In that instant he decided to grow a beard, get spectacles. 'Well,' he said, caving in, 'I'll have to work something out, won't I?'

'Yes,' she said sweetly. 'I'm sure that won't be the least bother. You're quite a guy, Frank. I can't see a couple of photographers getting the better of you.' And Frank, flattered, allowed himself to be persuaded. Which was naïve of both of them.

Duncreagh Listening Post *(archive)*
Daingean Council have refused planning permission for Coribeen House to be knocked down and a hotel and marina built on the site. A council spokesman says that 'It would be sheer vandalism to raze such an important landmark.'

Regression 8

Shay walked with me back to the cottage. There didn't seem to be much point in creeping about any more so we just went straight for it. An elderly man passed us on the lane. 'Grand evening, thank God,' he said, and touched his cap as though he knew us. I glanced over my shoulder and found he was doing the same. 'Who's that?' I asked Shay.

'Who?'

'The old bloke who just passed.'

'I didn't notice.' She looked round but he was gone.

'He seemed to know you,' I said.

'Well, it's a small feckin' island, so I suppose he would. What does it matter?'

After that we didn't talk much. My stomach was a bit upset; it might have been the huge fry-up we'd just sunk but it felt more like a premonition of disaster.

'Will you come in?' I asked, at the back door.

'No, I'd better get back or she'll come looking for me.' She giggled. 'Marilyn thinks the worst.'

'A minute?'

We were all over each other before we got inside. 'I have to go,' she said, every time we came up for air. I really wanted her but all sorts of fears grabbed my gut. She would go away and never come near me again once Marilyn had her say. Or if she did come back I wouldn't be able to make it. And if I could she wouldn't enjoy it. The place was so grotty and smelly. Not a bit romantic. I wanted more than a quick shag, but I was afraid she'd think I was soppy, stupid, clumsy. Uncool. I wanted her to hold me tight and love me and, most of all, I wanted to tell her everything about myself that I'd held back. But I knew I'd left it too late. Everything was scrambled in my head and I hadn't a clue where to start. I wanted to die. I didn't know what Marilyn would tell her or what Shay had guessed beyond the bare essentials I'd already told her.

There wasn't time to prepare her so I didn't even try. 'Will you come tomorrow?' I asked.

She pulled away, laughing. 'Seeing as there

isn't time tonight, you mean?' she said, all hard. But she looked like a rosebud.

I grabbed her and held her close. 'Listen, Shay. There are things I didn't tell you. Not things I know but what I've guessed, worked out.'

'You're afraid of my aunt, aren't you?' she whispered. 'You shouldn't be, Marilyn's sound.'

'Is she? I found her a bit scary. She doesn't like me much, does she?'

Shay giggled. 'It's not *who* you are, you sap, it's *what*. A big hairy ape, out for my virtue.'

'Well, she's right about that, anyway.' I kissed the tip of her nose. 'Promise me you'll come back.'

She stood up and brushed herself down. 'Promise.'

'No matter what?'

'No matter what?' Shay tittered. 'Don't push your luck, Sweeney.' She opened the door and peeped out. 'Coast's clear,' she whispered, and looked over her shoulder at me. 'You didn't like her knowing who you are, did you, Gil? You didn't like her calling you Sweeney,' she said, then darted away.

I sat in the dark for a long time, going over what had happened that day. I thought about the aunt's house, the garden. In that moment when I had stood in the river looking back at them, something had clicked in

227

my brain but as usual I couldn't find the right connections. That might have been because I'd got into the habit of shutting down whenever the past threatened to break through. Now I steeled myself to open up and invite the ghosts in. Solitary confinement in that dingy cottage was the ideal place for it. I lay down on the bed, emptied my mind of everything else – especially Shay – and allowed the memories to seep back.

A couple of hours later I got up again. It was dark and I couldn't stop shivering. It wasn't just external cold, it was more like I was chilled inside as well as out. A thing apart, nothing could touch me. I dressed warmly and went out into the night. This time I followed the open road to the old slipway. It was the long way round but that was what I felt compelled to do. I was on autopilot.

At first the night was pitch black, but after I'd walked a mile or so the clouds parted and a weak half-moon showed through. The rustling in the hedgerows was deafening and spooky. The closer I got to the slipway the more I felt I was retracing old steps, yet I couldn't remember walking along those narrow roads before. In the car, maybe, but never at night. Except that once. I was half dead with fear.

It was a clear night and the wind had died down. I sat on the Sullivans' upturned boat, watching the water softly lapping the shore while I worked up my courage. It was all different: too many hedges, the lights of too many bungalows. Yet that afternoon, when Shay and I had got into the Old Corn Store garden, I knew I'd been there before. At night. But I couldn't remember how I'd got there or why. When I stood up and looked around the moon had gone in.

Suddenly Gil, aged eight, materializes. He is sitting on the back seat of the Range Rover, his little white face pressed against the window. The car door is open and the driver's seat is empty. He crawls over it, climbs out and looks around. He is clutching one arm to his side. His face is bleeding. The image fades.

I walked slowly down the shingle to the riverbank and, keeping to the waterline, crept across the two gardens until I came to the boundary of the Old Corn Store. I slunk through the hedge and crouched in its shadow. The high roof was outlined against the sky and I let my eyes travel slowly downwards. The flickering light of the television danced around the edges of the curtains on the huge french windows.

Silence. Now little Gil is back. The light from the house runs nearly the whole way down the garden, over the sloping lawn. There's a table by the open french windows, a bench. A bottle on the table. My eyes travel up and down, searching, searching, and I catch a glimpse of dark figures hidden in the bushes at either side of the house. I cannot see them properly, but I sense they're there. A tiny glint catches my eye, further up from where I'm standing. Something big and black rustles the leaves – not at ground level but higher up, much higher than my head. I see the thin branches stir, then stop.

A woman comes floating through the window. She is wearing a long, light dress and it's fluttering in the breeze. Is she dancing? She stretches out her arms and twirls and twirls around like a ballerina. The dress falls open. I see her white breasts and the dark hair at her crotch and I feel hot and excited because I know who she is: the woman who always points at me when I'm in the boat with Tar. She's pointing now. I turn my head to follow her long white arm. Tar is walking up the garden, holding a fish in his outstretched hands. The silver skin glistens in the light. As the woman goes towards him, she faces my way and, for an instant, I see her lips move but before I can read what she's saying she turns back to Tar. She laughs, grabs the fish, and tosses it on the ground. They stand facing each other. I freeze. She holds her breasts in her hands, moving them up and down, up and down. Tar is coming towards her, nearer and nearer. He stumbles and she pulls his head to her bare breasts. I want to wee.

They are walking back now, up the garden, clinging together. Up, up the slope they go, towards the paving by the window. Someone is standing there, behind them, they cannot see. I notice the movement, but I'm distracted – I prefer to watch Tar and the woman. I am mesmerized by what they are doing. She's pulling down his yellow oilskin dungarees. The straps are holding his arms to his sides; he struggles to free them. Now she throws off her dress. Naked. His overalls are round his ankles and she's on her knees with his thing in her mouth. Oh, God. Suddenly he pitches forward on top of her. Pushing, pumping up and down, up and down. Up and down. I can't see Tar's face but the woman is happy because she's smiling, maybe laughing. Tar falls on his face, rolls off her and away. He rises to his knees and holds his head in his hands, as if he's crying. Then, suddenly, the thing behind the woman moves, grabs her hair and yanks her to her feet. The woman swings round but the figure in black pushes her away. Hard. She falls against one of the boulders by the house and lies still.

The other person stands looking down at her, then slowly turns towards where I'm standing. For a split second the light from the window catches her face. I see my mother.

I don't know what to do. The pee is running down my legs and all over my shoes. Tar has his overalls on now, he's pulling the straps over his shoulders. Mama runs to him. I can't look. The woman sits up. She looks round and sees Tar holding my mother's arm. Now she's laughing. She keeps doubling over, then throwing her head back. Why? I don't understand. They must be talking, shouting, but I can't hear them. The silence is thick and furry. Tar is pulling Mama away, down the garden to the water.

My legs won't work and I can't remember the way back so I crawl up the garden, keeping close to the hedge. A large brown muddy shoe steps on my ankle and a hand grabs at my shoulder. I wriggle free and escape through the hedge. I dash across the field without looking back and keep running till I get to the car. Something or someone is following me. I scramble into the car and lie face down on the back seat and cover my head. With one arm. I can't move the other.

Something hits the car. I wait for the vibration to die, then slowly raise my head and look out. Tar sees me. He has his hand on Mama's arm. There are tears pouring down his face. Mama looks at me and she's crying too. There is a huge cut over her eye and blood all down her face. And I suddenly remember why we're there.

Email from Sean Brophy to Fiona Moore
Fi, Change of venue and time and excuse, as a matter of fact. What about Roly's in Ballsbridge around nine p.m.? And did no-one ever tell you editors pay? Even – specially – on social occasions. Luv, Sean

Chapter 14

Grace and Cressida were delayed in leaving Oxford by heavy traffic and barely caught the overnight ferry from Fishguard to Rosslare. All the cabins were taken and they were forced to spend the night huddled under coats in the bar. Both were in sombre mood, preoccupied with the uncertainty of their individual futures. The crossing was mercifully calm, if uncomfortable, but it was pouring with rain when the ship docked at a quarter to seven. They headed straight for the Talbot Hotel in Wexford for a shower and breakfast, then pressed on. A few miles from Clonmel, Cressida, who had been quiet since leaving the ship, put her foot on the brake and pulled into the side of the road. She was sobbing.

'Cressie? What's the matter?' Grace was alarmed.

'Funerals.' Cressida sniffed. 'Too many funerals.' She pulled a crumpled letter from her pocket. 'I found this yesterday when I stripped the bed in Elsfield.'

Grace read the note from Frank's GP confirming an appointment with a cardiologist. 'Oh, my goodness, poor Frank's having trouble with his heart again?' Though Grace sounded surprised, she wasn't entirely so: she'd noticed how washed-out Frank had looked at the funeral. 'Lousy timing, isn't it? Didn't he say anything to you?'

Cressida shook her head and wiped her eyes. 'Oh, Grace, I feel terrible. I told him I was fed up with nursing. He must have thought I meant him.'

'But that's irrational. How could he, if he hadn't told you about this?' She reread the letter.

'You know, I keep thinking things come in threes. I'm so frightened. He's going to die, I know he is.'

'No, he's not, Cress. It's probably a routine check–up, but even if he has to have treatment, he'll get through. You both will.'

'What if it's another bypass?'

'You're jumping to conclusions, but even if it is it's a marvellous operation. I know several people–'

'How many do you know who've had it twice?'

'Two,' Grace lied, 'and both of them are hale and hearty and a good deal older than Frank. Cressie, shouldn't you go home? Abandon this, and just drive straight to Dublin?'

'No,' Cressida said, after a while. 'No.' She was curiously emphatic. 'I know you think I'm heartless but I'm not. I just don't feel I can face it yet. My head is all over the place, I can't think straight. I feel so bloody drained. I just can't seem to get a night's sleep.'

'I'm not surprised, you were up three or four times a night with your father for months. But, darling, wouldn't you both be better off together? Wouldn't it be easier?'

Cressida considered this. 'I'll ring Joe, our GP, as soon as I get to Clonmel. He'll give me the low-down. I'll make him give it to me straight. I want to know what we're in for.' She rubbed her cheek, then dried her eyes. 'I'm sick to death of being treated like a child,' she burst out. 'I want to be an equal partner. I'm not playing Frank's games any more.'

'Come again?'

'Frank thinks that if he tells me he's ill I'll only come home out of duty so he won't know if I really want to. Get it?'

'Oh, Cressie, come on.' Grace brushed back her hair wearily. Cressida might have been describing her own situation. It was too damn familiar. Did all couples have to go through these gut-wrenching convolutions? Pussy-footing around, afraid to be straight with each other and thereby making something fragile even more likely to break? 'What do *you* feel?' she asked.

'I wish he'd trust my love for him, but I don't know if *he* loves *me* enough for that. Or trusts me.'

'I don't think you're thinking straight, Cress.'

Cressida stared mutinously out of the windscreen. 'Oh, yes, I am. That night Halcyon attacked Katie May, Frank and I had a terrible row and that's when the rot set in. He accused me of putting our baby at risk and I knew he was remembering how it had been for Gil. He didn't say it, of course, but afterwards he wouldn't let Katie May out of his sight. It went on for months. Awful, awful. I hadn't realized he could be so angry.' She closed her eyes. 'It just seemed to fill the house, his fury. Like Val's. Gil was practically catatonic with shock. His face as he watched Halcyon almost kill the baby will haunt me for ever. That's when he began to go in on himself. He became terribly introverted. I couldn't talk to Frank about Gil or any of it. I was too afraid of losing Katie May.'

'Oh, my dear, I had no idea. No idea.' Grace put her arm around Cressida's shoulders and held her head to hers. Evangeline's poison, she thought furiously, touched us all. 'So why did you go on seeing Halcyon?' Grace asked quietly. 'It wasn't as if she ever noticed or communicated.'

'I couldn't abandon her, could I?' Cressida replied slowly. 'I suppose I thought of it as a sort of penance. Atonement?'

'How very Catholic. For what?'

'For Gil being OK when she was not. For my beautiful, perfect little daughter. It was my way of touching wood, all tied up with guilt about Val, I suppose.' She put her hand on Grace's arm. 'I hoped that if I did something good, something I found very, very difficult, then bad things wouldn't keep happening. It's hard to put into words but I had this superstition that Halcyon held the secret of what went wrong – with her and her mother and me and Gil. I had to get her on my side because I felt that somehow, if I loved her enough, she would ... she would ... disclose it, help me understand. Help me to stop feeling that the whole thing was my fault. Then Frank and I would be all right.'

'But, Cressie, love, Halcyon had no intelligence. She was mute. How could...'

'Oh, but she did. That day in the garden, I saw it on her face,' Cressida said intensely. She looked at Grace. 'You see, I always believed something in me made Val violent. But that day I realized he must have hurt

Halcyon as well. That it was his nature. It was almost as if she was re-enacting something that had happened to her.'

'That's what Murray's always believed,' Grace said thoughtfully.

'What?' Cressida swivelled round. 'Why didn't he ever tell me? Why didn't you?'

'Oh, Cress, how could we? None of us ever talks about any of it, do we? Not properly.'

'That's true. There's something I never told anyone except John Spain. Something Frank and Gil don't know.' Cressie spoke dreamily.

Grace tightened her hold on her friend's hands.

'I lied about Gil's deafness. I knew about it long before it was diagnosed.'

'Yes?' Grace kept her voice neutral. Cressida had never before discussed Gil's disability, which had steadily improved since Grace had first met him when he was about eight.

'People always said I never left him, that he was always at my side. But I did leave him once. He was about eighteen months, beginning to talk. The same age Katie May was that awful day. I'd put him down for his afternoon nap. Val had just come in from sailing and was having a bath. I asked him to keep an eye on Gil while I went to the supermarket. I left them alone in the house.'

'But what was wrong with that?' Grace

238

cried. She looked at her friend closely. 'Had Val started abusing you? Even then? So early on?'

'No. Honestly. Not then. But he didn't have much to do with Gil. Or me, for that matter. He was away a lot of the time. He never got involved with bathing the baby or feeding him or anything like that. Gil had to be clean, changed, all dressed up, before Val would pick him up. He claimed he was too old for "all that new man stuff".' Cressida made quotation marks with her fingers. 'Val couldn't stand mess.'

'Charming,' Grace said succinctly.

Cressida shrugged away the interruption. 'I took a bit longer at the supermarket than I intended. When I got back Gil was screaming. His nappy needed changing and I thought that was why he was crying, but when I picked him up there was blood on the side of his head, running out of his ear. Val was fast asleep on our bed, and when I faced him with it, he said he hadn't touched him, that Gil had been screaming since I left, banging his head on the side of the cot. I asked him why he hadn't changed Gil's nappy. I don't know why I bothered, Val never changed him, couldn't stand the smell. He couldn't stand the baby crying either. He told me off and went out.'

'What do you think really happened?' Grace asked quietly.

'I don't know. I can't be sure. Gil *did* sometimes bang his head on the side of his cot. He was quite a strong baby. He used to grab hold of the cot rails and shake and shake. I'd tied a little bell on one of the bars and he liked to hear it tinkle.'

'*Hear?*'

'Yes,' Cressida admitted, in a strangled voice. 'Oh, yes. Gil could hear.'

'But not after that?'

'I can't be sure,' she repeated. 'His nature seemed to change. He cried a lot and became very clingy. It took me a while to realize his hearing was gone or partially so. Weeks, months, even. I colluded with Val, didn't I?' she burst out. 'I should have followed my instinct and had Gil's hearing properly investigated immediately. Maybe they could have done something if I'd gone to the doctor at once, but I was afraid, you see. Afraid they'd think I'd abused him. It was ages before I took him to the clinic for a test. Five or six months. The nurse asked me a lot of questions. Then the doctor grilled me because they'd done the early hearing tests. They asked me if I ever lost my temper with him, shook him, things like that. I didn't have Marie with me that time, like I had with Katie May, but somehow I must have convinced them. I never again left him on his own with Val.'

'And Gil doesn't know?' Grace asked.

Cressida shook her head. 'Frank?'

'No, but...'

'What?'

'Gil asked me about it after Halcyon attacked Katie May. Not directly, in a roundabout way, but I knew what he was getting at. That strange expression on her face when she was holding Katie May in the air haunted him. He asked about her, not himself, but it must have been in his mind. How could I tell him? He doesn't know anything about his father. I could never bring it up. I wanted him to forget. Even now I couldn't tell him.'

'Oh?' Grace was sceptical. 'What about Halcyon? Does he know she was his sister?'

'Half-sister, if anything. It's only hearsay. No, he doesn't.'

'Surely he's guessed,' Grace suggested. 'Gil's extremely bright.'

'How could he? We've been very careful.'

'But don't you remember? *You* made that connection, Cress, the first time you saw her,' Grace said mildly. 'You told me so yourself. Isn't it possible that Gil did too?' She was afraid to say more.

Cressida looked at her fearfully. 'He couldn't. He was so little... Oh, Grace, I've been so frightened all my life. I have this feeling that some day a hand will grab my shoulder and ... and ... I'll be clobbered with all these awful, awful questions...'

As Cressida covered her eyes with her hands, like a child, Grace wondered how she had ever found the strength to make any sort of life. Yet in spite of, maybe because of, her uncertainties and fears, she was a devoted mother. And then the saddest thought of all occurred to Grace: she realized how much more relaxed Cressida was with young Katie May than with Gil. And yet when Gil had been the same age she was marvellous with him. Questions. *Cressie had just admitted that she was terrified of questions.* What questions? Pity welled up in her.

'Was that when Val started abusing you, Cress?'

'I kept asking what had happened to Gil. He slapped me about, said I was hysterical.'

'And it went on from there?'

'No, not for a while.' Cressida bowed her head like a penitent, casting Grace as confessor.

'Are you saying that your husband abused you and your child and *you* feel *you*'re the guilty one?' Grace shook her head in disbelief. 'Oh, Cress, your God is vengeful.'

She might not have spoken for all the attention Cressida paid her. 'Val was really ashamed. He kept telling me how sorry he was, didn't know what had come over him, promised he'd never do it again. He was very sweet for a long time afterwards.'

'Because you covered up for him?' Grace said.

Cressida blushed deeply. 'Maybe, but I didn't know for sure.'

'Oh, Cressie.'

'You sound just like Frank,' Cressida said, and restarted the engine.

Art experts from around the world gathered yesterday in Cork for a memorial service for the late Mrs Evangeline Walter. The ceremony was arranged by the late woman's friend and colleague, gallery owner Mrs Rose O'Faolain.

Regression 9

I don't know what time it was when I got back to the cottage and I didn't care. How the hell could I have got it so wrong? I was rigid with the fear and misery I knew I must share with my mother. All these years it must have been eating away at her. Why had she attacked the woman? Why was Tar screwing her? She'd wanted him to, I saw that; she'd forced herself on him, I remembered that as well. She was disgusting; she'd made him look like a fool. She'd pulled his trousers down round his ankles, trapped him, gone down on him like an animal. I hated it. I hated it. Who was she, the woman who laughed?

I couldn't stop shaking. My eyes felt like sandpits, wide open, staring into the dark. Shay would never come back. How could she? Until I had held her the thought of sex had always disgusted me. Now I knew why: I had seen the reality at its most brutal. But, even so, I couldn't understand the forces at play. How could I have forgotten so much? The more I thought about it, the more furious I became. Why didn't my mother trust me? Frank? Cowards, both of them. I should have been told. They had no right to keep it from me. How dare they? Did they think I was a complete moron? They must have known that one day I would go back. I banged my fists against my head and ranted and railed in the empty cottage until my anger died and reason crept back. I had balked at telling Shay more than the minimum. My mother had had to confront it all and much more was at stake for her. What could she possibly have said to make it all right – for either of us? *Gil Sweeney, murderer's son.*

Had she known there was someone else in the garden? As I asked myself that question I was certain she had not. I had the advantage of her: because I was deaf, my eyes had not been distracted. And my sense of smell has always been acute. What about Tar? I could hardly bear to think of him. I pictured instead the shoe coming down on my foot, the hand grabbing my injured arm, sending shooting pains through my shoulder into my head. For a moment I saw me, the little boy, sobbing and terrified, wriggling free, the

245

dead arm – the broken arm – hanging limp by my side. Eyes tight shut, I conjured up the muddy shoe. A brown shoe with stitching on the front. A brown brogue, like my father wore, and cords with caked mud on the cuff. Now I smelt his aftershave and I was even more terrified. What had my father been doing in that bloody garden? He had been after me. He had been going to hurt me again.

The broken arm worried me. It had some significance I couldn't fathom. I'd always known my wrist had been broken when I was a child because it was weak even now. But I'd been told the accident had happened after we left the estuary, some time before Katie May was born. Accident? What accident? I remember being in hospital, the doctor standing at the end of the bed with his stethoscope around his neck. He let me listen to my heart and told me my arm hadn't mended properly; it would have to be reset. He was a fat man with a huge, beaming face. I watched his big purple lips. 'Count backwards from ten,' he said. 'Can you do that?'

When I opened my eyes, the first thing I saw was Cressie sitting on the side of the bed, smiling at Frank. He had his arm round her shoulders. Later on it became family lore that I'd broken my arm when I fell out of an apple tree at the cottage.

'Reset' had meant nothing to me, but it did now. I went back over it slowly. My arm had been broken for the first time that night, which was why I couldn't move it.

My childhood was like a silent film: unless people were looking directly at me I couldn't read what they said. But I was always quick to sense when things were wrong, or about to go wrong. I still have that knack. Whenever my father went to hit me I'd duck just a second before he struck. My mother hadn't been so quick off the mark, or perhaps she had taken the brunt for me. The night in question we'd both got it, but I have a feeling that that particular attack had been meant for me. What had provoked it?

I put myself back into the Range Rover and wound back the film slowly as I tried to recall what had happened in the hours before we ended up at the slipway.

I am on the boat with Tar. My mother is away somewhere and he is minding me. We have our lessons, then I ask him to take me to watch the seals. He doesn't want to at first but I know if I keep nagging he'll give in. And he does, because I distinctly remember being on the boat with him.

The sun is shining on the purple mountain. Frank passes in his funny little sailing-boat, folded up like a big black stork. I laugh and wave and he waves back. A speedboat goes past and nearly capsizes our boat. We row along by the garden where the woman is standing. She has a basket in her hand. She waves and laughs. Tar looks sad and upset. The woman points at me and laughs again. There is another woman – a girl – running down the garden. She's wearing a long white dress and her hair is white too. But not as white as the dress.

We stay only a little while at the Crags, watching the seals. On the way back my father's yacht, *Azurra*, passes by, on the way out to sea. The motor creates a great wake that opens out in a giant V, and sets us rocking like mad. I am following the wake when something catches my eye. The woman and her friend in the long white dress are on the yacht with my father and another man. Tar touches my shoulder and points to where Frank is trying to right his sail. Distracting my attention, I suppose, but I sense he is afraid of something. Someone?

It's much later, the sun is setting, and now I'm in the car with my mother, bowling along the main road to Duncreagh. She always drives fast. She is pointing to a petrol station. She turns in too quickly and nearly crashes into a big black car waiting at the pumps. The driver jumps out and I see it's Mr O'Dowd, who is sometimes on the yacht with my father. He is furious. My mother gets out of the car and goes to talk to him. I climb out after her. They bend over the back bumper, their heads close together.

Suddenly, my heart was pumping. I knew what was coming. I sat upright and crossed my arms over my chest, rocking back and forth as I recalled the first time I saw Halcyon.

The girl in the white dress gets out of Mr O'Dowd's car and runs over to me. She starts to paw my face. I am afraid of her and back away. Mr O'Dowd straightens up, says something to my mother. I only make out one word he says, 'lady'. He looks at me then at the lady. I think it's her name. Lady. We are all standing very still. Each time he turns his head it seems to take hours. First at me, then at her. Once, twice, then he looks straight at my mother and he is smiling like always. I am by her side so I can see his face clearly, but although I watch his lips I cannot understand what he says. Something about the lady, I think.

When we get home my father is on the phone. My mother takes me upstairs and puts me to bed, but I don't go to sleep. I keep thinking of the lady in white. I get out of bed and go downstairs.

I am in the kitchen, in my pyjamas, holding my teddy. My parents are at the table opposite each other. My father is drinking a glass of red wine. He is wearing a navy blue jersey and light brown cords. One of his feet is resting on a chair and the brown brogues have left mudstains on the seat. He is smiling at my mother. I've been practising all the way downstairs. *Laaaaady, laaady, lady. Paaaapa.* I want him to smile at me. Tell me I'm a clever boy to be able to say the words. *Papa, I saw Lady*. It came out right. Now he will smile at me. I say it again. He shoves back his chair, but he's not smiling. His face is all twisted. He flings the glass down the table at my mother. She gets to her feet, her mouth open wide. 'Run, Gil.' She stretches out her hands, palms upright, pushing the air. 'Run. Run.' Suddenly I'm flying across the room and my face is pushed against the skirting-board. My mother is on the floor near me. I peep through my eyelashes and see my father raise his big brown shoe and bring it down on her head. He keeps kicking her.

Now I'm under the bed, curled up in a ball, holding my aching arm. My mother is lying on the floor trying to coax me out. One of her eyes is closed. Her face is covered with blood and she looks terrified.

Halcyon/Lady. Lady/Halcyon? They were the same. I'd always known her name but until now I'd forgotten the girl I'd seen that day in the woman's garden, on my father's yacht and later on the forecourt of the filling station. The oddest thing of all was that while I tossed and turned I kept seeing my father's yacht, *Azurra*, skimming along the

250

water in slow motion, with me in Tar's little boat riding the wake. When at last I fell asleep, the same image became part of my dream, repeating over and over, and all the time I was riding the wake I kept getting closer and closer to the stern until I could stretch out my hand and touch it. Thinking about it when I woke up, I remembered something very strange indeed. The name on the transom was not *Azurra* but *Halcyon*. The letters were dark blue, picked out in gold. I told myself it was a dream, that unconsciously I associated one peculiar detail with another. But, deep in my heart, I knew it was important.

Email from Fiona Moore to Sean Brophy
Sean, Bingo! I followed Recaldo from the school.
He was walking so it was easy. He kept stopping
and at first I thought he'd sussed me out but then
I realized he was short of breath. Not a well man,
I think. He lives about a half-mile from the school
in a rather miserable-looking semi. I didn't even
have to nudge Lulu in his kid's direction since
she's already fixated. They are the only new girls
in their class so they naturally cling together.
That's the good news, now the bad. That guy
O'Dowd turned up yesterday. God, he really
fancies himself and thinks I do too. Yuk. But he
has a story all right. It's been festering for years.
Just caught him at the moment of explosion. Well
done for spotting that house for sale. A
mausoleum, but a perfect intro. Sad and gay – is
that a contradiction or what? He's the type that
likes a bit of arm-candy and guess what? I've got
the job. I remind him of Vangie it seems. Must be
the accent. Have I got a story? See ya. Fi

Chapter 15

The Dublin newspapers were first off the
mark, and it was clear that the TV company
had already made contact with them, if not
his publisher. The journalist who rang was a

pleasant, youngish-sounding man called Sean Brophy. 'I'm going on holiday in a couple of weeks,' he opened. 'I just wanted to fix a date before you get too busy. You're going to be in great demand. I really enjoy your work,' he said. 'I sometimes review crime, under a different byline,' he added, and identified himself as the author of Frank's best notice. This, of course, broke the ice. The interview was set up for the following week. When asked which venue he'd prefer, Frank suggested the National Gallery.

'In London? Oh. I understood from your publisher that you'd be doing some publicity in Dublin,' Brophy said.

Frank gave private thanks that the journalist hadn't been told where he lived – when he should have recognized that Brophy was pumping him for information.

'That's true,' he said evasively. 'I can make it Dublin, if you like.'

'Great stuff. What about the coffee shop of the *Irish* National Gallery, then?' he returned, with a laugh.

Frank agreed. If a week wasn't long enough to grow a beard, he'd have to manage with designer stubble. Or perhaps it didn't rank as designer stubble if it was grey. He put down the phone with a sinking feeling that Fate was catching up with him.

For years he had pushed all memory of

253

those five fateful days out of his head but now it haunted him, day and night. He began to sweat as he recalled how carefully he had edited John Spain's story. How he had suppressed the vital clue of Cressida's presence in the dead woman's garden that night. When the two officers from the city, McBride and Coffey, arrived on the scene, they had rumbled him straight away and promptly placed him in the frame, if not for the murder then for leading the witness. Two uncomfortable days, and the tide, for no discernible reason, turned and Phil McBride swung to his side. How would things have panned out if he had not? After that false start, the two men worked well together and quickly unearthed damning proof of Sweeney's guilt. They'd been close friends ever since.

Frank opened the *Legacy* folder. He thought for a moment, then changed his own name to Hanrahan in an effort to stop picturing the *dramatis personae* as he knew them. That one change of name had a surprising effect: it altered his perspective and, as he reread the outline, the policeman took over from the writer.

Early one morning a woman is seen standing by a tree in her garden at the water's edge. An old fisherman approaches her to pass the time of day and discovers she is dead, covered in blood but still standing.

He lays her on the grass and calls the local policeman, who in turn calls his superiors at headquarters. By the time they arrive the fisherman's story is well rehearsed. In the new version Jack Hanrahan begins to sift through the evidence as presented: the fisherman is an ex-priest with a steamy past. He left the Jesuit order for the wife of the Spanish ambassador to Italy, and she later committed suicide.

He is friendly with a young Englishwoman and teaches her deaf son.

The dead woman has been spreading salacious gossip about them and also accuses the old man of paedophilia. She has a seventeen-year-old brain-damaged daughter, whom she keeps secret, locked away in a remote convent. The father denies the child. The woman has been stalking him for years. She has terminal cancer.

Putative murderer X is practically bankrupt. Victim Y buys his beloved yacht through a friend, under an arrangement which promises X use of it, but then she reneges on the deal and sells the yacht.

X discovers this the day before she's killed. At the same time, he meets his daughter for the first time since she was three.

Recaldo read back what he'd written and impatiently abandoned the Xs and Ys before going on.

Later that day, Cressida sees the girl and

realizes who she is.

Gil tells his father he's 'seen the lady'.

Gil spends the afternoon with Spain. Sweeney sees them together and threatens to report Spain for pederasty unless Cressida agrees to the sale of the house. When she refuses, Sweeney attacks her and his son. Later, he is seen going across the river towards Evangeline's house. Cressida goes to warn Spain, and finds him being sexually taunted by Evangeline in her garden. Cressida sees red, grabs Evangeline and knocks her out. In the struggle Cressida loses her comb. Spain drags her off and dispatches her and Gil to the city, where she hides out.

What happens then is unclear. The version Spain gives the police is that he stumbles upon the dead body. But eventually he admits revisiting the garden during the night, although he's evasive about how many times. He insists she is still alive around midnight, standing at the lighted window.

The dead woman's neighbour and friend, O'Dowd, claims to have heard Ella Fitzgerald's voice coming from Evangeline's house at around one o'clock that morning and believes her to be alive at that time. He, too, is suspected of knowing more than he lets on. Apart from Spain's later visits to the garden, Cressida eventually corroborates his testimony. There are other details but that is the drift. Reading through the statements, Hanrahan believes that Spain fudged the timing to give himself the opportunity to search the garden and tidy up a bit before calling the scene-of-crime officers.

The autopsy shows that the woman has had violent sex more than once and with more than one person before being fatally punched in the stomach, where she'd recently had surgery. The *modus operandi* inevitably points to the wife-batterer Sweeney, who is missing, though there is the small matter of getting the stories straight and producing concrete evidence. Which they do, but not before Sweeney and Spain are drowned.

Frank sat back and thought it through for the umpteenth time. Several things leaped out. The time-lag between Cressida's attack on Evangeline to the discovery of her body was a good eight hours. What else had Spain been doing during this time besides, as he claimed, sleeping? Cressida? It was too damn neat. A woman who was almost universally feared had been dispatched by a man everyone seemed to loathe? Who then, conveniently, drowns? *Or is drowned?* After a decade the loose ends were on the escape.

The whole thing stank. If Hanrahan were to carry out the investigation he would look more closely at Spain's and Cressida's evidence for a start, and he'd have Frank Recaldo off the case in double-quick time.

'Bah,' said Frank, and unceremoniously deleted his invented policeman. Remorse almost choked him. He rubbed his hand over his chin, lost in thought. There was no way he could write this book. If he did he would have to relive that terrible time and cast a cold spotlight on people he loved, not least the darling of his heart. Without further ado he consigned the entire file to the dump bin.

Troubles never come singly. The phone rang. Frank snatched up the receiver.

'Mr Recaldo?' It was his GP's secretary to say his hospital admission had been fixed for the week after next. 'Dr Boylan would like to talk to you.'

'Now? You want me to come to the surgery?'

'No, the doctor's on the line,' she said.

'Frank? How have you been?' the GP asked, and sweat broke out on Frank's forehead.

'Fine, Joe,' he said. 'No problems at all, in the last few weeks. The new regime seems to have done the trick.'

'What are you saying to me, Frank? You're not trying to postpone surgery again? Do you know how much trouble I've had trying to arrange it? Man, you're pushing yourself beyond the limit, not to mention myself. Is your wife home yet?'

'No,' Frank was forced to admit. 'She'll be here in a day or so.' He crossed his fingers. Cressida had to come of her own volition, choose to be with him again. Telling her he was ill would be tantamount to coercion and he couldn't bear that. It was not his style to be an object of pity.

'You haven't told her, have you, Frank?'

'No. How could I? She's been nursing her father for the last four years. How the hell can I tell her she's in for another marathon?' he asked plaintively.

Joe Boylan was made of sterner stuff. 'I'm afraid you're going to have to because you can't postpone this operation any longer. I'm sorry, Frank, it's very hard luck but you've had a good few years since the last one. How long is it?'

'Fourteen,' Frank mumbled. 'Next November.' He'd been thirty-eight then, unreasonably young to have a quadruple bypass. Now he was to have another. Dr Joe had first suggested it might be necessary seven or eight months before but Frank had refused to hear of it. It had been more difficult to ignore the increased ferocity of the angina attacks over the following months, and the attendant changes to his lifestyle. His libido had waned. He had stopped his long-distance walking, then couldn't manage even short distances. He had restricted all activity, drunk less, eaten less, slept less. Lifted nothing, hadn't flown unless he had to. But he had put off confiding in Cressida. How could he when he couldn't admit to himself how bad things had become? But in the past three or four weeks, when he had started having attacks at rest, the alarm signals had reached him at last.

'You have two remaining unblocked arteries. And one of those is iffy.'

'So I've been told,' Frank said drily. How had the cardiologist put it? 'You need a spot of replumbing.'

'Well, then?'

'I've been down this road before, Joe. Would it surprise you to hear I'm just a little apprehensive?'

'No, it would not then. It's a grim prospect, but the technology's moved on hugely. You'll find it much less traumatic this time. And once it's done you won't know yourself.'

Ah, but will my love know me? *Grá mo chroí.*★

'They'll keep you in for four or five days after surgery,' Dr Boyland said briskly. 'So, in on Tuesday, operation Thursday morning. You'll be home by the middle of the following week. If your wife wants to have a ... a chat, tell her to ring me. Any time.'

Frank thanked him and hung up.

★My heart's beloved.

Email from Fiona Moore to Sean Brophy
Sean You must be psychic. Ventry is Irish, though not the garrulous type. Bit of a recluse by all accounts. I was down in Waterford talking to that young film producer Ian Whyte. And what do you think? Not only has he optioned the entire Ventry oeuvre but has the first one in the can. He doesn't let the grass grow, that's for sure. It'll be screened in the UK in October and here a month later. He may also have sold it on – to France and to the States. Starts shooting second in the spring. That's the good news. The bad is that Ventry lives somewhere in Oxfordshire and absolutely refuses to give interviews. The J. D. Salinger de nos jours. Any ideas? Friday night as arranged, then? Fi.

Email from Sean Brophy to Fiona Moore
Fi, Not Oxford, Dublin. I rang Ventry to confirm the interview. He tried to pretend he lived in London. Wanted to postpone yet again. But I managed to pin him down. Tell you all tonight. Sean. PS S has lowered the boom, given me till next week. I've a headache even thinking about it. Any thoughts? S

Chapter 16

Evangeline's troublesome presence rampaged through his dreams. Frank tossed and turned all night, worrying about his health, Cressida, the children, the past, the future – in short, everything. Most of all he was weighed down by his failure to help Gil come to terms with his origins. When he had adopted the little boy he had voluntarily taken on that responsibility. He loved the child as if he was his own yet he'd never even begun to address the issue. Worse, he hadn't allowed the slightest room for manoeuvre. What he and Cressida had intended, what they wanted, was to create an environment of trust and affectionate acceptance in which Gil could approach, then deal with, the horrifying brutality of his early childhood. No use blaming Cressida: she had so much more to lose – at the very least the possibility of total alienation from her boy. It wasn't that they hadn't anguished about the problem for years: they had. But, in her confusion and terror, Cressida had allowed herself to be guided by Frank and he, poor man, was floundering in the dark. He had messed up.

Hidden in the universal pain, the murder was the most troublesome specific.

He was in a highly anxious state when he

got up next morning and freaked when he saw the messes Rafferty had made on the kitchen floor, which poor little Katie May was inexpertly trying to clear up.

He took the mop out of her hands. 'You take that yoke outside. Now. And don't let him in until I tell you.' He sluiced out the kitchen, which proved therapeutic, and made the breakfast. Afterwards he dictated a shopping list, which Katie May laboriously wrote out with Rafferty curled up on her knee.

When she'd finished, she and the puppy looked up at Frank with the same pathetic expression and watering eyes. 'You're not still mad at us, are you, Dad?' she asked.

Us? Frank looked down at her fondly and smiled. 'No, sweetheart, you were doing your best. Sorry I was such a grouch. I didn't sleep that well, but I'm fine now. Why don't you entertain his nibs while I do a bit of work? Then we'll change the beds and clean the place up for Mammy. What do you say?'

Katie May tied a length of twine to Rafferty's collar. 'I'm going to train him to walk on a lead,' she said confidently, and was not noticeably abashed when the reluctant puppy staged a sit-down strike and had to be dragged across the damp floor on his bottom. She picked him up at the door and carried him out to the garden for his first lesson.

Frank watched her through the kitchen window for a few minutes, and then, because he couldn't leave it alone, he sat down at the computer and resurrected the *Legacy* folder from the dump bin. He tried hard to persuade himself that after more than a decade hardly anyone would remember the crime beyond a few individuals in Passage South or Trianach, but he'd lived in Cloud Cuckoo Land so long that his thinking was askew. His alias was a well-kept secret and he'd always been ultra-careful about publicity. Now he regretted having ignored Phil McBride's advice to go the whole hog and drop Frank along with Recaldo. But who on earth would link the increasingly popular Frank Ventry with the lowly Garda Sergeant Frank Recaldo, as he then was, or with the murder? The hullabaloo had died down quickly, interest in the estuary shifted by a spate of terrorist-linked bank robberies in Dublin the week after the murder. It had been easy to assume that the general amnesia would last, though hardly wise.

So who would recognize the story? he asked himself. Apart from Phil McBride, devoted reader as well as friend. Like everything about Phil, his reaction wouldn't be easy to predict. Cressie? Cressie was another matter. She would be devastated.

She might even believe he was trying to get at her, punish her – for what? Her reluctance to come home? Frank pushed away the thought guiltily.

The oddest thing about all Frank's introversion was that until he abandoned, definitely, the *Legacy* plot, it didn't enter his mind that *he* might be a focus of interest. For years his considerable intelligence had been concentrated on protecting his wife and family, not himself For a man who could and did devise the most complex and chilling plots, he proved extraordinarily obtuse when it came to his own life: he couldn't see the woods for the trees.

And Gil? What about Gil? Through all Frank Recaldo's intellectualizing the small, silent figure of the child Gil intruded, stealthily, intermittently. But now he was at Frank's elbow the whole time. Gil the unconsidered, stifled witness. Even now Frank barely acknowledged that at no time did he or either of his colleagues try to discover what part, if any, the little boy had played. Or what he might have seen. Gil, who was never allowed out of his mother's sight. But, critically, the day of the murder Gil *had* been with Spain while his mother drove a friend to hospital in Cork. Images of Evangeline's garden floated in front of Frank's eyes, the dead woman on the grass at his feet. John Spain also kept materializing in the most unsettling way, mulishly sticking to his well-prepared story. 'When did you last see her alive?' he heard himself ask.

'Before I found her dead, you mean? Standing by that tree when I came in from fishing last night.'

'You were alone?'

'Why wouldn't I be?' No mention of Gil being with him all afternoon. Whenever he thought of Evangeline Walter, the same questions and the same dread came bubbling to the surface: Frank had not seen Cressida for a couple of days before the murder. In all, she had been missing for four days: two before, two after the murder. In his mind's eye he saw his fingers curling around the little tortoiseshell comb. She had loathed the American woman, whom she had suspected of having an affair with her husband, feared her vicious tongue for other reasons.

Frank put his head into his hands and closed his eyes. When Cressida had at last shown her face, it had been badly cut and bruised; Gil's arm was in a sling. It had taken longer for her to confess that she'd hit Evangeline over the head. Spain had reluctantly confirmed this, but claimed that Evangeline hadn't been badly hurt. 'She was lying there laughing at us when I dragged Cressie away. I saw her later on that night by the open window of her house. There was music playing. Ella Fitzgerald.'

'Where were you?'

'Out on the river, in the boat, of course.'

'You said you were in bed. Mind telling me what you were doing back there?'

'I wanted to make sure she was all right.'

The story had had to be dragged out of him almost word by word. What emerged was terrible. The night of the murder, Spain went to implore Evangeline to stop traducing him, but she laughed in his face and compounded the insult by goading him into a brutal sexual encounter that Cressida, who had witnessed it, later described as rape, with Evangeline as the aggressor. Cressida's account, too, had come in tiny painful instalments: earlier that day, by chance, she had encountered Halcyon for the first time. One glance had been enough for her to guess her paternity because the girl was the image of Val Sweeney. And this confirmed what she'd always believed: that Val was sexually involved with Evangeline. And, further, that it must have been going on well before and throughout her marriage. When she had confronted Sweeney, he had turned the tables by threatening to report her to the authorities for leaving their eight-year-old son in the care of 'the pervert priest'. The scene for violence was set. When Spain, and later Cressida, had made their way to Evangeline Walter's garden they were in despair and furiously angry.

When Frank had asked where Gil was at the time, Spain said he was in the car or in the cottage, catatonic after witnessing his mother being beaten to a pulp by her husband. And so the detectives had thought he was protecting Cressida. Had Gil been his main concern? And Evangeline Walter's sick interpretation of his affection for the little boy? Frank moved on and considered the evidence against VJ Sweeney, found in the boot of his abandoned car: the dead woman's blood-soaked clothes, Sweeney's similarly stained sweater and cords, a wooden chest crammed with her personal papers. And, most damning of all, wrapped in that day's newspaper, a tiny dictating machine, which, by luck or design, had been left switched on during a conversation between Evangeline and Sweeney. Phil McBride, rocked to his unshockable foundations, described it as a verbal snuff-movie, and it left no doubt of Sweeney's guilt. Convenient, to say the least.

One thing had always bothered Frank. Because of Sweeney's timely death, the tape-recorder was never produced in court so it had not been subjected to the rigorous forensic examination that that would have demanded. Neither was the conjunction of newspaper and tape-recorder ever thoroughly explored – at least, not to Frank's knowledge. It was not something he cared to query and, between himself and Phil McBride, the subject was, by unspoken agreement, taboo. Yet here it was, after ten years, still niggling away. Frank had never doubted that Sweeney killed Evangeline Walter; it was more that he wondered if the man had had help. But the question was, from whom? And why?

Little Gil was tugging at his elbow again. In praising Cressida for her devotion to her deaf son, every single witness had used almost the same words: 'He was always at her side, never out of her sight.' Jesus, Frank thought, supposing that was literally true? What then? That's enough, he thought, no more of this. *No more.*

Frank deleted the wretched file and switched off his computer. Once more Gil was pushed into the background. He had enough on his plate. His wife was on her way home, and he hadn't mentioned his heart or hospital to her, and he knew she would regard it as yet another example of him living in his head, when in fact he was unable to confront his own terror. He registered guiltily that he hadn't warned his publisher about his forthcoming surgery either. When Rebecca had said she'd cancelled her holiday in honour of his visit to London, he hadn't reacted. It hadn't been intentional, more a wish that, by ignoring it, he could will the operation away. He smiled wryly and ran his fingers through his hair, thankful that he was off two tiresome hooks, no previews and no celebratory dinner, and there was also the possibility that, if he played it cannily, he might somehow avoid the rest of the publicity as well.

It occurred to him that some sort of diversion might help them over the crisis, speed his recovery. Had he started the search for a new house instead of haring off to Kerry, they would, by now, have some options to consider. He looked around the dingy dining room and realized how dismal it was for Cressie to come back to. She'd always hated the house, the suburb, the proximity of the city. If he hadn't spoiled things that day by the river in Waterford, they might have found their ideal home; but the moment he had realized they were avoiding all mention of Coribeen, he feared no other house would ever live up to it and his courage had faltered. There was no going back. How could they? How could they ever expose the children to what had happened and face their judgement?

He shook himself out of his lethargy. There were thousands of lovely places they might go. And could probably afford. The production company had paid a substantial sum. The only worry was, how long would the bonanza continue? Like every writer, he worried how long his inspiration, and luck, would last. Frank crossed his fingers, pushed back his chair impatiently and called Katie May.

'Want to come into Dublin?' he asked the little girl. 'I need to do a few things but we'll have time for a hamburger. What do you say?'

'We should get some flowers for Mammy,' Katie May suggested.

'Sound thinking.' He put his arm round her shoulders and laid his parched cheek on hers.

Three hours later they arrived home with a huge bunch of red roses, a leather collar and lead for Rafferty, and a bundle of house-listings from five estate agents. Father and daughter sat at the kitchen table and trawled through them. To his astonishment, half-way through the pile he came to a lavish description and full-colour photo-graph of Coribeen. He stared at it then pushed it across the table to his daughter. 'What do you think of that one?' he asked.

'I like this better,' Katie May said, in a nice uncomplicated way, after a cursory glance. She held out a single sheet with a badly produced black-and-white photo of a beautifully proportioned house near Avoca in Co. Wicklow. 'Look, Dad, there's a kennel in the garden. Rafferty would love it.'

'The question is, little one, would you?' he asked. She nodded so hard that her head looked in danger of dropping off, and her enthusiasm woke Frank to the realization that somehow, somewhere, in his and Cressida's calculations, not just Gil but Katie May had been sidelined. 'Did you hate it in Oxford?' he asked gently.

Katie May looked up in surprise. 'Sometimes,' she said slowly. 'I didn't like the school much. The other children laughed at me. They said I sounded funny.' Her lip curled. 'Not half as funny as they did.' She gave him a wistful smile. 'I didn't have friends. Not a best friend, 'cos I couldn't have them home for tea or anything. On account of Grandfather.' She shrugged. 'I'm really, really glad to be home, Dad.'

'What about Grandfather? Did you like him?' Grandfather – such a grown-up word for a little girl. It spoke volumes that she never used the diminutive.

'Well, he was a bit cross, 'specially when I was little.' She looked at her father. 'He wanted me to be quiet all the time because he didn't like noise. But not always. Sometimes he told me stories. About the war.' Her eyes widened. 'Did you know, Dad? Grandfather was a soldier in Greece. All his comrades got killed,' she said. 'Dad, what are comrades?'

'Friends,' Frank told her. 'They were his friends.'

Katie May considered this for a moment. 'He used to cry for them and their immortal souls,' she parroted. 'Isn't that so sad? I didn't know old people cried. Then he'd get angry and shout at me to go away. He was a bit funny like that. You could never tell if he was going to be nice or not. Mammy said he didn't feel well because he was so very, very old.'

'But you liked him?'

Katie May wrinkled her nose. 'Not *like* exactly. He wasn't always kind, not like you and Mammy. I prefer being here with you, but it'll be nicer to have Mammy here as well,' she said, matter-of-factly.

Her father realized he had never put himself in the little girl's place, had never pictured what it was like to live at the whim of a capricious, curmudgeonly old man. He and Cressie hadn't meant to, but they'd made a mess, and he was the more culpable. He'd shut Cressie out. He'd used his work and Gil to give him space to pursue his new career. He had convinced himself that that was because he wanted to make a success for his family, but it was only partly true. He loved writing and wanted to continue because he knew he was good at it. Having come to it late, he cherished its freedoms all the more. But the inevitable fallout from publicity terrified him. As it did Cressie. Knowing this, was writing sheer self-indulgence?

The night before Piers Hollingsworth's funeral Cressie had accused him of always pushing her to the limit, perpetually setting impossible tests of her love for him, hurdles over which she had to jump. She had been right. And even if she didn't say it all again when she heard about the operation, she would see it as another failure. Of his love or hers? Why did he do these stupid things? Guilt. And humbug. She knew, as well as he, that the real reason he refused to live in Oxford was not just because he didn't get on with his father-in-law, but because he couldn't bear to start from scratch in a place where he had no history. It had not crossed his mind until now that his little daughter might have felt the same.

He got to his feet heavily. 'Come on, little one, let's go down to the pizza joint and get something for tea.' He looked dubiously at the puppy, who was taking apart an old T-shirt.

'He's coming too,' said Katie May firmly. She picked up Rafferty, then followed her father to the car.

When they got back, half an hour later, the VW Beetle was parked outside the house and Cressida was standing on the doorstep, looking anxious. Katie May tumbled out of

274

the car. 'Mammy, Mammy, Mammy,' she yelled, and ran into her mother's open arms, with Rafferty yapping at her heels.

'Who's this?' Cressida disentangled herself, bent down, picked up the puppy and held him to her face.

'That's Rafferty.' Katie May danced up and down with joy.

Cressida looked at Frank over her head. She blushed. 'I'm home,' she said quietly. 'Oh, my darling, I'm home. I can't believe it.'

Frank put his hands on her shoulders. 'You've cut your hair,' he said, and turned her round.

Freshly highlighted, short and stylish, it made her look boyish and young. 'It's lovely,' he said. 'You're lovely. Oh, welcome back, *a stoi.**' He took her into his arms and buried his face in her hair. It smelt of peaches.

*Darling.

Regression 10

When I woke up it was broad daylight. Someone was banging on the back door. I knew it wasn't Shay because she never knocked. I was stiff, cold and starving and I didn't want to see anyone, but it continued, getting more and more impatient. Then a voice called, 'Open up, I know you're in there.' A woman's voice. Marilyn Donovan. Blast.

I staggered to the door and let her in. She looked around and sniffed the foul air. 'Jesus,' she said, 'I won't ask you what you've been up to.' I felt like thumping her. If there's anything I hate it's middle-aged people trying to be all understanding and cool. In fact, I was right off adults. I gave Mrs Donovan my most challenging don't-mess-with-me stare but she just laughed.

'Well,' she said, 'I can see you're a ferocious bastard and all that, but I was wondering if you'd like a bit of breakfast? We need to talk. *I* need to talk to you, Gil Sweeney.'

'If it's about Shay—'

'Shay? Who the hell's Shay?'

'I meant Noreen. We weren't up to anything, as you put it.'

She sniffed. Pointedly. It got right up my nose. 'So, you call her Shay?' She laughed. 'Shay Donovan, star of stage, screen and the latest pop idol, I suppose?' She cocked her head on one side. 'The star is at school for once. I drove her there myself. So, if you're thinking of hanging around waiting for her, I wouldn't bother. Now, what about breakfast?'

'Do I have a choice, Mrs Donovan?' I asked.

'Yes, Gil. You have. You can come. Or not. Whichever you like.' She paused. 'Why are you so hostile?'

Without warning, and to my disgust, my eyes filled with tears and I heard this awful sobbing, which seemed to be coming from someone else. She didn't move, or put out her hand, or offer easy words. She stood waiting quietly until I had pulled myself together, then said simply, 'I can only imagine what coming back here has done to you, boy, but you've nothing to fear from me, I promise you. The car's outside.' She turned away and went to the door and, after a moment's hesitation, I followed her.

For once it wasn't raining, but it was overcast and the air was damp and chilly. We were driving along in glum silence when a black Mercedes saloon, as big as a hearse, came tearing round a corner and nearly ran into us. I got a glimpse of the driver and recognized him as the old bloke who'd passed Shay and me on our way back to Spain's cottage the night before. 'That fella will kill someone before he's finished,' Marilyn said sourly. 'He's got very erratic lately.'

'Who is he?' I asked.

She shot me a curious glance, her head to one side. 'Don't you know? That's Jer O'Dowd – otherwise known as Smiler.' My heart missed a beat but I was too busy trying to keep calm to respond, and Marilyn didn't say another word until we were sitting at her kitchen table with a big pot of tea and a heaped plate of thickly buttered home-made brown bread between us. To my relief, she made small-talk, giving me time to get myself together. She chatted about Noreen first, told me how clever she was: her parents had high hopes for her and wouldn't tolerate any messing. Noreen was funny and kind-hearted and great with young Liam. Then she said she had a daughter called Aisling who was studying to be a solicitor in Dublin. She talked about the jazz trio and told me Frank used to play with 'the lads' when he was a stationed in Passage South, and how he sometimes played the grand piano at the hotel to make a bit of extra money. 'He's a brilliant musician,' she said. 'And he was the most respected guard we ever had around here.' That was how she moved from the present to the past, effortlessly and kindly. In spite of my earlier suspicions, I could see why Shay was so fond of her.

'I worked for your mother, you know. In those days I was the charwoman supremo of the county.' She giggled. 'Full of myself. Do you remember me, at all?'

I shook my head. I didn't want to say I remembered her avoiding me but she must have read it on my face. 'You were a lovely-looking child, about two or so when I first went to Coribeen, but you threw temper tantrums all the time, cried, screamed, banged your feet on the floor. Sometimes your head. I was a bit afraid of you. To tell you the God's honest truth, I couldn't really handle it. I was never much good with little kids, even my own. I suppose that's one of the reasons I worked all hours. Aisling practically brought up Liam, I'm ashamed to say. But I enjoy them more as they get older.' She smiled at me. 'You used to go mad if Cressie wasn't in the room. I thought that was why she always looked tired and stretched.' She paused. 'It took me a long time to figure things out. What's she like these days?'

I shrugged. 'Much the same. Quiet, a bit vague. She's been in Oxford looking after my grandfather for the past four years.' Our eyes met. 'She allows people to take advantage of her,' I added.

Then she surprised me. 'Don't you believe it. The Cressida I knew had a mountain of strength as well as a kind heart. Don't look so sceptical. Your mother may be quiet, but she's strong – especially where her family is concerned.'

I didn't want her to go on. I didn't want her to tell me my father was a savage. 'Why did you leave?'

'I didn't leave,' she said bluntly. 'I was sacked. I made the mistake of commiserating with Cressie and she wouldn't have it. I understood that – I'd have been the same myself.'

'Did you tell Noreen all this?'

'Some of it. We talked for a long time last night. She knows how it was for you at Coribeen. She was talking about taking you there, so I thought she had the right. She's mad about you, in case you haven't noticed. As well as concerned. I don't want her hurt, d'you hear me?'

'What else did you tell her?'

'As little as possible. I was really trying to find out how much *you* had told her. She asked me about John Spain.'

'And?'

'What could I say but what I know? Which isn't all that much, mostly hearsay and gossip. You'd be better off asking Frank. I bet he knows the full story.'

I climbed down from my high horse. 'Will you tell me anyway?'

She poured herself another cup of tea. 'John Spain was here maybe twenty years or more. He was a great fisherman – indeed, when he first came he tried to pass himself off as one. He was humoured but he couldn't disguise that he was a well-educated man. I've no notion how his past was known, but it was. That's Passage South for you, the bush telegraph can be deafening. Spain was a Jesuit priest once, a university professor in Rome and after that in Harvard, so he must have been pretty hot stuff at the teaching.'

'What brought him to Trianach?' I asked.

'He was born not far from here, I believe, somewhere near Daingean. One day he just appeared, settled into the derelict schoolhouse and started trying to do it up. And a right mess he made of it – the poor man was hopeless with his hands. My father-in-law Des, God rest his soul, took pity on him and did a lot of the work, and got a few pals to help out. It was when Spain volunteered to teach the kids, my Steve and Noreen's dad, that Des got the wind up. That time the newspapers were full of scandal involving the clergy, mostly to do with the kids in their care. Some of it was true, of course, and a lot of it was way over the top, in my opinion, but it had an effect, all right, and not always on the guilty parties. Once it was known he was a spoiled priest, the rumours started and spread, until a couple of years after when Steve's aunt Molly came from Boston and gave us the whole story. She was full of it. Spain might have been a randy old goat but he was never interested in kids. It was women were his downfall. Didn't he only run off with some ambassador's wife and she committed suicide – something like that?'

'*Consuela.*' It just popped out.

'What?'

'Consuela was her name. It was written in gold letters inside the boat.' Marilyn stared at me, open-mouthed. 'He used to talk to her.'

'And you remember all that? God help us, isn't that the saddest thing?' She gave me a piercing look, her head to one side. 'It's the first time you've talked about it, isn't it?'

I didn't answer that. 'What happened then?'

'Molly said the woman left her husband and children for him. As well as her glitzy life. But they hadn't any luck, the unfortunates, nor a minute's peace. They were hounded by the press so much that the poor woman jumped to her death. Aren't those journalists the self-righteous hypocrites altogether?' She sat back in her chair and looked at me as if she was trying to work out how to go on. I waited.

'There's something you should know, Gil.' She spoke slowly, choosing her words with care. 'Shortly before John Spain was drowned all sorts of desperate stories started flying around about him and how he liked ... how he was a paedo-paedophile.' She stumbled over the word. Her face was scarlet. 'You told Noreen a woman was killed in this house, didn't you?'

'Yes. I'm sorry if that upset you. I mean, I can see–'

Marilyn waved me aside. 'That's not important. 'Tis well enough known. Anyone could have told her before now, it just happened they didn't. I don't allow myself to dwell on it, otherwise I'd never be able to live here, though I like it well enough. Me and Steve never discuss it. Never. I suppose we're both trying to forget it. It was a sorry business, all round. A lot of people were badly affected.' She fell silent again for a moment, then became businesslike. 'Anyway. What I'm trying to say is, the woman who lived in this house, the woman that was murdered? It was said that she was responsible for the rumours about John Spain. This is hard, Gil. She specifically accused him of molesting you.'

Why was I not surprised? Had I known about those rumours? Had Tar said something to warn me? Or my mother? I thought not because some other hardly-there association told me it had been neither of them. I closed my eyes but it wouldn't come. I could feel my face flush but I looked her straight in the eye. 'He did not. Nor did my father. I would not have forgotten if either of them had. That is one thing I am certain of. My father beat the living daylights out of me, but that is the only abuse I ever suffered and I remember it clearly. John Spain never laid a finger on me.'

Marilyn gave a sad little sigh and slowly shook her head. 'Sure didn't we all know that, Gil. The only reason I mentioned it was because I just didn't want you to get hold of those old stories and think otherwise. John Spain, God rest him, lived in these parts for years and years and, being who he was, people watched him, so if he'd ever done anything like that, I can assure you it would have been known. That woman was a twisted creature who had it in for him. Why, God alone knows, because I don't, though I've pondered it for years.'

'Thank you.' Shay had been right. Marilyn was sound. 'Did you know her?'

'Yes, I worked for her too. Sure didn't I work for practically all the blow-ins? I wonder now where I got the energy. She was American, some sort of art expert. She used to write the catalogues for the O'Faolain gallery in Daingean. Your ma worked part-time for Mrs O'Faolain as well – they were great friends. I suppose Mrs Walter lived here about nine or ten years.

The chill crept upwards from my toes. 'Mrs *Walter?*'

'Yes, Evangeline Walter.' She giggled and put on an American accent. '"You just call me Vangie, honey." Whenever she said it I couldn't help thinking vagina.' She chuckled. 'I should be ashamed of myself.' She sobered up. 'God rest her poor tormented soul,' she added piously.

'Tormented?'

'Yeah, I thought so, anyway, and I saw her every week. She was very solitary, completely self-absorbed, and never had a good word to say for anyone, even those who thought she was their friend. Very neurotic.'

'Had she many friends?'

285

Marilyn seemed surprised at the question. 'Not locally. She travelled quite a bit. I suppose Smiler O'Dowd – Jer O'Dowd that is – was closest to her. Thick as thieves, they were. The sleeveen,' she added, half to herself

'He was friendly with my father, wasn't he?' I asked tentatively.

Marilyn looked at me oddly. 'Well, now, I'm not sure friendly is the word I'd use, though they certainly did business some-times,' she said uncomfortably. 'They were on the board of the Atlantis Hotel in Passage South. It's closed down now, turned into flats.' I could tell she was holding something back, but I felt too nervous to press her.

'Was Mrs Walter a close friend of my mother?'

'Your mother?' Marilyn was astonished. 'No, I wouldn't say so. Mrs Walter wasn't what you'd call a woman's woman. Not by any means.'

I couldn't get my head round what she'd just said. The woman who had laughed at us was Halcyon's mother? If this was true, why had Cressie looked after her loony daughter all these years? But I couldn't ask because I didn't want Marilyn to comment on that or, more to the point, I didn't want her to confirm my other fear. I looked across the table at her. She was staring out of the window, mulling something over. I poured another cup of the tepid tea and sipped it while I waited. Strange how inward-looking you can get when what is going on in your head is a lot more interesting than what's being said. I wasn't really taking everything in. I kept thinking about the yacht, the name painted on the transom and the people who were on the boat that day. I could identify them at last: my father, Mr O'Dowd, his friend Mrs Walter, and the lady in white, Halcyon Walter.

'Had she a daughter?' I wanted it confirmed.

Marilyn swallowed. 'Yes,' she mumbled. 'I never met her myself, though I was told she was here the day before Mrs Walter was killed. Strange, that, because as far as I know she'd never before visited her mother. I believe she was backward. Mentally handicapped. When Mrs Walter moved here from New York the girl was put in a convent in Tipperary. With the nuns. They kept her there all the time.'

'Why did Mrs... Why did the woman move here?'

'Well, now, there you have me. It was a queer move, all right, for someone so interested in art, wasn't it? You'd think she'd have been more likely to live in a big city. I mean, apart from O'Faolain's the nearest art gallery must be in Cork city.'

'Why was the girl locked up?'

'I don't know, except there's few enough able to look after someone like that and I wouldn't say Mrs Walter was the type. They say you'd never know, to look at the girl, that she was ... well, backward.' Marilyn's wide, smiling mouth was pursed up.

We sat in silence while I tried to figure out why my mother had visited Halcyon all these years. Up to now, if I'd thought about it at all, I had assumed it was because our friend Murray Magraw was her guardian, and since he and his wife Grace lived in Oxford and we lived in Ireland... Now several other scenarios were buzzing around in my head as well as one troublesome detail I'd conveniently shoved aside but which was now haunting me: Halcyon and I had the same colouring, same eyes, even if hers were vacant. It doesn't take a rocket scientist to work that one out. *Gil Sweeney, murderer's son.* Had Halcyon something to do with the murder?

'Was there a big investigation?' I asked, and caught her on the hop.

'What? For Mrs Walter's murder? Yeah, it went on for a while, all right.'

'Who investigated it?' I asked.

Marilyn seemed puzzled by the question but that didn't stop her answering. 'Well, Frank, of course, since he was on the scene – the local garda in Passage South. There

288

were a couple of other detectives from Cork. One called Coffey – I never met him. The guy that interviewed me was from Dublin. McBride, his name was. A real Dub, bit of a smartass.' She warmed to the subject. 'Meeting him, you'd be inclined to think he was all mouth, full of wisecracks, but he was as sharp as anything for all his old guff. He didn't miss a damn thing. Not polished, like Frank, not educated.' *Oh, really? Three or four languages – only to read, old son, read and write. I'd never be able to disguise the old accent would I now, Magillacuddy?* 'Bit of a flirt, he was,' Marilyn said innocently. 'But not my type.' His partner Mark would be pleased, I thought.

Marilyn stood up. 'Would you like to go over to Coribeen, Gil? It's for sale, you know. I went into the auctioneer's this morning and borrowed the keys – in case you wanted to see it. I can take you if you like.'

I shook my head. 'No,' I said. 'No, thank you, not now.' *Not ever.*

She raised her eyebrows. 'You're not thinking of haring off there with Noreen, are you?' She was trying too hard to be matey.

'How could we?' I asked innocently. 'It's too far to row and...' I shrugged.

'It wouldn't be that Madam Noreen offered to borrow her mammy's car, would it? If it is, forget it. I had it out with her last night. But, if you prefer, we can go over when she gets home from school.'

'No, thanks, Mrs Donovan, I don't want to go there at all. I don't feel ready.'

Chapter 17

Frank couldn't bring himself to ask Cressida about Halcyon's funeral, certainly not while Katie May was hanging on their every word. They had supper together in reasonable, if strained, harmony, both concentrating their efforts on the little girl and Rafferty, who earned his keep by keeping them entertained. After Katie May had gone to bed, her parents stolidly unloaded the car, more slowly even than Frank's heart warranted. It was almost as if they were afraid to be alone together with nothing to do and without the diversion of the child.

When at last the car was empty and

everything was piled neatly in the hallway Frank suggested a nightcap, but Cressida said she'd prefer to get things tidied away. 'Otherwise we won't be able to move. It shouldn't take long.' When she added, 'You go and sit down for a bit,' Frank guessed she knew about the forthcoming operation. He went into the kitchen and sat staring at the wall, listening to her running up and down the stairs, his thoughts in turmoil, wondering how they were ever going to get on the same wavelength.

'I'd love a cup of tea, if you're making one.' Cressida put her head around the door after a fifth trip upstairs. 'I'm very nearly finished.' Frank switched on the kettle and made a small pot of tea, then impatiently put two glasses and a half-empty bottle of Hennessy on the table.

A few minutes later she slipped shyly into the kitchen. She'd brushed her hair and changed into an old pair of jeans and a scruffy green sweater he hadn't seen her wearing for four years. It emphasized how much weight she'd lost. 'You look nice,' he said.

Cressida laughed. 'We're like a pair of greyhounds,' she said. 'There isn't an ounce of flesh between us.' She sounded like her old self. The clipped English voice was softened by a return of the hint of Cork he loved. She took his hand in hers. 'I'm here for you, darling. I know about the bypass. Everything'll be all right.'

'How long have you known?' He couldn't look her in the eye in case he saw pity.

'Day of the funeral. I rang the surgery from Tipp – nothing to do with you.'

She didn't mention finding the hospital letter he'd left under the pillow in Oxford. 'I needed a prescription. The usual. I just happened to get Joe – his secretary was away,' she fibbed. 'He told me.' She laid his hand against her cheek. In fact Cressida had waited until after the funeral before ringing Dr Boylan to get the score. 'Don't crowd him,' Joe had advised. 'He's in denial at the moment. Keeps telling me he's fine. But with your help he'll come around. Cressida? You're going to have to be real strong for him, my dear. It's not going to be an easy time for either of you.' He promised not to mention to Frank that she'd been in touch.

'You've had four years of sickbeds,' he said stiffly. 'I didn't think you'd want any more of it.'

Cressida lifted his head. 'Aw, Frank, what are you on about? You didn't think at all. I'm your wife, for God's sake. I'm with you all the way.' She drew a long breath. 'Frank? Isn't it about time we talked?'

'Yes, it is.'

'Forget the tea, then,' she said decisively. 'Pour a couple of those.' She pushed a glass towards him with the tip of her finger and waited while he poured a stiff shot. She took a sip, then cradled the glass in her hands. 'Why didn't you talk to me?' she asked.

'I was afraid.'

'Of what? That I'd throw a wobbly? Or run away?'

'Well, you said yourself that you were sick and tired of nursing.'

'True. But that was duty. Daddy wasn't the easiest.'

'He should have sold those damn pictures and employed a live-in nurse,' he said harshly, and was surprised when Cressida giggled.

'He had a live-in nurse. He was much too mean to pay for one.' She looked at him seriously. 'The fact is, he was terrified of being alone. Afraid to die.'

'It wasn't good for us. He didn't think of that.'

'No. But it might have been good for me, Frank. I learned a lot about him and about myself in the last four years.' She smiled. 'I'm stronger. I can forgive. I get furious but I get over it. I'm not the poor forlorn creature I was, you know. Living with my father toughened me up.'

'At a price.'

'Yes. A big price. I realize that.' She leaned closer to him. 'He was frightened of institutions, and women too. I didn't count because

294

I was his daughter. He used women all his life, my mother, me and Marjorie. As long as you were compliant he was as sweet as pie, but I soon saw that he'd never really liked women. I think he had a weird idea that if he didn't control them they'd control him. Like Val. That was what amazed me – he was very like Val in his attitudes but, Frank, I wasn't afraid of him.' She sounded amazed. 'That was one of the things I found out about myself At first I was always trying to please him, the same as I did with Val. That's not your way, Frank, love, but maybe I had to go away to appreciate that. Learn to accept it. You're so grown-up, love, you give people room to make decisions. And mistakes. That can be very challenging – frightening for someone used to dictators. It's hard to be grown-up all the time, isn't it?'

'Why didn't you tell me all this before?'

'Why didn't you tell me how ill you are?'

'I'm not.'

'Stop it, Frank. If you're trying to protect me, just stop it. I've learned to take control. You have to learn to let up a bit. Listen to me. I'm here because I want to be with you but I'd really have liked you to ask – to have given me the choice.'

'Maybe I was afraid you'd say no.'

They looked at each other in horror. They'd got so close to the precipice before they'd drawn back. Cressida put her arms round him.

'Oh, my dearest love,' she said, 'we can get through anything together, can't we?'

They went to bed hand in hand and, for the first time in months, made love. Quiet, tender love. Afterwards, they lay awake for hours, chatting quietly about Frank's operation and where they would go from there.

'I want to tell you something, Frank,' she said, when he was almost asleep. 'After that I want to put it all away and concentrate on getting us back on the road. Together.' She snuggled into him. 'I've been down a very big hole, not just for the past few years but for ever. You've been very patient.'

'I've been a selfish pig.'

'Indeed you have, but maybe you earned the right? Anyway, there's a pair of us in it.'

Frank sat up, switched on the bedside light and traced the contours of her face with his finger. He kissed her nose. 'You've changed. Everything. You've changed.'

'Is it OK?'

'More than.' He held her close. 'Tell me.'

'It's about Halcyon. Something happened at the funeral. I was afraid Smiler O'Dowd might show up but he didn't. There were only a few people at the mass. Murray, Grace, me, and an old friend of mine, Rose O'Faolain.'

'Rose?'

'You know her?'

'I, er, met her. Nice woman. What was she doing there?'

'Bear with me, I'll tell you about Rose later. The mass was in a little chapel at the convent with the two remaining nuns, both ancient. It was very touching how they seemed to regard Halcyon as their child. Such kind women. They must be so lonely rattling around that old house with the life they knew all gone. They looked so tiny getting into the taxi to go home. The rest of us went back to the hotel afterwards and Murray got absolutely legless – and so maudlin. It was awful for poor Grace. When he started on about Evangeline, she went to bed. I stayed.'

'Why?'

'Because there were things I wanted to ask him. Things he wouldn't tell me if he was sober. I wanted to know exactly what was wrong with Halcyon and how Val Sweeney came into it.'

'And do you know now?' Frank asked gently.

'Yes. Once he started he couldn't stop. It was like it was all bottled up inside him, waiting to pop. Frank, Murray was there the day Halcyon was hurt. Val and Evangeline were living in New York, Murray was a young graduate at Cornell. He was staying with them. Halcyon was about two, walking, talking and a real handful. Always having tantrums. They never intended having children, he said, neither of them was any good with her. They were too impatient, giving in to her one minute then ignoring her, so she was running wild around the apartment.

'It was a Sunday. They joined some friends in Central Park for a picnic. Three or four other couples. Halcyon was the only child there. They drank a lot and were all lying about in the sunshine when Halcyon started to yell. Her parents ignored her. Murray changed her nappy and went off to dump the soiled one in a bin can. It was a good way off, but all the way he could hear Halcyon getting more and more hysterical so he dawdled. Next thing he saw Val dragging her along by the hand, still shrieking. Murray stood back behind a tree. He knew if Val spotted him he'd dump the child on him.' She closed her eyes and sighed.

'What happened?'

'Val was jerking the child up and down by the hand, bouncing her, the way you do to distract them. First couple of times she stopped crying but he kept on raising her higher and higher until she started to scream again. He was a big, strong man and she was tiny so he could raise her almost to his shoulder. And then he just let go and the child went flying through the air. Murray started running. She came down on the edge of a kerbstone. Val just stood looking down at her. A woman came over to help but the little girl seemed OK. She was lying quite still but her eyes were open. Murray picked her up and they went back to Evangeline who laid her on the grass and gave her a bottle and she went to sleep. But when they got home, she started whimpering and they noticed a lump and bruising on her forehead. Evangeline wanted to take Halcyon to the hospital to be checked over but Val told her there wasn't time because she had to drive him to the airport at once, otherwise he'd miss his flight.

'He'd arranged to fly to London that night. That was one of the reasons Murray was staying – to help Evangeline while Val was away. Evangeline thought the flight was at eight but Val insisted that it was "eighteen hundred hours, honey, not eight o'clock". The upshot was that Evangeline and Val set out for the airport and Murray was left holding the baby.

'She wouldn't eat anything so he put her to bed with another bottle. She was still whimpering, but she fell asleep. When Evangeline wasn't back after a couple of hours, Murray checked the baby and realized something was very wrong. She was snoring loudly and her face was flushed. When he turned her on to her side, she vomited. Murray was only young, he didn't know what to do. It was before mobile phones so there was no way of contacting Evangeline, and he knew from experience that she was quite likely to have gone off to visit friends or see a movie. He left a note for her, wrapped up the baby, ran out into the street and hailed a cab. She was deeply unconscious when they got to the hospital, with a lump the size of an egg and bruising on her forehead.

'The staff didn't believe his story, of course. They assumed he was the father, the abusive father. An hour went past and there was no sign of Evangeline. They kept accusing him of shaking the baby, or dropping her on the ground. They threatened him with the police.' Cressida began to cry quietly.

Frank tightened his hold. 'Shush, flower,' he whispered. 'You don't have to go on with this.' But he knew she must, that they were both thinking of Halcyon's attack on Katie May.

'All hell broke loose when it was discovered that the child's skull was fractured. Murray was held for questioning until Evangeline turned up four hours later. Then they were both grilled, day after day for almost a week, until finally the woman who had come to help in the park was located. Halcyon remained unconscious for a couple of weeks and all that time Val stayed in

300

London. In fact, that was the last Evangeline saw of him. Murray got the hell out as well. He didn't see her for years – seven or eight years, by which time she was on Val's trail.' Cressida shook her head in disbelief 'She knew everything about him. Even before I met him she was stalking him.'

'He was some shit.'

'Yes. And I always thought it was something in me that made him like that.' There was wonder in her voice. 'But he'd always been violent.'

'She punished him. She punished us all.' Frank spoke almost to himself.

Cressie seemed not to hear. 'I did the same as she did. I protected Val. I... I... If only she'd gone after him earlier... She should have...'

'What?' Frank asked gently. 'Had him charged?' He knew from his own experience how much easier it was to blame the parent on hand. How reluctant the police in any country were to get involved with domestic issues, how blurred the edges were. At the same time he wondered how Evangeline Walter had managed to wriggle free. By claiming it was an accident, probably. He noted that Cressida didn't believe it had been. She had known Sweeney's unpredictable temper too well.

She held him tight. 'I've so much more to tell you,' she said.

301

'And so have I,' he replied. 'But let's sleep on it. You've been on a long, long journey.' He held her away from him and smiled. 'You're so brave, and so wise. Next time I start pontificating, shut me up. Oh, my darlin' Cressie, welcome home, my love.'

Duncreagh Listening Post
Trianach businessman heads up board of the
Atlantis Apartments PLC in Passage South
and puts Coribeen House on the market.

Regression 11

I half expected Marilyn to come back, and indeed she returned to the cottage at about two thirty, looking flushed and upset. 'When are you going home?' she asked abruptly.

I bristled. 'I don't know. Some time.' Meaning, 'Get off my case, it's none of your business.'

The message must have come across loud and clear. She glared at me. 'God, you're a touchy son-of-a-bitch, aren't you? I don't think I deserved that.' She looked as if she was going to storm out but when I apologized she changed her mind. 'Right so. I'll make it snappy. I presume you're in touch with your parents. And before you get all uptight, I'm not asking for their phone number. I just want you to give them a message from me. Will you do that?'

'Yes,' I said humbly. 'And I'm sorry for being so rude. I–'

'It's all right, boy. You're overwrought. Forget it.' She gnawed her lip. No lipstick, I noticed absently. 'I was over at Coribeen. The auction is next week. Now, listen to me carefully because I think this may be important. Does Frank write those detective books? Is he Frank Ventry, by any chance?'

I didn't know what to say – that's one thing Frank has forbidden us to discuss and I was beginning to understand why. Marilyn watched me closely, reading my face. 'I see I'm right,' she said. 'Tell him there was a woman – a journalist – with the auctioneer. She had a bit of an American accent but she's Irish, all right. He showed us round together. Mind you, he ignored me. Well, he would, wouldn't he? I'm not a serious contender. I just trailed after them. She didn't seem interested in the house either – and this is what really spooked me, she kept bringing the conversation around to your family, Gil. *And* Mrs Walter's murder,' she added pointedly. 'I nearly dropped dead when she started talking about being here at the time, and meeting "that drop-dead handsome Garda Recaldo". How he was hard to forget with that exotic name, and did we realize that he was writing detective stories, these days, as well as the travel books. She had it all down pat, the nosy bitch. Now, this is the important bit. This is what you have to tell him. She said she was writing a series about unsolved crimes for the magazine section of the *Daily News*. Well, working for that rag I could see where she was headed, right enough. Gil? She's trouble. I took the auctioneer to one side and asked him who she was. Tell Frank Fiona Moore was in Coribeen today. I couldn't place her but I dropped in on Aoife Hussey below in Passage South on my way back. Aoife reminded me she was here at the time of the murder, asking a lot of questions about John Spain. She seemed more interested in him than she was in the murder. Remember the name, *Fiona Moore*. Aoife said that someone once told her it was Fiona Moore wrote about him for the American papers when he left the priesthood.' She looked at me as if she was about to tell me all about it but I didn't want her to. I wanted her to stop gossiping about Tar.

'Did you meet her when she was reporting the murder?'

'No, I was sick. I lived next door to the pub then, and Aoife kept me up to date, but she never let on that I worked for Mrs Walter. Neither did her husband, Michael. Nor Frank, of course. Otherwise I'd have been destroyed. I could never keep my mouth shut. They'd have made mincemeat of me.'

That seemed unlikely to me. I started to

ask a question but she brushed me aside. 'That isn't all. Just wait till I tell you what happened next. I thought I might make a few enquiries of my own so, like the know-all I am, I offered her a lift, but she said she had one. Next thing, Jer O'Dowd comes puffing up the drive. Now we know where he was off to when he nearly ran us down this morning.'

'Is he interested in buying Coribeen?'

'Buying? Of course he's not, boy. He's selling. Wasn't it him bought the place from your mother? Didn't you know that?' I shook my head and she was off. 'Oh, indeed. Isn't Smiler our very own property tycoon? And sharp with it, as I know to my cost. We thought we were getting a nice secluded property but didn't that greedy bastard chop away the two fields on either side of the Old Corn Store before we completed, and next thing he built four houses – eight if you count the ones built on the site of his own house. Feckin' shark. Instant neighbours are all very well but it wasn't quite what we had in mind.' She snorted. 'But Smiler O'Dowd was never one to pass up a bargain. He got stung on Coribeen, though.' She chuckled gleefully. 'He had all sorts of great plans for it – marina, hotel, golf course. But the laugh of it was, shortly after your mother sold up, the county boundaries were changed and instead of the Duncreagh planning authority, which was in his pocket, he had to deal with Daingean and that was a different kettle of fish entirely. Coribeen bested him, and I have a horrible feeling he blames it all on your mother. I'm not sure Smiler's the kind I'd like to cross – there's a spiteful side to him. Of course, the cute hoor is only selling about half an acre with the house, so God knows what he intends doing with the rest.'

'Are you going to buy it?'

'Indeed and I'm not then. It's in an awful state, completely neglected,' she said impatiently. 'And I can tell you something else. That Fiona one hasn't the slightest notion of buying it either. So I ask myself what the hell was Smiler up to, chauffeuring her around. All pally like. "Hiya, Fiona," he said, when he got out. "I see you've met Marilyn. She'll tell you all about the Sweeneys." The cheek. "Wasn't she their cleaning lady?" I turned on my heel but he wasn't finished. "And didn't she work for poor Evangeline Walter as well?" She started saying something, but I ignored her and got into my car. I'll only kill that fella when I see him.' Marilyn swept her hair off her flushed face. 'The whole caper was weird. D'you know something, Gil? I had a terrible feeling I'd stumbled into some sort of set-up. I swear O'Dowd knew I was at Coribeen. The

307

auctioneer must have tipped him off. Is that paranoia? God, I don't know, but whatever it is, I could kick myself for going there at all. That Fiona one was all over him like a rash. Jer this, Jer that. All feelie-touchie. For a minute I was reminded of Mrs Walter. Made my flesh crawl, it did. He's always been a terror for the women. Never local girls, mind you. Smiler likes something more exotic. A man for Sundays only, not a weekday bloke at all. The lord of the feckin' dance, he thinks he is.'

Marilyn was getting up a head of steam. 'That reporter will be down on top of me any minute now with her feckin' questions. Why the hell does she want to go dragging it all up again?' she burst out. 'O'Dowd won't have any qualms about giving her my address either. I'm going to make myself very scarce, up sticks and stay in Noreen's house for a few days, and the family with me. So my advice to you, Gil, is to do the same and get the hell out of here.' She gave me an awkward little hug. 'I don't know why I feel so upset. There was something very peculiar going on. D'you know what he shouted after me? "Didn't I see you this morning with the young fella that's squatting in Spain's old cottage? I've a feeling I know him from somewhere." He grinned at your one when he said it. With a what-did-I-tell-you look on his self-satisfied mug. Then he burst out laughing. Sounded a bit demented, to tell you God's honest truth. Thinks he's so feckin' clever. But I hope he knows what he's doing because that is one woman I would not like to cross. So go home, there's a good boy. Please. I've always been wary of that fellow and maybe you should be too.'

'Why? He doesn't know me or where I've been staying, whatever he says. I've been really careful.'

'Hmm. Not careful enough, I'd say. Same as young Noreen. Ye're not invisible. Several people have remarked on your presence to me. I'd say Smiler has you pegged, all right.'

'What does he look like, Mrs Donovan?' I asked quietly.

'Didn't you see him this morning when he almost ran into us?'

'Not really, just a quick glimpse.'

'That'd be enough for most of us. He's always got a big bloody grin on his face, all the time wandering around in that great big car of his, with his feckin' sunglasses and the cap to hide his baldy head.'

I had seen him. The first day in Hussey's, the night I met the Sullivan brothers, and then with Shay. Damn! 'Where does he live?'

'He used to live next door to the Old Corn Store, now he's over the other side, but he still has property on Trianach.' She fell silent for so long I thought she'd forgotten I was there. 'I didn't intend to pass this on,' she said reluctantly, 'because I'm not sure I understand what that creep was getting at. So I'll just repeat what he said after he claimed to know you from somewhere. "Mrs Walter's daughter Halcyon died last week, did you know that, Marilyn? Now there's an unfortunate could tell a story if she hadn't been so dumb. I hear Mrs Sweeney that was, Mrs Recaldo that is, showed up at the funeral in Clonmel. Isn't that the strange thing altogether? *Maybe poor Evangeline is going to get justice at last.*" And he took Ms Moore by the arm and led her to the car.' Marilyn gnawed her bottom lip. 'Mark my words, that journalist is going to rake over the whole mess again.' She nodded slowly. 'You'd better get away from here fast, Gil. Today. I'm sorry things haven't turned out for you, boy, but maybe you'll come back some day?' She smiled faintly. 'Otherwise Noreen will have my guts for garters.'

She left me in such a spin, I couldn't begin to sort out my feelings. Up to then, I'd stowed my mother away for the duration. She was supposed to be safe in Oxford or Dublin. The news of Halcyon's death didn't really affect me: I hadn't seen her for ages and, anyway, I'd never liked her, but the thought of Cressie on the loose, and not far away, made me realize just how out of touch and out of control I was.

After Marilyn had left I tried to ring home several times but nobody was there. I didn't leave a message. I went back over Marilyn's story, and worked out a plan. I got out my mobile again and rang Chief Inspector Phil McBride at Garda Headquarters in Dublin.

I was put through immediately. He must have sensed that something was up because he was unusually serious. No jokes, no nicknames. 'Gil? What can I do for you?'

'I need to talk something over with you.'

'Shoot.'

'No, not on the phone. Could we meet?'

'When?'

'Tomorrow?' I had worked out how long the journey to Dublin would take if I took Marilyn's lift.

'You still in France?'

'No, I'm back.'

'But not at home?' He sounded more guarded. 'I can't see you tomorrow, Gil, I've something on. I could make it later in the week or the weekend.'

I took a deep breath. 'I'm in West Cork. Trianach.'

There was a long silence. 'And your folks don't know.' It wasn't a question so I didn't answer. 'Is that what you want to see me about? You'd be better off talking things over with your parents.' What could I say? That they had had their chance, ten years of chance, and blown it? That I had questions they might not want to answer? 'Phil, please, I need to know what happened.'

'Need? You talk to anyone down there?'

I hesitated. 'Yeah. Marilyn Donovan.'

'What about?'

'The American woman's murder.' I didn't want to admit I knew her name.

'Oh. Right. Make contact with anyone else?'

'No.'

'No? So what's troubling you, exactly?'

'Being here brought things back. I went to the Old Corn Store. Phil? I remember what happened in the garden that night. My mother was there, John Spain… Cressie…' My voice wobbled. Shit, I was turning into a right cry-baby.

'I know all that. Listen to me, Gil. Whatever you remember, or think you remember, your mother didn't do it.' He spoke firmly and calmly but didn't give me a chance to butt in. 'Gil? Think carefully. Can you recall seeing anyone else in the garden?' His voice seemed to come from miles off.

'Yes.'

'Yes? Yes? Do you know who it was?'

'I only saw his feet.'

'Oh.'

'Brown brogues, same as my father's.' I

said it aloud for the first time and felt like Judas. 'I smelt his aftershave.'

'Jaysus.' He let out a low whistle. 'I'll meet you in the back room of Boswell's Hotel in Molesworth Street. Two o'clock. If you get to Dublin sooner give me a ring. Here or at home. Gil? Go straight there. Don't talk to anyone else. Not anyone. Do you hear me?' He put down the phone before I could ask if that included my parents. I packed my things and sat down to wait. Shay came to the cottage at about six, just when I'd given up hope of seeing her.

She saw my backpack the minute she came in. 'You're going?'

'Yeah, I have to. I can't hack it. I have to sort my head out. I'm sorry, Shay.' I felt numb.

'There's nothing I can do, is there, to change your mind. Will I see you again?' she mumbled.

I put my arms around her. 'I hope so. I'll write. Email. Phone. I've decided to travel for another year. Far away – Australia, the States. Maybe we could start college at the same time.' Fantasy, fantasy.

She snorted. 'And I suppose you expect me to... Ah, feck it, Sweeney...'

'Please don't call me Sweeney,' I said quietly. 'Please.'

'It was just, it was just – oh, Gil, I didn't mean anything by it.'

'I know you didn't, but it makes me very uncomfortable,' I said, as calmly as I could, then immediately lost it. 'Ask your aunt about the Sweeneys,' I shouted. 'Ask her. She knows more about us than anyone. Ask her.'

'Shush.' She put her head against my chest and rocked back and forth. 'Come and lie down for a bit. It's too late to go tonight. I'll get the aunt to give you a lift to Duncreagh tomorrow morning.' She giggled. 'She doesn't trust me to get to school on my own.'

Duncreagh Listening Post *(archive)*
*EXTRAORDINARY SCENES AT PAS-
SAGE SOUTH AS FISHERMAN HERO IS
BURIED AT SEA*

Regression 12

Shay stayed so late that I was surprised
Marilyn didn't come after me with a
shotgun. After she left I allowed myself to
doze for an hour or so, until it was too late
for her to come back or for any of my
invisible neighbours to be out and about. I
felt odd, as if I was travelling outside my
own body, when I slipped out into the
velvety dark night just as I had on the night
of the murder.

My mother had been sleeping, curled up
on the bed, still wearing her black sweater
and jeans, when I followed Tar out on to the
lane. He had gone ahead and didn't seem
aware that I was after him. For once he
wasn't wearing his overalls so he was harder
to see in his old navy Guernsey and cords
with his tattered sailor cap on his head. I hid
behind a rock until he got into the boat and
rowed away. Then I climbed the spit.

When I get to the top he's coming round

the other side, a little way out and pulling hard against the current. That's when my father's launch glides away from the bank further on and cuts across towards Cori-been. Tar has his back to it, but I suppose he must hear it. He turns his head.

I sit watching him struggle with the tide for a long time, and when he's far enough ahead I slither down the side of the spit and run after him along the shore. At first I can't find him in the dark, but then the moon shines through the clouds and I see he's already left the boat, which is bobbing between the oars that he'd somehow wedged upright into the mud between me and the woman's garden. There's a full moon but it's cloudy, so that one minute the garden is all lit up and the next it's plunged into darkness, like lights going on and off, and I see what happens in minuscule disjointed episodes.

Tar is running, crouched, up the hill towards the house. The huge french windows are wide open but the lights are out. The woman is lying on the terrace close to the window, exactly where my mother left her. There is something around her head – a scarf? – but otherwise she is naked. She is lying on her stomach with her bottom in the air like I do when I've a pain in my belly. There is something white, maybe her dress, lying a little to one side. Tar bends over her for a long time. I cannot see what he's doing. He straightens up and disappears into the house, leaving the woman where she is. He doesn't help her or anything so she must be dead. Cressie killed her! No, no, *no*. I start shaking and crying. No! Please, God, let her not be dead. The moon goes in. Nothing happens for a long, long time. The tide is beginning to run and soon I won't be able to get back to the cottage on foot. I wade out to the rowing boat and climb aboard. There's a folded tarpaulin under one of the seats. I pull it out and try to wrap it around myself but it's stiff and cold. I lie on my stomach with my good arm holding the side and wait for Tar. I can't keep my eyes open.

I don't know how long I remain under the tarpaulin. I keep expecting Tar to come back but he doesn't. When I peep out again, moonlight floods the garden. Now the woman is covered with a blanket or something. A big square thing standing on the terrace by the open side gate catches my eye. It's too far away to make out clearly but I think it's a big box, or a trunk with brass handles. It glints as the light catches it. Next thing I see Tar walking up – up? – the garden, and he must see the box as well, because he goes to it. He doesn't touch it but stands looking down at it until the headlights of a car light up the drive outside the open gate.

Tar scarpers sharpish, although I can't see where because I'm busy watching the headlights get nearer and nearer. The car turns: I see the rear brake lights and then the white reverse lights come closer and closer to the opening. I gasp when I see my father come round the back of his silver Lexus. He goes over to the box and picks it up. It must be heavy because he staggers and almost falls down. He puts it into the boot and goes back for something else that is still lying on the grass, which he tosses in beside the box. As he stands at the open boot I notice he's changed into something dark – a suit, maybe. He walks across to where the woman is lying and stops dead. He looks around then bends down and lifts what's covering her and holds it in the air. It's a white dress or something but she's not under it. She's gone. I sit bolt upright. She isn't dead. The woman isn't dead. My mother didn't kill her. I want to shout it out, I'm so relieved.

But what is my father up to? He tosses the cloth on to the table and goes into the house. The lights come on, lots of lights. I can see right inside. He walks around and around as if he's looking for something. Or someone. My heart is in my mouth for fear he'll find Tar and there'll be a big fight. But it doesn't happen. The light from the open window reaches well down the lawn, and just where the steep incline flattens out, Tar is lying face down on the grass, with his arms covering his head, trying not to be seen. I don't know how long my father stays inside the house – a few minutes, no more. When he comes out he stands on the terrace. My heart begins to thump. Now he'll see Tar for sure, but he doesn't seem to. Yet he's looking in the right direction, facing the river. He raises his arm and waves. Waves? I turn to see who he's waving at and there is the woman leaning against the tree with a long scarf trailing in the breeze. When I look up to the house, my father is gone.

I watch the headlights go off into the distance before Tar moves. He is stiff when he gets up, and it takes a moment for him to straighten. He goes over to the woman. The scarf is tangled in the low branches of the tree. I can't make out what's happening, what he's doing by the tree, but he must be talking to her because when the moon comes out again I see she is standing beside him and his arms are still round her. That makes me angry because I thought we didn't like her, that she's bad. They fall backwards on to the grass. Oh, no, oh, no, I don't want him to start all that kissing stuff again. I shut my eyes tight, tight. When I look again, Tar is going into the house but the woman is lying on the grass near the tree, stretched out, like she's asleep.

Tar is inside for a few minutes and when he comes out he's holding a bucket and sweeping brush. He throws some water on to the terrace and brushes it down just as it starts to rain. He goes back in. I keep expecting the woman to run in out of the wet but she doesn't. And suddenly I know it's because she's dead. Really dead. But how come I didn't see it happen? Did I fall asleep when she and Tar were rolling on the grass? He killed her, he killed her. I don't know how, but I'm relieved it wasn't my mother. But what was my father doing? Why was he there? I hold my swollen arm close. He could hurt a person without even trying. Why did he wave at Tar? Because he knew the woman was dead? Oh, God, he's going to come after us again, he saw me in the garden. Now he'll kill me for sure.

What's that? There's a shadow at the top of the garden. The house lights go out. A shadow? I peer into the half-light and for a split second see someone all in black running across the window. Not Tar: he is still in the house. Smaller. Mama. What is she doing? She's gone. Maybe I imagined it. I might have. Now I'm so frightened I wriggle down well into the boat and keep very still. After a little time a small bundle is shoved in under the tarpaulin beside me and the boat sinks down into the water and begins to move. The tide is roaring in and the rain is lashing down.

I touch the bundle with my free hand, cloth with paper wrapped loosely around two small hard things. I feel them all over but I can't figure out what they are. The boat stops. I feel Tar climb out. I wait. His hand feels under the tarpaulin and pulls out the bundle. I stay very, very still. Maybe I dropped off to sleep? When I next peep out it's pitch dark. The rain has stopped and Tar is nowhere in sight. I pull back the cover and climb out. The ground underfoot is slippy. I'm half-way to the cottage when I remember I didn't fold away the tarpaulin. I run back and trip over a rock. Next thing I know I'm being carried into the house by my mother. Tar is walking beside us, holding on to her. My arm is throbbing.

I left the spit for the last time and walked like a zombie up to John Spain's cottage. It was three o'clock in the morning. I closed the door and shot the bolt. Then I lay on the sofa and ran back over everything that had happened to me since my return to the estuary. I knew I had missed something, perhaps many things. And I knew that I couldn't leave the cottage until I'd worked it out. But I was bushed. I dozed and woke and slept again. I got so cold I crept back into the musty old bedroom, unrolled my sleeping-bag and wrapped it round me. It smelt of Shay. I snuggled down in it and at last fell asleep.

I had the weirdest dreams, all featuring Tar, and he was desperate to tell me something. We were together on the boat, watching the seals slither off the Crags. We were hauling a fish basket up to the cottage door. We were in his car delivering lobsters to a restaurant. We were in the cottage at the table doing our work. I was writing in my copybook and he was at the sink. At first he was standing with his back to it, pointing out something. Next he had his back to me. He bent down under the old Belfast sink and after a minute or two straightened up with something in his hands. Something for me. Now I am hunkered down beside him and he is pointing under the sink to where there's a hole in the wall. He pulls out a Mars bar and laughs. 'Magic,' he says, and gives it to me.

I was shaking when I woke up, with cold and fear. It took me a little time to work up the energy to get up and brew some coffee over the paraffin stove. I was frozen, hungry and filthy. I needed a bath and something big and fatty to eat. But not yet.

We had this game. He would say a word: *Beano*, toffee, biscuit, and when I worked it out, I'd find whatever he'd named in the secret hiding place. Magic. I knelt down

322

beside the sink. It was smelly and mouldy underneath and first off I plunged my hand into a nest of mice. I nearly threw up at the sight of the naked wriggling little bodies – there seemed to be hundreds of them. I gritted my teeth and moved my hand along the wall behind the U-bend where I could feel the edges of one brick standing proud of its neighbours. It came away easily because the mortar was damp and crumbly. I put my hand into Tar's secret hiding place and felt around gingerly, afraid of finding more mice. I drew out a small package – a plastic sandwich bag with a bunch of keys and an old mobile phone wrapped in a bit of newspaper. With my heart in my boots I opened the scrap of the *Irish Times* and looked at the mobile. The screen was missing. It was about three times the size of mine with what looked like a rechargeable battery attached to the back. Quite a weight in your pocket. I'd no idea why it was there. I examined the keys. The leather tab with the makers' mark had almost completely perished but the metal Lexus emblem was intact. I searched the back of the cavity again and found a second bit of plastic stuck fast to the floor. I eased up one corner and gradually worked my fingers underneath until I could wrench it free. This bag was folded over and sealed with perished Sello-tape. Inside was a small yellowing envelope with faded writing on the front, which I brought over to the window. My name was faded but still readable. Inside was a letter from Tar. Three or four pages written in pencil so that it would survive the damp. Clever Tar.

My dearest Gil, I write in the event that you return, as I believe you will one day. For the past three days I have been in my boat writing, writing. It is hard to say goodbye, not to see you and your mother again. You have been the most precious joy of my last years.

My boy, I have lately been accused of corrupting you, and your dear mother has been accused of colluding with me. I can hardly bring myself to speak these things or defend myself. For what defence is there if the poison has already gained ground? I pray you know with the same certainty as I that abusing your mother's or your trust in me would be the very last thing on earth I would do. I swear you were always safe with me. But protestations are useless, useless.

The architect of this calumny is dead, and very soon so shall I be. Would that rumour died so easily. I killed her. Oh, yes, it was I. I may not have given her the *coup de grâce* but I struck the first blow. I didn't intend it, but that is what happened. What troubles me more than what I've done, or am about to do, is that you may have witnessed more than any of us realized. I write to set the record straight.

The girl with the strange name, Halcyon Walter, was the catalyst. Your father's first, unacknowledged child. The poor innocent creature was in the care of an order of nuns in Tipperary, of which my own sister is a member. On the day Evangeline Walter realized this, she knew she could keep the girl secret no longer and turned on me. It was suspected that Halcyon's condition had been caused by neglect or abuse and, in your father's absence, the blame fell on Evangeline. She'd been after him for years. When you lost your hearing and speech, and it became known around the township that your father was abusing you and your mother, something seems to have snapped in Mrs Walter: her resolve to destroy Sweeney hardened.

She attacked him every way she knew, financially and personally. Others may be able to explain how, since I don't know the details. What I do know is that the more she goaded him, the more he went to pieces. When his business failed, his attacks on your mother grew more and more ferocious.

When he was forced to sell his beloved yacht, Mrs Walter bought it, using Smiler O'Dowd as her go-between. Sweeney must only have realized who was behind the scheme when she changed its name to *Halcyon*. She did it as soon as she came out of hospital, terminally ill with cancer. It was then she arranged a sailing party to introduce her deaf-mute, brain-damaged daughter to her father and, incidentally, to the neighbours. Anyone looking at the two together would know exactly who she was. I did, O'Dowd did, Cressie did. And, so my dear Gil, did you.

If a murder has a beginning, that was it. You mentioned seeing her to your father. He threatened to have me charged and you taken into care. He beat the living daylights out of you and your mother, then lit out for Trianach in the launch. Despite her and your injuries, Cressie came to warn me but I had already gone to plead with Mrs Walter myself. Cressie followed me with you in the car, and the whole thing spiralled out of control.

I'm filling in this background because, over the past few days, I'm worried that if indeed you saw what happened in that accursed garden, you may misinterpret it. If so, you will surely read this. I killed Evangeline Walter by forcing myself on her two weeks after she had had a major stomach operation. She was high on medication and drugs and I was beside myself with anger. I lost control and violated her savagely. Cressie tried to save me and inadvertently knocked Mrs Walter to the ground. I believe your father was also concealed in the garden and saw what happened; his launch was tied up at the old slipway.

After I got you and Cressie safely back to this house, I went back – again, as I think you know. Between the two visits, Sweeney must also have used her. This I learned later from Frank Recaldo, who is frantic about Cressie. I went back to the garden to check that Mrs Walter was all right. I never for a moment thought that Cressie's blow had done more than momentarily stun her. I've told Frank and the other detectives that I wasn't the one who killed her but they won't believe me. I can't work it out. My head aches.

I heard the launch roaring across the estuary as I came close to the garden. I found her dead on the terrace, blood all over the place. I held myself responsible. I *was* responsible. I became so frantic I didn't know what I was doing. I carried her down to the cold river to try to revive her or clean her, but of course it was hopeless. Then Sweeney came back. I threw myself down on the grass and watched him put a pile of stuff into the boot of his car. When he found Mrs Walter's body was gone, he stood searching the garden. I thought he was looking for the body, which was still lying by the tree at the water's edge, but I believe it was me he was seeking out. He couldn't have missed me lying on the grass near her. He gave a loud laugh and waved. Then he went into the house, switched on all the lights and turned on the CD player. Ella Fitzgerald in top cry. It was obscene. He must have known she played music late at night. I often heard it.

I began to panic – not for myself alone but for your mother. The woman had been left on the terrace when Cressida felled her. I was sure he was trying to set her up for the killing – wife catches husband *in flagrante* and attacks his lover – or her and me both, even better. I set about cleaning things up, obfuscating the evidence. I went inside the house and saw at once that the floor was damp, as if it had been mopped. The place looked undisturbed, neat and clean, but I wiped all the surfaces, anyway. I found a small tape-recorder under a folded news-paper on the coffee table which he somehow overlooked and her mobile phone which had dropped behind the sofa. I listened to the tape until I could bear no more. Dear God. She was sick in mind as well as body. She goaded him into doing what I started. We are all damned. I never intended to evade justice, Gil, but I didn't want your mother dragged down in the mire.

We found you lying unconscious in the

cove at three that morning. As soon as we had strapped up your arm, I sent you and your mother off to the hospital in Cork. She was in a dreadful state; she kept telling me she'd lost the comb she used to hold back her hair. I promised to go back and look for it but instead I drove my old banger to Coribeen. The house was in darkness but the Lexus was outside. I let myself in at the back door, which was never locked. Sweeney was snoring on the sofa, a half-empty bottle of whiskey on the floor beside him. He didn't wake up when I fished the car keys from his jacket pocket. I drove the Lexus away and hid it on an abandoned farm where it wouldn't be found. I threw mud at the car until it was well covered and went back on foot for my own.

It was nearly five o'clock when I got home. I changed into my overalls and rowed back to the garden to do a final check before I called Recaldo. I used her mobile phone. I forgot to look for the comb.

I am afraid, and afraid of what this might do to you. And that is why I have to make sure there is no trial. For if any of the three of us stands accused, then the stories about me will be taken for fact and Cressie will surely lose you. I am damned anyway. If I can die a hero's death it will staunch the flow, and both Sweeney and I will get what we deserve. It will be justice of a kind.

Justice without charity. Forgive me.

It is now five thirty on Saturday morning. I have been watching Coribeen for days. Sweeney's been hiding in the attic and one of the boats moored on the estuary whose owner is away. The police are closing in. The loss of the car has unnerved him, as I intended. Now he'll be forced to flee by yacht, leaving the car and evidence behind, and that's what I gambled on. Earlier, when there were few people about, I drove the Lexus to the supermarket car park in Duncreagh, which is always packed on a Saturday. I want it to be found, but not for a few hours. Another gamble. It's unrecognizable, caked all over with mud and dung. I am so tired.

I have the keys of the motor launch, and three spare cans of fuel. I hope it's enough. Sweeney went out to the yacht last night and is still there, so he is about to make his move... I will go to *Consuela* for the last time and wait. Goodbye, my boy. My house is yours, should you want it, otherwise let it go back to the earth. Tar.

I rolled up Tar's things in one of my T-shirts and put it into my backpack. I took one last look round and let myself out.

Email from Fiona Moore to Sean Brophy
Sean, Saw the charwoman as well but she's
keeping mum. There is a gallery owner I might
tap into. The daughter died. Brain-damaged,
abandoned. According to Slimer, the image of
the half-sibling. Mrs Recaldo showed up at the
school this morning. You'll never guess who she
turns out to be. This is good, this is great. The
copper married the murderer's wife. Oh, boy! We
have it sewn up. Fi

Chapter 18

The Recaldos were having a strange and wonderful interlude. Something miraculous had happened between them since Cressida's return home: the tension had lightened. Superstitious about enquiring too closely into the causes of this blissful hiatus, or discussing it, they put all their previous problems and disagreements down to their prolonged separation. Now that they were together, things would work out fine.

Next evening, Frank opened a bottle of Brouilly and he and Cressida sat at either side of the kitchen table going through the estate agents' bumph. 'Thanks for giving me space, Frank,' she said, 'and for getting this stuff.' She put her hand on top of the pile and sat back in her chair. 'But I'm not sure this is the best time for a move. I know I've been banging on about it, but Katie May seems to like the school and now that Gil is away this place doesn't seem so small, does it?'

'He'll be back.' Frank laid his hand on hers. 'You're thinking of me, aren't you? The operation.'

'Well, yes, of course I am. It helps to be near a decent hospital and a good GP. We have both here. I think we should at least bear it in mind, don't you?'

'I think the same, but I don't like this place any more than you do. I've always seen it as a transition stage. I never thought we'd be here so long.' He took a long draught. 'This is good, I could get used to decent wine, couldn't you? Look, love, moving Katie, if we do it quickly enough, won't be a problem. She's very enthusiastic about living in the country. We talked about it a lot while you were away. As long as there's a kennel for your man Rafferty, she'll be fine.' He rubbed the back of Cressida's hand. 'Oh, Cress, my darlin', I'm that pleased to have you back. When I think—'

'Of how we were both feeling and behaving a week ago? Yeah, me too.' She

332

leaned across the table and kissed him. 'I love you, Frank Recaldo, you know that? Everything's going to be fine.' She leafed through the particulars until she came to a glossy folder marked 'Coribeen' that Frank had placed in the middle of the pile. She looked up. 'Where did this come from?' she asked. She seemed neither surprised nor upset.

Frank watched as she read through it and studied the picture. 'I didn't realize it was there till we got home. We picked up so many and I binned most of them. Can we talk about it, Cress?' There was a moment's hesitation before Cressida got up and, without a word, went into the hall. That's torn it, he thought.

But, no, she came back almost at once, carrying her voluminous shoulder-bag. She gave him a rueful smile as she plunged her hand into it and brought out an identical prospectus. 'Yes,' she said. 'We do need to talk about Coribeen. Or, at least, I do. You've always wanted to, but I've been so ... repressive.' She smiled wanly. 'Still am. But the time has come.' She took his hands in hers. 'I've been on a pilgrimage to the holy shrine. That's what it became, you know. I could never get it out of my head. I resented leaving it so much that I lost sight of what it did to me, what it represented. Frank? I went back. I've seen it.'

'When?' he asked, though he'd already guessed.

'After Halcyon's funeral. I told you Rose O'Faolain showed up. I was so surprised to see her, but apparently Murray asked her to help. I hadn't realized she'd arranged a memorial service for Evangeline Walter a few months after we left.' Cressida's voice wobbled on the dreaded name but, after a moment, she continued: 'I'm not sure Murray realized Grace kept in touch with Rose. I certainly hadn't, but I was glad to see her. She had the details with her. She thought we'd be interested because it was so cheap. And, of course, I was. I couldn't wait to see it. So we drove down after the funeral. She borrowed the key from her pal the auctioneer that evening after hours and we viewed it early next morning.' She paused. 'The whole thing was a terrible mistake – but maybe it wasn't. It was certainly a shock. Nobody's lived in the house since we left and it's had no maintenance either. It's almost back to how I first found it. Not quite, but pretty bad. O'Dowd was never able to get any of the planning permissions he wanted. He's hived off the land and restored the old path to the main road. Otherwise it's as it was. I only got as far as the front hall, Frank.' Cressida was trembling. 'Rose waited outside. I stood inside the door, and all I could remember was standing holding Gil's little hand and the two of us shaking like leaves. The smell of fear is still there. I'm not imagining it. I thought of how desperately unhappy I was, not about how much I loved it. I thought about Gil, too, and I couldn't get out fast enough.'

Cressida's head was down, her hands clasped. 'Frank? Oh, Frank. I realized something terrible. I kept saying I loved Coribeen, but I used it as an excuse not to leave Val. I told myself it was my anchor, my security. Frank, I sacrificed Gil to a pile of bricks.'

'And yourself too, *mo chroí*. You were afraid of losing Gil. Don't forget that. You did what you thought best at the time.' Ponderous platitudes, he thought and tried again: 'Cress, you were absolutely paralysed with fear. Don't underestimate what that did to you. The man was evil. Cressie, he was a bully, he controlled you. That's what abuse does.'

'But how could I have exposed Gil? Look what Val did to Halcyon.'

'You didn't know that at the time,' Frank said reasonably.

'I knew Gil was in danger. I should have taken him away. How could I have put all that out of my mind? I mourned that house for years and years, looking over my shoulder for so long I couldn't see what was in front of my eyes. This is the hard bit, Frank. I blamed you for taking me away. I can't believe it now. You did everything for us, provided us with love, shelter, a home,' she waved her hands around the room, 'and our beautiful daughter. All I could do was whinge on and on about how dismal this place was.'

Frank burst out laughing. 'Oh, come on, don't be tragic about it. It *is* dismal. And I don't remember all that much whingeing. You think I like it? Of course I don't. But, darlin', we've been happy here, haven't we? In our fashion? In our way?'

But Cressida didn't laugh. 'Oh, yes,' she said fervently. 'I didn't appreciate how happy until I went back to Coribeen and remembered what my life was like before I met you.' She brightened. 'It broke the spell. Even the view is different. There are new houses everywhere. There isn't a square inch of space on the Passage South side. That beautiful view? Gone. I was glad of that too. I think her house must have been knocked down, you know. There seems to be a hotel or something in its place, covered with balconies.' She shivered. 'I wouldn't stay there. Not for anything.'

'Cressie, love, one of these days soon we have to talk to Gil about it all.'

'I suppose so,' she agreed reluctantly. 'But, darling, Gil doesn't remember any of it.

He's never once asked in all these years.'

'That doesn't mean he hasn't any memories, Cress. Haven't you noticed how withdrawn he's become in the past couple of years?'

'Adolescence?'

'Oh, Cress, he's eighteen, he should be past that. We're going to have to find a way. Together.'

'He hasn't said anything to you, has he?' she asked anxiously. 'God, how could we begin?'

'I suppose we could just make it easy for him to talk, ask questions.'

'But we've never stopped him, have we?' she asked, and Frank didn't want to spoil the mood by telling her that the bond between her and her son was so strong that Gil would do anything to spare her anxiety. So he let it lie. 'You didn't see O'Dowd?'

'No, thank God, I didn't see anyone. Didn't want to. And I don't want to go back. Ever.'

'What about John Spain's cottage?' he asked, treading on eggs. 'Gil will have to be told about that some time soon.'

'I couldn't bear to go near it. It would bring it all back.'

'But he left it to Gil. The boy should at least be told, Cress – he's eighteen.'

'How can we? Oh, Frank, that gossip about poor John Spain has never really died away. Rose told me.'

'But you know there's no foundation in it. You know that, I know that, and I bet if you asked Gil, he'd say the same. John Spain was a good man. Gil adored him. That kind of trust doesn't come through fear.'

'I know. When he comes back for university I promise, Frank, I'll talk to him. I'll sort it all out. But whether Gil wants to or not, I'm never going back.'

'Right, then,' Frank said, and poured more wine. 'So that's Cork out, is it?'

Instead of answering, Cressida dug in her bag again and passed him a one-page estate agent's listing. 'Would you consider Wexford?' she asked shyly.

'You went to Wexford as well? You have been buzzing around.'

'Rose again. She suggested it. I had the watercolours from Elsfield in the car and I showed them to her. They aren't her sort of stuff but she has a nephew who deals in watercolours and small works of art. He has a gallery in Wexford town. I took a huge detour on the way home and dropped in on him. Rose came too.' She was bursting with excitement. 'He's looking for a partner. They suggested I use the collection to start me off. There are fifty good paintings and about as many prints, so enough to start buying and selling. I'd like to give it a go. What do you think?'

'Good. Seems so obvious, when you think about it. Everything you've done, your years working for Rose and then Grace, all seem to lead the one way.' He got up, took her in his arms and they waltzed languidly around the kitchen. 'Wexford, eh? I'd really like that. It's a great idea. The opera festival. Good sailing.' Frank was excited. 'Estuaries galore. Let's ring Gil and tell him.' But Gil's mobile was switched off.

'He's probably out crewing,' Cressida said.

It did not occur to either of them that he had taken matters into his own hands. But that was about to change.

Chapter 19

On the Friday after Cressida got home Katie May's class was taken on an outing to Dublin zoo. That afternoon while Cressida waited with a group of parents outside the school gate the headmistress came out and told them that the bus was delayed in traffic and wouldn't be at the school for at least a half-hour. Cressida set off to a nearby park for a stroll and returned about twenty minutes later.

On the way back she passed Gil's old school with a sense of *déjà vu*, and thought about her early years in Dublin, when Gil was little and the fear of being hounded by the press was intense. The brouhaha about the TV and Frank's forthcoming book had brought it all back, especially when he told

340

her how much publicity he was expected to do. And although his illness had given him an excuse to back out gracefully, she worried that someone would rake up the murder and make the connections that she and Frank had gone to such pains to hide. 'My love, it's a long, long time. I've been very careful, always.'

'We've got Daddy's money, Frank. You don't...' she was afraid to ask him to retire but as usual he knew what she was thinking and did a skilful detour.

'Ah, Cressie, love, how long do you think that will last after we pay off Gil's school loan? It'll hardly cover the rest of Katie May's fees – they're going up all the time. And then there's Gil's university and the move.' Listening to this middle-class *angst*, so unexpected coming from Frank, made them both laugh.

'Oh, Frank, what's happening to us?'

'Pathetic, isn't it? But all this won't last. It might, but the chances are it won't – at least, not at this level.'

'We don't need to move, not yet anyway.'

'But you said–'

'Yes. A load of old guff. We'll manage, as long as we're together.'

After the turmoil of the previous months, she was still amazed at how glad she was to be home. She didn't like the house but somehow the realization that it wasn't going to be for ever made it more acceptable. Katie loved her new school and was quickly making friends. It was hardly an ideal moment to up sticks, but Frank had taken the Wexford proposal on board and seemed determined to make it happen. Cressida suspected that it was his way of clinging to the future while he tried to come to terms with the forthcoming operation, so she played along.

That Frank had been so fearful of telling her, afraid she couldn't handle looking after him, appalled her and awakened her to how dismally she'd treated him over the past few years. When she saw how terrified he was, her previous resentments turned to remorse. He had a phobia about hospitals, which wasn't surprising considering his family's medical history – his father and elder brother had both died of coronary disease. The knowledge that Frank had been too proud to ask for her help broke her heart and highlighted the sad state of their relationship. His previous marriage had foundered during his first bypass, and they had come dangerously close to the same edge.

Watching Grace and Murray drifting inexorably towards the rocks had shown her how much she loved Frank, needed him, and wanted to be with him. All their other problems, including the fear that his fame would draw down unwanted publicity, were nothing compared to losing him.

She had been shocked by his appearance when she got back, partly because she'd ignored the danger signals. He'd been irritable and tired in Oxford when she had been too preoccupied with her own grievances to notice how defeated he seemed. She was further bamboozled by how much more himself he'd been in Waterford, buoyed up by the excitement of the TV film, perhaps. But even then she, poor goose that she was, hadn't observed how he avoided activity. There had been none of his usual vigorous walks with her and Katie trailing miles behind. They'd strolled by the river a couple of times but nothing more. Watching him try to disguise the effort of moving stuff from the car on the night she got home had been another matter. He had seemed to be thinking and moving through molasses, sluggish of speech and action. The Grim Reaper shifted position.

Cressida walked along the suburban street looking neither left nor right. I could be waiting for death, she thought, waiting for it to stroll round the corner and grab him. At night, in the darkness of their bedroom, they talked for hours as they faced the best and the worst. The previous day he'd done an interview with a journalist from the *Daily News*, a man called Sean Brophy who seemed to know too much about him, and Frank had come home upset. 'I'm effing useless at dissembling. I was a complete eejit to allow myself to be talked into it. I'm not doing any more,' he promised. 'I don't give a fig if it affects the sales or not. Cress, would you be an angel and ring Rebecca and tell her to cancel everything? She won't argue with you if you tell her I'm not well.'

'I've been trying to get hold of Gil, Frank. I'd like him to come home.'

'He's due any day, isn't he? But maybe it wouldn't be a bad idea to get him to come a little earlier?'

We should tell him. We should have told him many things. It was in both their minds. One day soon, she resolved, for the umpteenth time. When Frank is out of hospital, I'll take my lovely boy away for a couple of days and tell him everything.

'If you can get hold of him,' Frank added. 'He seems to have become very elusive. Did you tell him about Halcyon?'

'No, I couldn't reach him and I didn't want to leave a message.'

Now, as she strolled past Gil's old school, in the warm autumnal sunshine, she remembered she hadn't spoken to Gil for a couple of weeks. He had left snappy little messages on her mobile or on the answer-machine at home, at odd hours, which he explained was because he was now crewing and had little time to himself. She presumed he'd met a girl. She clung to that thought. He'd stopped sending Katie May postcards. Definitely a girl.

She was almost in sight of the school when she heard someone call, 'Mrs Sweeney.' Her heart lurched but she walked on resolutely. But there it was again. 'Oh, Mrs Sweeney.' This time the voice was low, insinuating, as if spoken down a long tube, giving a sense of distance. Cressida froze. Nobody used surnames any more, did they? She must have imagined it. Then she heard it again. 'Oh, Mrs Sweeney.'

After a decent pause Cressida turned casually and looked up and down the street. Bumper-to-bumper parked cars, a few with the drivers still inside, a couple of young men wheeling bicycles, obviously headed towards the school, a few pedestrians. She glanced at the group of women chatting outside the school gate. One, catching her eye, nodded vaguely in her direction. Cressie smiled back but made no attempt to join them. Instead she pulled her mobile from her bag and pretended to make a call while the crowd at the gate gradually swelled. Nine women, four men so far. Had the voice been male or female? Hard to tell since it had been little more than a whisper. Maybe it was inside her own head?

She was blasted into reality by a loud

squawk. 'Oh, rats, don't tell me the bloody bus is late.' A woman, who had just run her car half on to the pavement, barely avoiding Cressida, leaned out of the window.

'It should be along in about ten minutes,' Cressida replied.

'Ten minutes? Are you sure?' The newcomer opened the car door and struggled out. 'I'm going to be late. Damn.' She tugged nervously at her watch. 'I have a dental appointment.' She was plump, good-looking and carelessly but fashionably dressed in black. Like many of the parents, she looked a bit long in the tooth to be the mother of a ten-year-old. Cressida looked at her more closely. Dishevelled with purpose. The light wool suit was a bad fit but managed to give a hint of expense and would have suggested 'cool', were it not that it looked as though it had recently been recycled from a full laundry basket. Her shoulder-length dark hair was well cut and shone. She wore full makeup and an expensive-looking silver neckband.

'The headmistress came out a while ago and said the bus was held up in traffic. The driver phoned in,' Cressida murmured. She'd never seen the woman before and wondered who she was.

'You're Katie May's mum, aren't you?' There was something vaguely familiar about her face but Cressida couldn't place her.

'Lulu talks about her all the time.' She smiled.

'Lulu Stephenson?' Cressida looked at the woman with interest. Katie May was smitten with her daughter Louise – known as Lulu – whom Cressida had not met.

Her companion started rubbing her jaw. 'This tooth is driving me insane,' she said. 'If I miss this appointment, it'll take weeks...' Cressida knew what was coming. 'Would you mind?'

'I could take Lulu home to play with Katie May,' she offered grudgingly.

Mrs Stephenson practically fell on her neck, 'Oh, you wouldn't, would you? You sure?' She smiled broadly. 'That's really kind. I'll do the same for you some time, promise. I'm Fiona, by the way,' she said, and held out her hand. 'You're Cressida Recaldo, aren't you? I love your name,' she gushed.

Icy fingers clutched Cressida's heart. *How the hell does she know my first name?* 'I prefer Cressie,' she said coldly. 'Where do you live?' she asked, quickly enough to catch the other woman on the hop.

'Blackrock. I'm still waiting to complete on a house.' She named a street close to the school. 'It's taking an absolute age. Meanwhile I've rented a grotty little flat that costs the earth.' She touched her cheek again. 'It shouldn't take long, an hour or so.

347

I'll ring you as soon as I'm finished.' Another big smile. 'I'll just jot down your number.'

'Blackrock's very convenient,' Cressida said blandly. 'I can easily drop Lulu home. Matter of fact I have to collect something from Merrion Road around six. So, if you'll just give me your address?' Game, set and match. She watched Mrs Stephenson leap into her car and drive off. She'd stopped rubbing her jaw. Cressida smiled ruefully. I'm too bloody suspicious, she thought. She relaxed. Nevertheless, long practice and innate caution made her note the make and colour of Fiona Stephenson's car. As well as the registration.

Email from Fiona Moore to Sean Brophy
Sean, The old toothache act worked wonders.
But she was too canny to give me the phone
number. Lucky I spotted Frank that day or
what? I've given O'Dowd the bird. If I hear
another word about the wrongs done to him by
all and sundry I'll scream. The canonization of
the saintly Vangie continues. Yuk. Fi. PS I've
come up with another subject – a real peach and
a load of sex. Luv, Fi

Chapter 20

Katie May appeared to be both overwhelmed and dazzled by Lulu Stephenson's
robust personality, but Cressida was less
enamoured. Frank dealt with the rise in
decibels by shutting himself in the dining
room, which had been converted to a study
in Cressida's absence. Rafferty alone was
full of enthusiasm and the two little girls
played with him for most of the afternoon.

Cressida delivered Lulu home well before
the arranged time. Amazingly self-pos-
sessed, the little girl sat in the front seat
beside her and kept her entertained all the
way. She was nothing if not informative and,
without any prompting from Cressida, gave

out a good deal of her family history. She had been born in San Francisco but had lived in London, Cape Town and other places whose names she couldn't remember. She had a big brother who was at Cambridge. Katie May was her best friend ever, in the whole world. She loved Rafferty and when they moved, which would be soon, she was going to get a puppy just like him. She rambled on and on, long after Cressida had tuned out her squeaky little voice. Or almost, since it was quite piercing. Her mommy had a new friend, a nice man who might, one day, become her new daddy. She'd had quite a few in different places but Sean was the nicest. Cressida was dying to ask the child what her mother worked at that took her to so many far-off places, but knowing how outraged she would be if Katie May was pumped for information, she put temptation behind her.

'Could I play with Katie May tomorrow?' Lulu asked. 'I love going to your house. Rafferty's only gorgeous.' And she was off again, but Cressida was distracted, looking for the apartment building. 'It's over there,' Lulu shouted. 'Look, there's Mommy.' She pointed to her mother at a second-floor window.

As Cressida looked up and waved, the woman stood up. She bent over behind a curtain, then straightened and waved back.

Something about the sequence of her movements made Cressida wonder if she'd been working at a computer, shielded behind the half-drawn curtain.

'My mommy's writing a book,' Lulu said proudly, as they walked, hand in hand, to the porch. 'She writes for a newspaper as well.' Cressie froze. 'Come on, Mrs Recaldo, there she is.'

Mrs Stephenson was standing at the door holding her hand to her cheek. Her speech was muffled as she thanked Cressida, and took delivery of her irrepressible child. She didn't ask Cressida in or offer her a cup of tea – not that she would have accepted. But as she walked away stiffly from the apartment building, her relief at not being asked in did not blind her to how offhand Lulu's mother had been compared with her hail-fellow-well-met friendliness outside the school. Somehow or other she didn't think it had anything to do with toothache.

When she got home she didn't mention the incident to Frank, who was cooking pasta. Katie May was sitting at the kitchen table, ostentatiously doing her homework. Later, while Cressida cleared away, Frank put his daughter to bed and read her a story. When he came downstairs, he had Rafferty in his arms. He dumped him unceremoniously into his basket. 'The kennel woman told me he was trained,' he said. 'Disgusting

little brute's just peed all over the bath-
room.'

'Maybe Lulu will take him off our hands,'
Cressida said absently.

Email from Sean Brophy to Fiona Moore
Fi, The article is fantastic. Double-page spread.
Talk about throwing a grenade. It will be
interesting to see what results. I got the pics you
asked for. Oh, and tickets for the Point for
Friday. She's thrown me out finally. Now why
am I pleased? Luv Sean.

Chapter 21

On Tuesday morning the Recaldos over-
slept. Plans to go house-hunting in Wexford
while Katie May was at school were
scrapped over a rushed breakfast. Which
was something of a relief to Frank, who
hadn't slept well. The previous day Phil
McBride had told him about Gil's phone
call and he had lain awake half the night
trying – and failing – to find a way to break
the news to Cressida. After all their
resolutions he had failed at the first jump
and, as a result, he felt stressed out and was
desperate to get out of the house for a
breather. 'I'll drop Katie May off, Cress, you
stay and finish your breakfast,' he said.
Father and daughter were just going out of
the door when the phone rang. Frank
listened in silence, then hung up. 'Cress?' he

called. 'That was Phil, he wants to talk over something.'

'But didn't you see him yesterday?'

'Yeah, that's what he wants to talk about,' Frank said truthfully.

Cressida came out of the kitchen, drying her hands. 'What a nuisance. D'you have to?'

'Ye-es, I must.' He thought for a moment. 'Look, why don't you go to Wexford on your own? If it's any good we can all go down at the weekend. I'll pick up Katie May so you won't have to rush back.'

'Oh? That'd be good. Are you sure? It'll certainly be less of a rush if I don't have to be back for the school. You won't forget, will you?'

'Aw, Cress, what do you take me for?' He smiled. 'Don't forget your mobile.' He patted his pocket. 'I've got mine. Keep in touch.' He kissed her lips tenderly. 'We'll have supper ready when you get back.'

'Any idea how long you'll be with Phil?'

'He said a couple of hours or so.'

Cressida laughed. 'That'll be the whole day, then. I'll see what I can find in Wexford.'

'Daa-ddy! I'm going to be late,' yelled Katie May.

'Coming. I'm coming, coming, coming,' Frank shouted, though he seemed curiously reluctant to leave. ''Bye, darlin'.' He kissed

Cressida again. 'I love you,' he said quietly, as she hugged him close.

Cressida went back to the kitchen and poured herself another cup of coffee. She calculated that the rush-hour traffic wouldn't clear for another half-hour or so, sat down at the table and opened the morning paper. It was book day. She glanced idly through the arts section to see if they'd run Sean Brophy's interview. They had. *Man of Mystery*. The photograph was poor. Frank had cleverly sat with his back to the light so that his face was in shadow. He also wore a derby she'd never seen before – it made him look shifty and absurd, like an out-of-work bookie. But definitely unrecognizable. Relieved, she began to read the interview.

The first couple of paragraphs were mainly about the quality of his writing and the forthcoming TV series; after that came the personal stuff. She read on with some anxiety. Frank's whole working history was laid out in some detail, though his real name wasn't mentioned. But anyone who knew Inspector Frank Recaldo well would surely recognize him in Frank Ventry, even though Brophy had been skilful in fudging the edges and there was no mention of his sojourn in Passage South. His early retirement was put down to ill-health. The travel series was mentioned in passing, though not by the name under which Frank published it. It might have been worse, but she knew Frank would dissect it, hate it.

She neatly reassembled the broadsheet, slipped the review section inside the main news and folded the newspaper in two. As she placed it on the table something caught her eye. The narrow banner on the front page had a running headline: 'Review: Starting today: True Crime: Unsolved Murder Mysteries by Fiona Moore.'

Cressida opened the paper for the second time. The top was damp and the first two pages were stuck together, which was probably why she hadn't noticed the article before. She eased them apart and laid the paper flat on the table. The title ran over both pages: 'The dead woman left standing in her own garden – the unsolved murder of the decade'. Underneath the byline was an inch-square photograph of Fiona Moore. Cressida stared at it for a second or two before she realized she was looking at Lulu Stephenson's mother. She drew in a sharp breath and collapsed on a chair.

At first she couldn't focus on the dancing print but she forced herself to read it several times, from the twee opening, 'This is the story of an abandoned woman, her gay lover, her murderer, their mentally handi-capped child, the handsome policeman, the

deaf boy and the unfrocked priest.' There
followed a description of Evangeline
Walter's murder as told to the author by her
closest friend and partner, 'who every day
lives with the pain of his beloved's death'.
Although the names had been changed,
including Cressida's, it was perfectly
possible to recognize Smiler O'Dowd as the
narrator. The gay narrator. His history was
briefly outlined but with deadly accuracy.
Cressida, who had never liked Smiler,
nevertheless found herself hoping that the
poor man had outed himself before Ms
Moore had so comprehensively done the
job for him. Had she been less shocked on
her own account, she might have wondered
how the journalist had wormed her way into
his confidence then mercilessly exploited his
vulnerability. But that appeared to be her
stock-in-trade. The details of the murder
were alarmingly accurate, as were the
conclusions. The article managed to be both
salacious and holier-than-thou. Ms Moore
started with the difficulties of working single
mothers, through the abandoned handi-
capped child, then neatly paired the rest of
the characters. There was a snide innuendo
of how John Spain had driven his wife to
suicide then turned his attention to little
boys, specifically the alleged murderer's son
– she was careful about the finer points of
law – while his wife was banging the local

357

policeman. She read on, appalled, as her carefully constructed world caved in on her.

Exposed and defeated, she sat staring into space. Images that she thought she'd buried crowded in on her. One above all: Gil, lying still and injured at the cove that terrible night. She'd got back to find Spain asleep, face down at the kitchen table, and crept unseen into the bedroom. *Gil was gone.* She'd screamed and run down to the estuary where she stumbled across him, huddled awkwardly against a rock, soaking wet. As she bent to pick him up, she heard Spain cry out: 'Oh dear God, he must have followed me.' His despair matched hers. She should have walked into the water with her child in her arms, which was her instinct. Walk while Gil was still unconscious, walk until the waters closed peacefully over them. But Spain dragged her away. Once too often she allowed her actions to be dictated by well-meaning blunderers.

The newspaper article had shattered all her hopes for a happy future with Frank. The same dead feeling of inevitability that had kept her at Coribeen all those years seeped back. Now as then, her soul cried out for someone to help her through the darkness, but even her beloved Frank couldn't save her this time. Fiona Moore had damned them all.

Cressida Recaldo closed the paper and

nervously folded it in two, uncreasing it with trembling hands then refolding and refolding it, over and over. After a long time she went upstairs like a sleepwalker, collected a warm jacket and left the house. She didn't carry a bag and left her mobile phone lying on the kitchen table.

Dublin Daily Post

New unsolved murder series starts today by award-winning journalist Fiona Moore. Review section, pages 2-4.

Regression 13

I left well before seven the next morning and picked up a lift to Cork about a mile out of Duncreagh. I was dropped off at Glanmire station and had breakfast while I waited for the train. I spoke to no one. As I went to buy my ticket, I was stopped in my tracks by a read-all-about-it billboard. 'Award-winning Fiona Moore's new series starts today: Unsolved Murders – True Crime.' Fiona Moore. I had a premonition about it before I picked up the *Daily News* and read: 'The handsome policeman, the deaf boy and the unfrocked priest.'

I got fully acquainted with the deadly Miss Moore on the train. I read her nasty snide article three times and each time I felt more and more exposed. Scum. One thing was for sure, I didn't want to discuss it or see my parents for a very, very long time. I pictured their reaction and felt sick. After that I shut down and stared out of the window. I stopped feeling very much and stopped thinking completely. I felt my life was over and that there was no way back for me.

I walked slowly along the south bank of the Liffey all the way from Heuston station. The day was fine, I think. At least, it wasn't raining. I turned into Temple Bar and cut across College Green, through Trinity College to the Nassau Street gate and from there up Kildare Street. I counted off the streets from a list in my head, like a zombie.

I'd never been in Boswell's Hotel before and arrived a little before the appointed time. It was opposite the Dáil – the government buildings on Kildare Street. I remembered that it was well known as a haunt of politicians and journalists when I saw two or three recognizable faces from the telly while I hovered in the foyer, trying to pluck up courage to approach the bossy-looking woman at the desk, who instructed me to leave my backpack with the doorman. She'd obviously been forewarned of my arrival because when I said I'd an appointment with Inspector McBride I was shown into a small room off the lobby. A couple of minutes later a waiter came in with a pint of Guinness and a plate of sandwiches. 'D'inspector said you'd probably be hungry.' He grinned.

I was deadly calm by the time Bridie showed up, a quarter of an hour late.

Looking at him, the last thing you'd think would be 'senior police officer'. Not the most senior at the Phoenix Park, but pretty nearly. When Bridie was promoted to chief inspector, Frank reckoned he'd hit his glass ceiling and that, being gay, he'd never make the top job. He was the opposite of camp: he looked more like a successful businessman than anything else, but with a bit of an edge. He had a strong Dublin accent, shaved head and an ever-expanding paunch. But he was a sharp dresser: mid-grey Italian suit, dark shirt buttoned to the neck, no tie. And, to confuse you further, he wore a narrow gold band on the third finger of his left hand. He and his partner, Mark, who was a senior nurse in St Vincent's Hospital, had been together as long as I could remember. As Shay would have put it, Phil McBride was sound.

'Howya, Magillacuddy?' Bridie had a nickname for everyone. Frank was either Amigo or Troilus, for obvious reasons, Katie May was Cutems and Mark was Suze, don't ask me why. 'Not hungry, then?'

'No. Thanks.' I pushed the Guinness across the table. 'I don't feel much like food.'

He sat down. 'Understandable, old son, understandable,' he said, as the door opened and Frank walked in.

I got to my feet furiously. 'No,' I shouted. 'No.'

'Calm down,' Bridie said sternly. 'This is too important for tantrums.' I threw myself back on to the sofa and squeezed my eyes shut to stop the tears that had seemed ever ready in the last week. I was humiliated at being treated like a child and confused because I didn't know how I felt about Frank any more.

When I looked up he was still standing just inside the door. His face was as white as a sheet. Bridie got up, took him by the arm and led him to a seat opposite me. In spite of my anger, I was struck by how gentle and affectionate he was and how frail my dad looked. I'd thought he looked pretty seedy at Grandfather's funeral but now I realized he was ill. 'I'd like to stay, Gil, please,' he said quietly. 'I think this concerns all three of us. But if you insist, of course I'll leave.' Frank never forgot his manners or how to give you space – though, God knows, I've really put him through it in the past few years. The only time I ever saw him lose it was at that dingy old wake. I wished I'd talked to him that day. He'd tried, but I'd pushed him off. I couldn't help myself.

'Stay, if you like,' I said ungraciously. I couldn't look at him. 'You seen today's paper? Seen what the bitch said about Tar?'

'Yes,' he said. His face turned green and I knew he was thinking of Cressie and her reaction, but he didn't mention her.

'You should have told me all this stuff years ago,' I burst out. 'You shouldn't have left me to work it out myself.'

'We thought – we hoped you'd ask when you were ready,' Frank said. 'Me and your mother.'

Solidarity or what? 'Hoped I wouldn't, more like,' I growled. 'Hoped I'd forgotten.'

'Stop whining, Gil.' Bridie took command. 'You asked for this interview, remember.' His voice softened. 'I realize how difficult all this is for you, how threatened you must feel. So, can you tell us what you think you found out?' he said. 'Take as much time as you like. What made you go to Trianach?'

'I've been thinking about it for a couple of years. Longer even.' I glared at Frank. 'Christ, I didn't even know who my father was until Grandfather talked about him one day. I didn't even know my own bloody name, for God's sake.'

'I am your father, Gil. You are my son, Katie May's your sister. I've never thought of you otherwise.' Frank looked so sad.

I fought back more tears. 'I know, Dad, but there's also Gil Sweeney, the murderer's son, isn't there? Halcyon Walter's brother?'

'Oh, God almighty.' Frank put his head into his hands.

'Half-brother – if that,' Bridie cut in. 'Let's cut the dramatics.'

I swivelled round. 'You could have done a

DNA test,' I snarled. Bloody stupid, really, since neither of them was denying it.

'To what purpose?' Bridie asked mildly.

'So I'd bloody well know whether I was half-witted as well as ... as...'

This time I couldn't control the tears. I heard Frank say, 'Jesus Christ, Phil, what are we going to do?' And then, as usual, when I'm stressed out, I blanked out sound. Frank knew immediately. He came over to me, took my face in his long, slender hands and looked straight into my eyes. 'Start at the beginning, Gil.' He formed the words carefully. 'When did you get back from France?'

'I only stayed there a week or so after the funeral,' I mumbled. Then I pulled myself together. At first I spoke into silence, but slowly I began to hear my own voice and Bridie's, when he had a question or let out a string of expletives.

Frank didn't say a word until I finished describing what had happened in the garden, then he simply said, 'You thought your mother murdered her? It's not true.' Frank shut his eyes and tried to control his breathing. 'You've got to believe me, Gil, Cressie did not kill that terrible woman.'

'But she thumped her, knocked her down.' Neither of them looked surprised. *They knew?*

'And that's all she did.' Bridie spoke slowly

and clearly, as if he wasn't sure I could hear him properly. 'Your mother didn't kill Evangeline Walter. The wound to her head was superficial. We thought it might be important but the pathologist put us right. There was absolutely no doubt that a blow to the stomach killed her. Look at me, Gil. The autopsy was conclusive. The evidence against VJ Sweeney was incontrovertible.'

He spoke the name as if it meant nothing to him and should mean nothing to me. But it did. 'My father?'

'Yes.' He looked away.

'So either way, according to you, I'm a murderer's son.'

'I'm sorry, but better him than your mother,' Bridie said roughly, in police mode. 'That bastard was never much of a father to you, Gil.'

Somehow he managed to lower the emotional level. Thank goodness he didn't try to make me feel better, because had either of them touched me or commiserated I don't know how I'd have coped.

'I want you to tell me about the investigation,' I said stiffly. 'That's why I'm here.'

They exchanged glances. Frank sat on the opposite side of the room and Bridie paced up and down. He did the talking. He spoke as if he was reporting the investigation to a colleague or even a superior. He was completely unemotional and factual and he got it wrong. At least, that was what I was struggling with. Because as far as I could remember all three of them, my mother, father and Tar, had done their bit.

'When did you realize that Mrs Walter was Halcyon's mother?' Bridie broke in on my thoughts. I don't know how he knew that that piece of information was critical to me, but I suppose that that sort of intuition makes him a good copper. It took me a while, but somehow or other I told them about seeing her at the filling station and carried on to what had happened when we got home. I described my father throwing the glass at my mother and knocking me over.

'Now, can you explain to us what happened when your mother took you away from the house?' I told my long, rambling, incoherent story. Frank looked stunned. It was Bridie who asked me about seeing my father in the garden. 'Go over that bit again,' he said. So I did, starting from the shoe coming down on my foot. This time I remembered that the colour of the muddy cords had not been brown but buff. They exchanged meaningful looks.

'Why is it so important?' I asked, and they told me how they'd found the evidence against my father in the boot of his car. *Including* the tape-recorder, though they didn't know who'd put it there, and I didn't enlighten them.

'His clothes?' I asked.

'Yes. Her blood was all over them,' Bridie replied, and I remembered that my father had a lot of clothes, sometimes duplicates, and that Tar was in and out of the house.

'What else?'

'Her laptop, bag, that sort of thing.'

'And a big box?'

Frank's jaw dropped. 'Yes,' he said. 'A painted Italian chest from her house. How do you know that?'

'I saw him put it in.'

I thought Frank was going to leap across the room and shake the information out of me, but Bridie put up his hand. 'What happened *after* you left the garden?' he asked. 'Can you remember?'

I closed my eyes. 'Tar's cottage. Cressie and me lying on his bed. She fell asleep. In the morning he carried me to the car.'

'But before that you went back to the garden, didn't you?' he said softly. 'Did you follow Tar?'

Well, I'd got myself into that one, all right, but I was afraid of what he'd drag out of me. I felt I was seeing him for the first time – the tough copper – and I was afraid. He was much cleverer than I'd thought, and a hell of a lot smarter than me, so I felt I had no choice but to tell it like it was – I knew he'd keep at me until he got the full story. The only thing I kept back was all mention of my mother. I simply implied she was sleeping when I left and when I got back.

'What did he do with the bundle he took from the house?'

I shook my head. 'I don't know. I didn't see.'

And, like before, he moved on as if he'd lost interest. No chance. 'What happened in the morning?'

'He carried me out to the car. It was in a field, I think. We drove a long way.' It was only then that something else came back. 'A hospital. We were in hospital. Talking to a woman. She was sick, lying in bed.'

'Marilyn Donovan,' Frank said.

'That was Marilyn? Oh.' Another with her own agenda: she hadn't said a word about us coming to the hospital.

'She'd had a miscarriage two days before the murder,' Bridie said. 'Your mother drove her to the Bon Secours in Cork.' He was silent for a while after that, which made me even more tense. 'In all, you were in the garden twice?' A faint smile. 'I'm a bit confused. Let's go through it sequentially, will we?'

'I'm the one supposed to be asking the questions,' I said. 'Why are you interrogating me?'

He wasn't in the least put out. 'You think this is interrogation, old son?' He laughed mirthlessly. 'Look, Gil, I want to help you understand but it's your interpretation that's to cock. I can't clear it up until I hear what you think. OK?'

I nodded but I really hadn't a clue what he meant. At the same time I wanted to stop playing games, to clear it up in my mind. I think I wanted him to make the decisions.

'So. Go back to the cottage after you got back first time. You fell asleep?'

'No,' I said, feeling my way back into the dark bedroom. 'Cressie fell asleep. John Spain was next door, drinking whiskey at the table.'

'How do you know?' Bridie asked.

'I could smell it.' You could have heard a pin drop. 'I got out of bed but I didn't go into the living room. I peeped round the door and watched him. He was crying. His shoulders were shaking. After a while he got up and went out.' I looked at Frank. 'I crept out after him. I tried to call him, but I couldn't get the words out, so I followed him down to the cove. He took the boat out. I climbed up on the spit to wait for him.'

Bridie looked at Frank. 'What spit?'

'It's a rocky outcrop, quite high, edging the cove, where he kept his boat.'

'They call it Spain's Cove now,' I said inconsequentially.

'Go on,' Bridie ordered brusquely but the spell had been broken so he made me start

370

all over again.

'My arm was hurting and I kept slipping. By the time I got to the top, Tar had disappeared. I was just going to run back to the cottage when the launch came shooting out of the night and across the river.'

'Launch? What launch?'

'My father's launch.'

'Are you quite sure? You heard it?'

'I saw it. He was at the wheel. There was a full moon. It shone on his hair.' I touched my own. 'Like mine, same colour. He wasn't wearing a cap. Dark sweater, no coat. It was cold.' I was talking to myself.

'Then what?'

'I sat down again and waited for Tar.'

'You weren't afraid of him after what you'd seen earlier?' Bridie asked gently.

I was surprised myself. But maybe that was looking at it from an adult's point of view. As me, aged eight, I'd had no fear of him whatsoever. I just wanted him to come back and look after me. 'None, except the fear that he wouldn't come back for us.'

'How long did you wait?'

And back over it I went, adding the detail. There no longer seemed any point in leaving things out. Except for that one thing. I didn't tell them I thought I'd seen Cressie.

'And Spain was there next morning?' Bridie said, when I finished.

'Yes. But I don't know if it was morning –

it was still dark. He carried me out to the car.'

'I'm sorry you had to do all this alone, Gil.' Frank broke a long silence.

'Yeah, you really blew it, didn't you? Why didn't you tell me?'

'Oh, for crying out loud, Magillacuddy, get real. How the feck were they supposed to tell an eight-year-old or a ten-year-old or a twelve-year-old all that stuff? How? You want to tell me that? Look at me, son. You think they knew how much you saw? How much you were taking in?'

'I should have been told about Halcyon, about my father,' I said stubbornly.

'I'm sorry,' Frank said. 'Oh, Gil, I'm so sorry. Cressie and I agonized over it, all the time, but when it came to the point, we were afraid of what it might do to you. We screwed up.'

'Oh, stop it!' Bridie exploded. 'Weren't you only trying to protect the child? You did your best, Frank.'

'It wasn't good enough, though, was it?' I said.

Bridie gave me such a dirty look that I was glad I wasn't a criminal. 'Maybe you could have done it better. Put yourself in their place, lad. Ask yourself how you would tell Katie May now, aged ten. Where would you begin?'

That got to me more than all the rest

because I suddenly saw Halcyon send my baby sister flying through the air, damn near killing her.

'I don't normally do this, Gil, but I want you to hear the story from my point of view.' Bridie talked for nearly half an hour, starting from the moment he had arrived with his superior from Cork to take charge of the murder investigation. He went through the whole process, ending with the burning of Tar's boat. And when he'd finished, he told me that Frank, Tar and my mother had all been suspects, at one stage or another. Tar and Cressie for the murder and Frank for fudging the evidence. I pricked up my ears at that. 'He nearly scuppered it, you know, with his bloody meddling, and very nearly ended in jail himself, trying to save your mother. Thought I was a feckin' eejit.' So they'd thought Cressie did it too. But not now? Why were they so sure?

He said it was only when they got their wires uncrossed and worked together that the real evidence was found. That was when they'd believed Tar's story of seeing Sweeney in the garden later that night. 'The story you've just corroborated, Magilla-cuddy. You're a bloody great witness, d'you know that? We could have done with you at the—' He put his hand to his mouth. 'Aw, Jaysus, what am I saying?'

'I don't think I'd have been much good, would I, at the time? Seeing I couldn't really talk all that well. Or hear.' I put my hand on Frank's arm. 'Anyway, I was terrified of my father. He damn near killed me and Cressie the same night.' I swallowed hard. 'Yet my mother lived with him, stayed with him. For what?' Even to my own ears I sounded hysterical. 'For the sake of a fucking house?' That silenced them. 'I have a question.' I couldn't look at either of them. 'Was Tar trying to save him when they drowned?'

Bridie turned to Frank. 'Over to you, Amigo. What's your take on that?'

Frank hesitated. I had a horrible feeling he was going to get all pious but I should have known better. 'Spain went to pieces after the murder. He practically lived in his boat. We realized too late that he must have been lying in wait for Sweeney.'

'We found out that Sweeney sold his shares in the Atlantis Hotel in Passage South – forty Ks' worth in hard cash. Evangeline was after them, but he sold them to someone else a couple of days after the murder. It was my opinion Sweeney had already got away by car,' Bridie put in. 'But Frank always thought that if he was going to make a run for it he'd use the yacht and Spain must have been thinking along the same lines. The yacht slipped anchor on the Saturday morning around six. We missed it, but Spain was right there. He took the motor launch and gave chase. They were caught in a storm.'

'Cressie thinks he might have nudged the yacht on to the rocks,' Frank said.

The man they were discussing was my father. I kept telling myself that, and it hurt like hell that they talked about him as if he was a wild animal. 'Why does she think so?' I asked, although I knew what he was going to say.

'He'd have done anything to protect you. I believe he figured that if a trial could be avoided, then the scandal would die.'

'In a manner of speaking.'

It hadn't worked for him, had it? Marilyn had told me how 'everyone knew John Spain wasn't a paedophile', but the fact that she'd felt she had to say it was damning in itself. Ten years after his death, the same old lies were being denied and that didn't seem to me to be much different from making an outright accusation. Either way the dirt stuck. For a split second I was glad that the bitch who started it had been killed. But there was still one more. Moore.

'Why did Mrs Walter make up those terrible lies about Tar?'

'Well, now, that's the feckin' million-dollar question,' Bridie said, but at last he got to the reason for the murder. He confirmed what Tar had said in his letter.

'She was trying to get at Sweeney, destroy him and everything he had, including his family.' Frank seemed to be thinking it out as he spoke. 'Sweeney used those stories about Spain to threaten Cressie. He said he'd inform the Social Services if she didn't give up the house. I'm not sure that was what Evangeline Walter had intended him to do but that was the effect. She and Sweeney weren't having an affair, as everyone, including Cressie, thought. Not an ongoing one. They had been lovers but he abandoned her when Halcyon was a baby. Murray admitted to your mother last week that Sweeney was responsible for her condition. Evangeline certainly believed so. She stalked him for years, looking for revenge. For herself? For the brain-damaged child? Cressie and I've thought about it a long time,' Frank said, 'but we still can't figure it all out. She publicly humiliated him. She bought the yacht–'

'The name was changed to *Halcyon*,' I said. I drew in a deep breath and quietly placed the clapped-out mobile phone I'd found in the cottage on top of the plate of sandwiches.

Bridie leaped on it.

'Where did you get that?' Frank whispered.

'Tar left it for me to find. In a place only I knew about. He knew I'd go back. It's hers,

376

isn't it?'

'Probably. Hers certainly went missing about the same time Spain seemed to have acquired one.' He turned it over in his hand. 'We'll never know now, if there were any significant messages on it.'

Frank came across the room, put his arms around me and held me tight, like he used to when I was a child. We both cried. He asked me if I'd go home with him. 'No,' I said. 'I couldn't face it. I'll go away for a while.'

'Where? What about university?'

'What about it? You think I could hack university after all this? You've had ten years to bury it. I'm just beginning so I'm heading out. Back to France for a while, then I'll probably go to Australia or somewhere.'

'You'll need money. I'll put some in your account.'

I stood up and headed for the door. 'No, I'm OK. If I need it I'll ask. Thanks. I'll ring in a day or so and let you know my plans. OK?'

Frank came after me. 'Cressie will be very upset. Won't you come and see her before you go?'

I shook my head. 'I'm sorry. Tell her I'll be in touch when I get my head together.' To his credit, Frank didn't try to change my mind. And he didn't play the heart card either. He just stood looking at me. I noticed he was stroking the beginning of a beard.

'You can come and stay with us for a few days, while you get sorted,' Bridie suggested.

'No thanks,' I said. I was almost at the door when I turned back to face them. 'You got a few things wrong,' I said, and held out the car keys with the Lexus symbol prominent. 'I found these with the phone. See if you can figure out what he was trying to tell me.'

I turned and crashed into a waiter. 'Turn on the television, sir,' he shouted. 'New York's just been bombed.'

Duncreagh Listening Post
Trianach businessman Jer O'Dowd, after five attempts, finally gets permission to develop new marina and clubhouse at Coribeen.

Regression 14

I slipped out unnoticed. I didn't bother with my backpack. The foyer was full of people gawping at a television screen mounted above the reception desk. In the couple of minutes it took me to push my way through, I saw the aircraft fly into the World Trade Center twice. It seemed unreal. I didn't linger.

Out on the street people were hurrying towards public buildings looking for TV sets. Several times I heard voices cry out, 'Did you hear? Did you see?' I walked swiftly down Kildare Street and along Nassau Street where I found a hairdresser and watched the newsreel while I had my hair cut close to my skull.

After that, I rang the hotel I'd worked in before I went south and they said they could give me a room for a couple of nights at half the going rate. I bargained a bit more and Fred, the guy at the desk, eventually said,

'Ah, you're all right for a couple of nights. You've heard the news? I bet we're in for a mountain of cancellations. You mightn't get sheets but.' Which was fine by me. I headed for O'Connell Street, which was crowded. Either the word hadn't spread or people had other things on their minds. As I had. I went straight to the newspaper office where there was total chaos. Phones were ringing, staff were flying about, two of the girls behind the reception desk had headsets clamped to their ears. If I'd planned it myself I couldn't have done better. I took my hearing-aid out of my pocket and stuck it into my ear. There was no need to switch it on.

The front of the huge counter had a series of posters, some with pictures of the star reporters, others announcing forthcoming features. Bang in the middle was 'The murdered woman left standing in her own garden – the unsolved case of the decade. Read award-winning Fiona Moore's great new series: Getting Away with Murder. The Unsolved Crimes of the Century. Exclusive to the *Daily News*. Starts Tuesday.'

I took an envelope from my jacket pocket and waved it in front of a receptionist's nose. I'd printed 'Fiona Moore' prominently across it in big letters. 'Urgent,' I mouthed, and twisted my head, bringing my aid into full view. She smiled and scribbled, 'Third floor, room four' on a Post-it label, attached it to the envelope then picked up another phone and shouted into the receiver.

I took the stairs two at a time. The third—floor corridor was deserted but every room I passed had men and women standing open-mouthed in front of televisions. In rapid sequence along the corridor I saw one of the twin towers collapse, read the flash at the bottom of the screen – 'Pentagon hit, thousands feared dead' – then saw it all over again. Neither image impinged on me. I pressed on.

The door of room four was wide open. Just as I reached it a red-haired man came charging towards me and slid to a halt at the open door. 'Fiona,' he shouted.

A woman peered out. 'Come in, Sean,' she said. 'It's totally unbelievable.' She was older than I expected, big and busty with huge brown eyes and a lot of makeup, dressed in black from top to toe. Her hair was dark, shoulder-length. Neither of them paid me any attention. I held back until they went inside, leaving the door wide open, then I sauntered past. The man had his arm around her and was nuzzling her ear as they watched a TV mounted on the wall above her desk.

I went back down, this time by the lift. The ground floor was even more crowded, but stunned. I removed my hearing-aid as I left the building, went into the Starbucks next door and nursed a double espresso for an hour or so until Fiona Moore came racing past. I followed her to the Tara Street DART station and on to a southbound train. She didn't pay me any attention. She put on earphones as soon as she sat down. I took a seat half-way down the carriage, pretending to look out the window. She got out at Blackrock and went to an apartment block on a quiet road about a quarter of a mile from the station. Five or six minutes after she'd gone into the block, she came out and got into a green Saab parked outside. It was four o'clock. I found a convenient low garden wall and sat down to wait. At five fifteen she came back with a blonde child, about the same age as my little sister, and an older woman. The kid never stopped talking as they went inside.

On the supposition that journalists work in the evening, I waited for another hour and a half. It was growing cold and started to drizzle. I pulled up the hood of my jacket and strolled slowly up and down the road. I felt a bit conspicuous until people started coming home from work and I melted into the background. By seven the light was going when a young guy, about my age, came out of the apartment and drove away in the Saab. That was my main worry out of the way. I stepped back into the dubious shelter of a nearby hedge and hung on.

There were cars parked on either side of the street by now. A big black Mercedes with dark windows and the name of a Cork dealer on the rear window had been there on and off since I arrived. I noticed the windscreen wipers switched on once or twice so I knew someone was sitting in it. And I had a good idea who. I was almost certain it was the same car that Marilyn had pointed out to me the day she gave me breakfast. Having read Fiona Moore's article I wouldn't have been surprised to see the legendary O'Dowd hop out of it. But maybe I was mistaken because, on reflection, I thought it more likely that the poor guy would have disappeared into the woodwork to lick his wounds. I would in his position. There was also a VW Beetle of the same beige colour as my mother's half-way down the road. But I couldn't make out the number-plate without showing myself. I could see that it was empty. I almost weakened at the thought of poor Cressie, alone and worrying about me, about all of us. But anger and resentment swiftly overcame sentimentality.

At last, at half past eight when the rain was lashing down and I was soaked, she came out. I didn't mind; the weather was perfect for my purpose – people slipped on wet pavements all the time. Railway platforms were even better – and that was what I had in mind. I wondered vaguely how many people the DART killed every year. She stood in the doorway looking up, then went back inside for a few minutes and returned with a big black umbrella. She was wearing flat shoes and was a lot shorter than I'd thought. I held back until she had gone about fifty yards or so down the road in the direction of the railway station, then started after her. The Mercedes went past in the opposite direction, sending up a huge filthy spray. The pedestrian light at the main road was against her. I held back, waiting for it to change, but Fiona stepped fearlessly out on to the road and wove in and out of the traffic. I followed. We passed the super-market at the corner and went down the quiet local-traffic-only road into Blackrock village. She held the black umbrella low over her head, against the wind. I was bent over holding on to my hood, about twenty paces behind her but catching up. As we turned the corner, the station was ahead across a deserted car park. I was close to her now: if I had put out my hand I could have touched the umbrella. Something made me half turn my head. The black Mercedes was bearing down on us. Fast, too fast. Out of control. The driver's face was huge, grinning at me. I gave an involuntary scream, and then I was slammed against the wall.

Chapter 22

'Phil?'

'Frank. What's up?'

'Cressie hasn't come home.'

'But it's only six o'clock – she's probably glued to some television set like the rest of the world. It's only desperate, isn't it?'

'Phil, she didn't take the car.'

'What? I thought she was going to look at houses in Wexford? Maybe she went by train. Did I tell you I think you're both mad? What do you want to bury yourselves in Wexford for?'

'Phil, listen to me. The car's outside. Cressie left the keys on the table. Her mobile as well. She's gone.'

'That's why you couldn't get hold of her. Oh, my God, Frank. The paper. She must have read that feckin' article. I forgot all about it with the Trade Center thing. Fifty thousand dead, they're saying. Cressie is probably–'

'You already said that. I should have come home. I didn't even see the bloody newspaper until after Gil– God, why didn't I...'

'Any sign of him?'

'No, no.'

'Well, then, that's probably it. I bet he came straight home to see her. They'll be together somewhere.'

'No. They won't. She's been gone eight hours. My next-door neighbour saw her leave the house this morning. On foot. Her bag's in the kitchen.'

'Calm down, Frank, I'm on my way. What was she wearing?'

Dublin Daily News, *Thursday 13 September*
Dublin Gardai are appealing for witnesses to a fatal incident on the approach road to Blackrock station on the evening of 11 September around nine o'clock, in which a woman was killed and a young man seriously injured as they crossed the road. A large black car was seen leaving the vicinity shortly afterwards, make and registration unknown. Anyone who saw the incident or has any information about the car or driver should contact the duty officer at Blackrock or at Pearse Street Garda Station.

Moore, Fiona *11 September*
Victim of a hit and run incident at Blackrock, Dublin. Fiona (48) beloved mother of Sebastian and Marie Louise (Lulu), and dear daughter of Brian and Annie Moore of Daingean, Co. Cork. Funeral details to be announced.

Chapter 23

Five days after Gil was admitted to hospital, he was moved from the intensive care unit into a single room, though he was still hooked up to a phalanx of monitors at the head of the bed. His head was swathed in bandages and his right arm and leg were in splints. His face was deathly pale and his breathing barely perceptible; he appeared to be asleep. Mark, appalled, stood inside the door and tried to calm himself before approaching the bed.

'Gil?'

'Mark?' Gil opened his eyes groggily. 'What are you doing here?' His speech was slurred.

'I might ask you the same. I brought a few grapes.'

'Not sure I can eat. My jaw hurts like hell.'

'Poor Gil.' Mark sat close to the bed and took Gil's hand. 'We'll look after you, kid,' he said.

'Hmmm.'

'What happened? Did you see what hit you?'

'Not a thing.'

'So Bridie says. He also said you're taking another year off, is that right?'

'Not sure what I'll do.'

'If you're free, what about coming to work for me?'

Gil managed a laugh. 'Doing what? I've a broken leg, arm and my head feels like a balloon.'

'I have a plan. Come on, it'll be great *craic*.'

'Is that right? I hope you can wait. What

had you in mind?'

'I've given up the nursing. Feel like a bit of a change. I'm opening a restaurant so I'll need a good waiter. You're it.'

'You're off your head.' Gil sounded a bit more lively. 'When?'

'Oh, in about six months, you'll be well better. But I'll want a bit of help in the planning stage too. We could start on that, pronto. It'll be a laugh.'

'Where is it going to be?' Gil asked cagily.

'On the waterfront.'

'New York?'

'Don't be an eejit. Ringsend, of course. I'm going to call it Wagner. Get it?'

'Not yet, but I'm sure you'll tell me. I was going to go to Australia or somewhere.'

'So your dad said. I'd be really pleased to have a pal around at the beginning, Gil. I'm begging. On my knees.' He laughed.

Gil blinked back the tears. 'I'd be no good. I'm only out of school.'

'You're the best I'm likely to get for what I'm paying,' he said.

'I'll think about it. If you don't mind waiting. Thanks, Mark.'

'Seen the folks yet?' Mark asked casually.

'Yeah. Dad's been here a few times. Cressie's in and out the whole time.'

Mark choked back a cough. 'Oh? Was she here today?' His voice was strained.

'Not yet. She usually comes at night when

389

Katie May's in bed. She's got a new dog.'

'Who? Your mother?'

Gil's eyelids drooped again. 'No. Twink.'

'Cressie in good form, then?'

'Yes. The usual. She never says much but it's nice ... bit like it was when I was little. Her sitting at the end of the bed, smiling. Old times. She understands why I went back to ... to...'

'So everything's OK? Gil? You awake?'

'Sleepy. I promised her I'd go home for a while.' He opened his eyes and made a feeble attempt at a grin. 'Bit ironic, really. Now that she's rid of Grandfather she's lumbered with me. Doesn't seem fair, does it?'

'No, but I'll help. I'm moving in for a few days when you come out of hospital. Might as well make myself useful, as long as I'm out of a job.'

'Mark?'

'Yeah?'

'Why does Bridie call you Suze?'

'Ah, now, that would be telling,' Mark said as the door was tentatively pushed open and a wide-eyed girl edged into the room. Just as Mark had done, she stood with her back to the door, using it for support. Mark stood up as the girl began to weep very quietly, wiping her eyes and nose with the back of her hand. She appeared to be rooted to the spot. 'He's just dropped off to sleep,' Mark whispered. 'Come and sit down.' When she didn't respond he went over to her, put his arm around her shoulder and led her to the bedside. 'I'm Mark – a friend of the family.'

She turned her head to him. 'Is he going to die?' she whispered.

'No, he's going to be OK. It'll take a while, but he's strong.'

'Does he know about his mother?' she whispered. Mark put his finger to his lips and shook his head.

'Shay? Shay?'

The girl knelt beside the bed and held her face to Gil's hand. 'Ah Sweeney,' she said softly, 'look at the cut of you, sure you're not fit to be let out on your own.'

Dublin Daily News, *Saturday 15 September The body of a woman washed up on Sandymount Strand yesterday morning has been identified as mother of two Mrs Cressida Recaldo (43), who was reported missing by her husband, ex-Garda Frank Recaldo, on Wednesday. Mrs Recaldo's son Gil was seriously injured in the hit-and-run incident that killed award-winning journalist Fiona Moore late the previous evening. Mr Recaldo is the popular crime writer Frank Ventry.*

The publishers hope that this book has given you enjoyable reading. Large Print Books are especially designed to be as easy to see and hold as possible. If you wish a complete list of our books please ask at your local library or write directly to:

Magna Large Print Books
Magna House, Long Preston,
Skipton, North Yorkshire.
BD23 4ND

This Large Print Book, for people
who cannot read normal print,
is published under the auspices of

THE ULVERSCROFT FOUNDATION

**Other MAGNA titles
In Large Print**

ANNE BAKER
Merseyside Girls

JESSICA BLAIR
The Long Way Home

W. J. BURLEY
The House of Care

MEG HUTCHINSON
No Place For A Woman

JOAN JONKER
Many A Tear Has To Fall

LYNDA PAGE
All Or Nothing

NICHOLAS RHEA
Constable Over The Bridge